THE DAMASCUS COVER

THE DAMASCUS COVER

HOWARD KAPLAN

E. P. DUTTON & CO., INC.,
NEW YORK

Library of Congress Cataloging in Publication Data

Kaplan, Howard
    The Damascus cover.

    I. Title.
PZ4.K17328Dam [PS3561.A558] 813'.5'4   76–40311
ISBN 0-525-08850-4

Published simultaneously in Canada by Clarke, Irwin & Company
Limited, Toronto and Vancouver

For my parents
ALBERT and CLAIRE KAPLAN

ONE

SEPTEMBER 21

Dov Elon sat in the dirt in his cell leaning against the whitewashed wall. The cubicle, three feet by five feet, was windowless. The air stank of urine. A can, his wash-basin, lay on its side in one corner. A thin blanket covered the mound of damp straw piled in the other.

Dov's eyes rested on the food trap in the door. Not long before he'd heard the banshee cry of the muezzin beckoning the Moslem inmates to prayer. He assumed a bowl of jasmine tea would soon be pushed through the food trap, but he wasn't sure. The previous day he'd been transferred from Tadmor Prison, near the ancient Greek ruins of Palmyra in the north, to Sigin al-Mazza, on the outskirts of Damascus. He didn't know if his new guards would feed him regularly or at random intervals. So he waited, listening for approaching footsteps, not moving—for every shift in position arched pain through his bruised body. After awhile he closed his eyes. The minutes fell away. There were no sounds. The silence hummed in his ears.

With the grating of wood against metal the heavy door swung open, jarring Dov out of a semi-conscious stupor.

"Get up," the guard said in Arabic.

Although the Israeli understood his captor perfectly, he didn't respond.

"Stand up!" The guard gripped his kurbash, a leaden whip made from the coarse hairs of a bull's tail.

"My pleasure," Dov said, struggling to his feet, refusing to let the pain rippling through him register on his face. Several of his ribs were cracked and the open wounds on the backs of his legs, inflicted by palm frond lashings, festered with infection.

Haltingly Dov followed the guard through the dimly lit underground corridor, past two narrow passages lined with the fourteen *al-Aadem*, death row cells; then past the damp *muabed* section, containing those serving life sentences; until they reached an iron gate. The guard fitted a single key into the lock. The bolt clattered and the metal squeaked loudly as he pushed the gate open.

Farther on, the corridor walls changed from gray to white. As they mounted a flight of concrete stairs the temperature rose. By the time Dov was led into the second-floor interrogation room lines of perspiration glistened on his brow.

In the center of the room stood a high straw stool supported by wooden legs. Opposite it was a desk, uncluttered, with an upholstered chair. The plaster walls were bare; the lone window closed; the blades of the fan overhead, still. The guard motioned to the stool with the butt of his kurbash. Dov moved toward it and sat. His legs dangled; neither they nor his back had any support. Outside the sun beat down on the desert. The sweat began to trickle from Dov's body, dampening his brown prison shirt. According to a thermometer by the door the room temperature stood at 102 degrees.

Moments later Suleiman Sarraj entered carrying a copper tray loaded with iced drinks. He set it on the edge of the desk, removed a tan folder from the top drawer, and

2

sat down. The guard stationed himself against the wall at the prisoner's back.

"How are you, Dov?" Sarraj asked, with the familiarity developed during previous interrogations.

"Just fine. I'm in a beautiful suite on one of the lower levels. It's got everything—a blanket, a gallon can, room service, meals delivered directly to my door. You ought to stop by sometime."

"Oh Dov," Sarraj said, shaking his head. "I thought a few weeks at Tadmor would convince you further resistance is quite futile. Evidently I was mistaken." He took one of the drinks in his hand and almost spilled it. The condensation on the outside of the glass made it slippery. "Or maybe my men have been too gentle. In any event, it seems they've failed to show you exactly how serious I am."

A drop of perspiration rolled down Dov's nose and onto his shirt. The dry heat invaded every cavity of his body. There was pressure on the sockets of his eyes. His mouth was viscid. His nostrils parched. His throat felt like someone had run sandpaper along its inner walls.

"Give me a drink, Sarraj."

The Second Bureau chief set his glass down. "I'm sorry I can't do that, at least not yet. But as soon as you begin cooperating you shall have a glass of Kortisan. It's a local specialty, made by soaking licorice roots in water for several days. The result, chilled, is quite delicious. I'm sure you'll find it . . ."

"Why don't you just kill me and get it over with!" Dov shouted.

"I'm afraid that would do neither of us much good. Besides you are too young to lose your life. Believe me, at twenty-six you've barely begun. I know, I have a son and daughter about your age." There was paternal warmth in his voice. "I don't want to see you dead. As

3

I've told you before, I want to help you, to send you back to Israel. In fact, let me do something now, as a gesture of good faith." Sarraj reached behind him and flipped a switch on the wall. The whine of an electric motor sounded overhead and the black blades of the fan suspended from the ceiling gradually picked up speed. Dov shivered as a stream of hot air glanced off his sweaty brow.

"Is that better?"

He nodded.

"Good. Now, tell me—what do you know about the former Nazis living in Damascus?"

"Which Nazis?"

"How did you penetrate the German colony here?" Sarraj demanded impatiently.

Dov's lips curved into a smile. "I just asked where I could find the best knockwurst and sauerkraut in town."

Sarraj strummed his fingers on the desk. "If you persist in this manner, I'll have the answer beaten out of you. I will ask just one more time. How did you penetrate the Nazi colony?"

A long silence followed.

Sarraj stood up. "You are a fool. You will regret this, I promise you." He motioned to the guard and left the room.

The soldier closed the door behind Sarraj, then turned toward the prisoner.

"Over here," he said.

Dov lowered himself to the ground and looked over to where the Arab pointed. Two wrist shackles were bolted into the wall just above the casing. As he moved near, the guard grabbed his shoulder, pushed him face forward against the door, lifted his right hand, locked it inside the manacle, then did the same with his left. Dov hung over the door. The wood felt warm where it pressed against his cheek.

He heard the sound of the kurbash beating the air, then abruptly the first blow ripped into his infected calves. The bull's hair shredded his prison garment and the outer layer of his skin with one stroke. Dov bit his lower lip hard. Again and again the guard lashed at the back of his legs, cutting through tendon and muscle, bloodying his whip. Dov tore at the shackles, writhing in agony. Streams of sweat ran down his face. He smelled the salt odor of tears in his nose. The guard paused for a moment, stepped to his left, then sent the ends of the kurbash slicing through the side of Dov's knee. The second blow struck the exposed peroneal nerve. Excruciating pain clawed down Dov's leg and exploded into his foot. His tongue caught in his throat. He screamed without restraint.

The door opened. Sarraj stood there for a long time, studying the boy's face. Finally he spoke in a soft voice:

"Have you had enough?"

Dov turned his head away.

"Take him down," Sarraj said to the guard.

When Dov was seated on the stool, Sarraj reached into his desk and withdrew a gun. It was an FN Browning .45 caliber High Power Automatic Pistol manufactured in Belgium under license as a copy of the American original. He circled around the desk and faced the young Israeli.

"I have lost my patience, Elon. I did not bring you to al-Mazza for you to waste more of my time. We have reached the turning point in our discussions. Either you begin cooperating or you will not leave this room alive." His voice was flat.

Dov felt the control of his mind slipping. His head

throbbed. And the thirst. "Sarraj, give me something to drink," he cried out.

Sarraj sensed that he was on the verge of victory. He lowered the Browning to his side. He had now only to apply the *coup d'grâce*. But he would edge toward his final threat. He knew better than to spoil his advantage by proceeding too quickly.

"Why did the Colonel send you to Syria?"

"Please, Sarraj, my legs. Let me lie down."

"In a minute. There's a doctor waiting in the next room. As soon as I have the information I want you shall have treatment, a bed, food. Now, tell me, how did you penetrate the Nazi colony?"

"No," he whispered, weakening.

Moisture built in his eyes.

"Come on, Dov, talk and it will be over for you. In a few days you'll be home. Think about it, no more beatings, an end to the pain."

Dov licked his lower lip; it was bleeding.

"Nobody ever holds out under prolonged torture. You've been here for five months. The Colonel will understand. Nobody will blame you. You'll be considered a hero for lasting as long as you did. Please don't make me use the pistol. You made a special effort to seek out the Nazis. Tell me, did Ludwig Streicher help you?"

"I can't," he shouted, burying his head in his arms—waiting, wanting to die.

Sarraj moved next to the chair, gun in hand. "You leave me little choice."

Dov looked up.

The pistol was pointed at his elbow. In one terrible instant he realized Sarraj was not threatening to kill him.

"You wouldn't . . ."

"The bullets for this pistol are forty-fives. Notches

have been sliced into the ends. They'll shatter on impact. Why did you come to Syria?"

"The Colonel sent me."

"I know that," Sarraj said, the anger in his voice scratching his words. "Why?"

"I can't tell you."

"I'm not bluffing!" Sarraj pushed the muzzle of the Browning against Dov's skin. "Who is your contact in Damascus?"

"I have no contact here."

"You're lying! Who is Operative Sixty-six?"

At the mention of the highly placed Israeli agent terror swept through Dov. How had Sarraj known? It was impossible. But no time to think now. He had to focus his will against Sarraj. Defy him. Resist. That's all that mattered.

"I'll give you one last chance. I want the identity of Operative Sixty-six."

Silence.

"I want his name!" Sarraj screamed. "Now!"

Dov stared into his eyes. "I'll never tell you," he said, gritting his teeth.

Sarraj pulled the trigger. The sound exploding in such close quarters was deafening. Pieces of flesh splattered the wall. Blood gushed from the open wound. Dov's arm, hanging from the elbow by a piece of membrane, swayed in the air. Then the skin tore and it fell to the ground.

"Get a doctor," Sarraj shouted at the guard. "I don't want him dying."

THE PREVIOUS SPRING

TWO

APRIL

THE MAN KNOWN as Hans Hoffmann cried out in his sleep.

Jarred awake, Michelle shook the naked body beside her until his eyes opened. Slowly he stirred. Drawing his hand from under the covers he touched her cheek, seeking palpable proof that she was real and the dream was not.

"Qu'est-ce qu'il y a?" Michelle asked in French.

For a split second Hans didn't understand her. The dream had been in German, that dream from his youth was always in German.

"What do you mean, is anything the matter?" he said, adjusting his thoughts and words to her language.

"You cried out."

He shrugged and turned onto his back. "I must have been dreaming. It's nothing to worry about. An occasional nightmare is healthy, it releases tension."

Comforted by an explanation, she smiled and hooked her foot around his. The night air brushing through the curtain bore the damp odor of the sea and the pines outside. Though Hans's eyes were open, the dream was still there: the mud, the barking dogs, the barbed wire. Michelle sensed his thoughts, still clinging to the night-

11

mare. Helping the only way she knew how, she drew him close and brought their lips together. Her mouth worked, arousing him. Strands of her long black hair embraced his face and she felt his response to her breasts. Slowly she rolled her tongue from his ear to the base of his neck and back again. He reached for her; the memories had been put back in their place.

In the morning, awake early, Hans and Michelle stood in front of the white hillside cabin looking down at the Cyprus coastline. Ten miles to the east lay Kyrenia, a hamletlike fishing village, plaster and red tile roofs. Below the town fishing smacks and small boats were sheltered inside two arms of a sea wall that formed a miniature harbor. On one arm stood the Virgin Castle. The other arm was a quay with a lighthouse at the end. Anchored outside the harbor, flying a red flag with a gold crescent, was the 3,500-ton *M. Feuza Cakmak,* a World War II vintage destroyer stationed there ever since Turkey first landed six thousand troops on the island in July, 1974.

The white cabin Michelle had rented stood in the midst of a forest of pines and acacias. Behind them rose the Kyrenia mountains, whose terraced vineyards and olive orchards reflected the early morning light. Above the orchards, atop a three-thousand-foot peak, St. Hilarion's Castle stood guard over the rolling hills to the west. Though inhabited more than seven hundred years earlier by Richard the Lion-Hearted and his beloved Berengaria, its royal apartments, great halls, monastery, and fortifications have been preserved, intact.

On their way down to the beach Hans and Michelle saw no one. She had chosen the cabin with care. The nearest neighbors were several miles away. Michelle wanted to stay away from any place where they might be seen. She said she was married. Hans didn't mind one way or the other.

As they moved along the water's edge Michelle noticed, and not for the first time, that he had an attractive physique. He was strong—she had discerned that the night before—but now walking without his shirt, she could see the muscles in his arms and shoulders. A shade under six feet, his small blue eyes, charming manner, and ability to put strangers at ease made people remember him when they returned home from a crowded party. Occasionally it struck those he was close to that they really knew little about him. His name sounded German and indeed in most Berlin nightclubs he was given the best table. But that meant little, for he was known equally well by the maître d's in Paris and Buenos Aires. At Christy's in London, his checks, drawn on an obscure Argentinian bank, were accepted without question. After hundreds of grueling hours with teachers and tapes he'd mastered four languages, all without the trace of an accent. He was difficult to place. In fact, natives of England, Germany, France, and Argentina all assumed he was born in their country. It would never have occurred to them to think otherwise.

Hans and Michelle continued to walk for a long time without speaking. When they finally reached the beach he stopped.

"I'm going for a swim. Would you like to come?" he asked, placing a kiss on her forehead.

She shook her head. "I'll just lie out in the sun for awhile."

"Fine, I won't be long."

As he shed his sandals and watch, Michelle removed a blanket from the wicker basket she carried and carefully spread it out, smoothing down the lumps of sand with her hand.

Hans walked into the Mediterranean and dove headfirst into a churning wave, the saltwater filling his mouth. With a series of powerful strokes he propelled himself away from the shore. When he was in quiet water, out past the waves, he flipped onto his back and floated, offering no resistance to the drop and lift of the swells. Though his eyes were shut, the glare of the sun penetrated his skull. The water felt cold in comparison to the warm air. After awhile Hans almost succeeded in purging himself of all thoughts. Almost. He knew he should return immediately to his apartment in Nicosia. He should not be away when the weekly transmission was due in from Damascus; but the trip to Kyrenia was worth the risk. For months the cable traffic had been routine, and Michelle was a telephone operator at the Syrian Embassy—cultivating her favor might produce large rewards. Besides, he was tired, he deserved a rest. This weekend trip would cause no problems. Or so he tried to convince himself.

In the evening while she prepared dinner he built a fire in the pit outside the cabin. When the wood began to burn freely he sat on the ground and listened to the sounds of the surf pounding the rocks scattered along the coastline. He'd met Michelle several weeks ago. He'd seen her half a dozen times at the Ottoman Bank on Stasinos Avenue, a block from the Syrian Embassy; but it was not until he discovered she worked at the Arab legation that he approached her and struck up a conversation.

When Michelle brought out the skewers of souvlaki he took the handles and held the rows of beef, green peppers, and onions over the crackling flame. He liked his meat singed on the outside but rare on the inside. It

14

reminded him of people, encased by a shell of defenses, which when permeated leads to a soft, tender core.

"I've got Cokinelli and Pella," Michelle said. "Which would you prefer?"

"Pella," he answered immediately, choosing the semi-dry over the very dry Greek wine.

She returned in a moment with a tray bearing a tomato, cucumber, and avocado salad as well as the Pella. She lowered it to the grass area in front of the cabin, poured the red wine, and set the full glasses down by the settings she'd already arranged on wooden placeboards.

"The meat's ready," he said, moving toward her. As he slid the beef, onions, and peppers off the skewers and onto their plates, she dished out the salad. The smell of the souvlaki filled the air.

Michelle bit into a piece of meat causing the juice to trickle down her chin. She smiled and wiped it away with a napkin. Hans speared a large chunk of beef with his fork and popped it into his mouth. His face contorted, he grabbed at the Pella and drank, mixing the cold wine with the hot meat.

"Did you burn yourself?"

"No," he said, smiling.

She took a segment of green pepper off her plate, leaned over, and slipped it into his mouth. He chewed it slowly.

"Are you married?" she asked suddenly.

Hans thought about his wife and their childless union. It had been over three years since he'd seen her. He promised he'd try and be home for his fiftieth birthday six months ago, but he'd been unable to make it. At least he'd called.

"No, I've never been married," he said.

"A wise decision."

"Maybe."

15

"Have you ever considered marrying? I mean, you must meet dozens of attractive, intelligent women in the import-export business."

"Like yourself?" he teased her.

She laughed. "You forget, I'm already married."

He snapped his fingers. "It completely slipped my mind."

She put her knife and fork down and playfully lunged at him, pushing his shoulders to the grass and pinning them there.

"What do you intend to do now?"

Michelle smiled. "I don't know. I haven't thought that far ahead."

"Well I have." He kissed her, tasting the Pella on her breath, and reached for the zipper at the back of her blouse.

"Let me help," she said.

He nodded and she rolled to the side. They undressed in silence, the light from the fire creating shadows that danced among the trees.

The night air felt warm against their naked bodies. Hans lay on his back with her head on his chest, but for some reason his thoughts were elsewhere. Shattered specks of light pierced the heavens. He stared into the sky, made out the constellation Orion and tried to distinguish the colors of its four perimeter stars. Failing, he closed his eyes and listened to the interminable silence of the dark hunter, who seemed somehow to be trying to tell him something.

"What's the matter?" Michelle asked.

"Nothing."

"Are you sure?"

"Yes."

She kissed his shoulder and silently ran her nails along his spine. She really didn't care if he told her what was on his mind or not. Her assignment was not to understand him, not to extract information from him; but to keep him occupied, away from his apartment in the heart of Cyprus, away from his radio transmitter, away from the message he should have been receiving.

THREE

MAY

PRESSURE BUILT in Hans's ears and he felt the landing gear lock into position. Preparing for arrival, he took the white plastic coffee cup off the tray in front of him and handed it to a passing stewardess.

"How soon are we due in Frankfurt?" he asked her.

"We'll be landing at Rein-Main Field in seven minutes."

He thought about the ever punctilious Germans. It would not do for a Lufthansa stewardess to say five minutes, or ten minutes, when the precise figure was seven.

Three weeks had passed since Hans was ordered to liquidate his assets on Cyprus and fly to Germany. He wondered if he was to be reassigned immediately. He supposed he was. Agents simply were not presented with vacations or sabbatical leaves. Not that he minded; he couldn't think of anything he would want to do with time off. There was a ping above his head. He fastened his seatbelt and sank deeper into the cushion. He lacked any feeling of well-being now that the Cyprus operation was over. He thought only of the next mission.

Karl Richtman met Hans at the terminal, quickly ushered him into a small, beige Mercedes 250c, then sped out of the airport, accelerating rapidly onto the autobahn. Hans knew the route well. It was a short six miles along the Main River to the city.

"Where are you taking me?" Hans asked, as they raced through the wooded German countryside.

"Nowhere. I'm just going to drive long enough to make sure you weren't followed, then I'll head back to the airport. You have a flight to catch in less than an hour."

Hans hesitated before asking the next question.

"Where am I going?"

Richtman looked sideways at him. "You're going home."

Hans's face bore no expression of the emotion he felt. "For how long?"

"I haven't been told." He paused for a moment. "Would you like it to be permanent?"

Hans looked out at the tree-lined highway. Tall cypresses bent and straightened in the breeze. "I don't know. I haven't given the idea much thought."

"There is a limit to how long one can stay out there. I've been in Germany for two years and I can hardly wait to get home. You must be tired."

"Not too tired," Hans snapped.

"I didn't mean that," Richtman said apologetically. Hans sensed that he did. "We just heard there was some trouble on Cyprus."

"Is anyone following us?"

Richtman looked into the rear-view mirror. "The green Volkswagen's ours. It's the all-clear signal."

"Good."

Richtman swung the Mercedes off the autobahn and proceeded to the airport via a secondary highway. A strained silence separated the two men as the car darted through the traffic. Finally Hans turned and placed his hand on Karl's shoulder. "I'm sorry if I was short with you, but you hit me with quite a surprise. It's been awhile since I was home."

Richtman smiled. "I understand. It must be a long time since you've seen your wife."

"Three years, and then it was only for a month."

"It's rough. You know, I missed my son's graduation from the university." Richtman paused for a moment. "Maybe men like us have no right to marry."

Hans didn't respond.

As they parked in front of the departure terminal Richtman reached into his coat pocket. "Give me your Hans Hoffmann papers and I'll give you your own."

He nodded, reaching for the dark blue passport Richtman extended across the seat. Holding it in his hand, he fingered the gold embossed letters on the vinyl cover.

"You haven't forgotten who you are?" Richtman said jokingly.

"No."

Major Ari Ben-Sion of the Mossad Haelion Lemodiin Ubitachon, his country's supreme intelligence agency, slipped his Israeli passport into his coat pocket and headed for the El Al departure lounge.

As the Boeing 707 inched its way over the Aegean Sea, Ari took a final sip of his J & B, then lay back and closed his eyes. There was so much to think about, so many loose ends to tie up in Israel; but he preferred not to deal with any of that before he landed. He would sort out his life later. Now he would sleep.

He was jarred awake as the tires, locked into position below the wings, banged down on the concrete runway. The plane surged forward in the air, bounced, and began

20

to slow with the application of the engines' reverse thrust. Looking out the window, Ari saw that the lettering over the terminal read BEN GURION INTERNATIONAL AIRPORT. It had been LOD AIRPORT the last time he'd landed.

As he cleared customs he noticed the young men in olive uniform, short-muzzled Uzi submachine guns in hand, stationed at strategic points throughout the terminal. Not everything changes, he mumbled to himself, heading for the car rental desk. He gave the clerk his name, signed a form, and she handed him the keys to a car parked in stall number fourteen, directly across from the Egged bus stop. The Colonel, knowing Ari preferred to come in alone, always left him a vehicle.

Outside the odor of jet fuel hung in the air. Pushing a shopping-cart-like baggage carrier, Ari threaded his way past the *sheirut* drivers, loudly beckoning arriving passengers to share a taxi to Tel Aviv or Jerusalem, and headed toward the bus stop. The yellow and blue number 401 bus, idling in the street, black exhaust spewing from its rear, was loading passengers for the twenty-minute ride to Tel Aviv. Behind him at the Wimpy stand, hamburger patties were cooking on a greasy grill. Though Ari had slept through the meal on the plane he wasn't hungry. With the grinding of gears the bus pulled out and sped toward the security checkpoint just before the Petah Tikvah-Ramla highway.

Ari looked across the street. At the end of a row of empty stalls were two cars, a Peugeot 504 and an Israeli Susita. The numbers painted on the ground along the stalls had worn away and were illegible. Ari pushed the cart toward the Peugeot, his hands vibrating as the wheels rolled over the rough asphalt. Reaching into his pocket, he pulled out the keys the receptionist had given him, found the round-ended one, and inserted it in the lock. It wouldn't turn. He tried the other one. The result was the same. Looking at the keys more closely, he saw that the imprint on them was in Hebrew. He took hold of the cart and pushed it toward the Susita. The Colonel must be economizing.

Speeding into the Ramla junction, Ari veered to the left, choosing the familiar road that wound below the Latrun Monastery's terraced vineyards. Bypassing the highway that cut through the Arab village of Abu Gosh, where David had kept the Ark of the Covenant for two decades waiting to enter the holy city, would delay his arrival in Jerusalem by twenty minutes. But the Abu Gosh route was new—for that reason he avoided it.

On both sides of the road pines soared abruptly above the flat kibbutz fields, silent sentinels marking the entrance to Bab el Wad, the Gate of the Valley. From there Ari entered a narrow gorge and for twenty-five miles the ribbon of concrete climbed and twisted through rock and forest, cresting two thousand feet above the coastal plain. At several points on the side of the road lay the scorched steel skeletons remaining from the convoy that broke through to Jerusalem in the 1948 War of Independence. In a country where the past is a national obsession, they were constant reminders to what almost happened.

It was dark by the time Ari reached the outskirts of Romema and entered the city. Driving down Weizmann Street, he noticed that a new, cylindrical building, appearing about twenty stories high, had risen across from the central bus station. Though he'd never seen the windowed tower before, he knew it was a Hilton Hotel—he'd stayed in an identical structure in Nairobi. Turning into Ruppin Street, he proceeded into the rocky valley watched over by the Hebrew University on one side and the Knesseth, the Israeli Parliament, on the other. Ari

22

halted in front of a row of brown government buildings, built of stone, and left the car by the curb, under a sign that read NO PARKING AT ANY TIME. A few lights dotted the façade of the end building, nearest the Knesseth. One of them would be the Colonel's. He always worked late.

Ari bypassed the steel-reinforced front door, certain to be locked now, and moved down a narrow concrete walkway to the side of the Ministry. As he opened the unmarked night door and headed into the enclosed stairwell, a yellow light flashed on the security guard's desk in the lobby. Looking up at his overhead closed-circuit TV screen, the army sergeant followed the intruder's movements. Moments later Ari entered the small, dimly lit lobby and faced the boyish-looking sergeant.

"Ben-Sion to see the Colonel," he said.

The security guard pointed a commanding finger at the stranger. "Wait right there." Lowering his arm, he reached for the cables on the switchboard behind the desk and dialed the third floor. It took a few seconds for the Colonel to answer and tell the guard to send the man up. When he turned to do so, Ben-Sion was gone.

Ari walked hurriedly through the quiet corridors, not wanting to slow down and let the memories catch up with him. Reaching the Colonel's office, he paused for a moment, then entered without knocking. The Colonel moved out from behind his desk, and the two men hugged, holding each other close.

"It's been a long time," the Colonel said, breaking the embrace.

"Three years."

"It seems even longer." He reached for a small box on his desk and held it toward Ari. "Will you have a cigar? They're Dunhill Montecruz, hand-made in the Canary Islands and most mild. Take one." Ari withdrew one of the cedar-lined aluminum tubes, unscrewed the cap, and slipped out the cigar. But before he could strike a match the Colonel produced a lighter. Ari took it from him, lit the cigar, and handed the lighter back. "Excuse me, you must be tired," the Colonel said apologetically. "All the traveling and time change. Do sit down." As the Colonel moved behind the desk Ari dropped into a chair and cautiously faced the pudgy, balding man who was responsible for the security of the State of Israel. There had been no time change, Ari thought to himself; the hour he'd lost flying to Germany he'd regained by crossing back into the Middle East. The Colonel knew that.

"There were no problems with the flights, were there?"

"No."

"You met Karl in Frankfurt?"

Ari nodded. Of course he met Richtman in Frankfurt, how the hell else would he be in Jerusalem now.

The Colonel rose and moved to shut the window behind him. "We had a horrid winter this year—five feet of snow and no equipment to move it. The city was virtually paralyzed."

"I heard about it," Ari said, trying to push the impatience from his voice. The Colonel was exactly as Ari had remembered him: the slight smile, the verbal banality, the talking of trivia. He'd continued that way, probing for weak spots until his victim was caught off balance and easily tripped up.

"I hope they've warned you about the inflation; you're going to find food prices up something frightful since you were here last. We've been forced to devalue the pound nine times in the last twenty months."

Ari nodded dutifully.

The Colonel sat down, pushing aside the red-bannered afternoon edition of *Maariv* he'd not yet found time to read. "You know, Ari, I remember when you first entered the Service. You'd been at Deganya less than a year and already you were bored with kibbutz life. Running the British blockade three months after being liberated from Dachau had its effect. You'd caught the smell of adventure, martyrdom, nobility. Those qualities were no good to us, but we found beneath all that crap there was a sense of mission, of survival. So I took you, and my hunch proved to be right. Within two years you became one of my most valuable agents."

There was an uncomfortable pause, the silence broken only by the sound of an electric clock buzzing on the wall behind the Colonel's desk. Finally, Ari took a deep drag on his cigar and spoke.

"I was away from my receiver the twelfth of April when the weekly transmission came in from Damascus."

"Indeed," the Colonel said, as if Ari's words contained information he did not already possess. "A bit unlike you," he added, lighting a Montecruz for himself.

"I was following a lead near Kyrenia."

The Colonel screwed the top back on the cigar tube; he saved them for his grandchildren. "Did anything come of it?"

"No. It was a dead end."

"I see."

"It happens!" Ari said.

"Yes, it does." The Colonel nodded understandingly. "Dead ends eventually confront us all." The Mossad chief placed his glasses on the desk, rubbed his eyes, then looked up. "Ari, I was wondering if you'd had enough?"

"I don't understand."

"I was wondering if you were worn out, tired, if you wanted to quit spying."

He couldn't believe what the Colonel was saying. "You mean, do I want to stay in Israel?"

25

"Yes."

There was a long silence, each second seeming interminable.

"I'd rather not," Ari said finally.

The Colonel puffed on his cigar, then allowed the smoke to drift from his mouth. "I thought you'd say that." He knocked a short length of ash into the wastebasket at his feet. "Ari, I've got only three operations that are worth anything, and Hans Hoffmann is one of them. Your work's been of tremendous value to us, but even the best agents can't remain out there all the time. Everyone has to come in periodically, otherwise the loneliness—it becomes too strong to fight. Then, inevitably . . ." The Colonel stopped in midsentence and put his glasses back on. "Maybe we've made a mistake, maybe we've neglected you for too long. Maybe it's time."

Ari thought about all the airports and train stations he'd been in, the all-night vigils he'd undertaken, the gallons of coffee he'd drunk trying to stay awake and warm while his adversary slept in a heated apartment across the street.

"Time for what?" Ari said at last. "I don't understand what you're saying. What is it you want me to do?"

The Colonel leaned back in his chair. "I want you to take a few refresher courses—physical exercise, instruction in the use of some of the new explosives, that sort of thing. Ari, I want you to keep sharp. There are a lot of young agents on the way up who are begging for field assignment. I can't keep them in the background indefinitely." Ari said nothing so the Colonel went on. "And of course while you're here I'll want to make use of your experience; you might think about giving a few lectures and possibly you could spend some time in Operational Planning. I wouldn't be surprised if you came up with a suggestion or two. Some of those armchair theorists on the first floor have never been out of the country." Abruptly the Colonel ground out his cigar. "But enough of this for now. You just got in. You haven't even been home. We can talk again another time."

"Does Yael know I'm here?" Ari asked.

The Colonel nodded. "I had one of the girls phone a while ago and tell her you were due back this week. She's pretty shaky. I thought it best she had some time to prepare herself."

Ari rose. "Is that all?"

"I should think so." The Colonel moved across the room and accompanied him to the door. "Take as long as you need; when you're ready, report to Yehuda Shamir in room 312. He'll debrief you and arrange those refresher courses I mentioned."

"I'll be in tomorrow," Ari said flatly. Opening the door, he stepped into the hall, then turned back. "What about the car?"

"Oh that. Keep it for a week or so—until you're settled."

Ari nodded and moved slowly down the corridor.

Outside, he pushed up the collar of his jacket and walked along the empty street, listening to the echo of his footsteps. Lights shone from the windows of Givat Ram, the dormitories at the back of the Hebrew University campus. Ari wondered what it would have been like to attend a university. He kicked at an empty Goldstar beer can and sent it spinning into the rocks and weeds along the side of the road. Such speculation was pointless; he was only stalling. He shrugged and retraced his steps back toward the Susita. The Colonel had been even vaguer than usual. Ari wondered why.

Driving down Yafo Road into the heart of the New City, he turned left on Straus Street, passed the Bikur

Holim Hospital and headed into Mea Shearim, the orthodox quarter of Jerusalem. Though it was late, and the streets were virtually deserted, while Ari waited at a red light two frail men wearing long black gabardine coats and round fur-edged hats stepped off the curb and crossed in front of the Susita. Strolling arm in arm to lend each other support, they prodded the pavement with their sticks as they walked. Buried from dawn to dusk in the timeless world of books it was only at night that they ventured out for a breath of fresh air. After they'd passed, Ari eased down on the accelerator. Minutes later the street climbed the steep hill that opened into the northernmost tip of the city—Ramat Eshkol, a fashionable suburb built on land taken from Jordan during the Six Day War. Ari parked the car in front of number 12 Mitla Pass Road and ran his eyes along the rows of five-story stone buildings and manicured flower gardens, so characteristic of the newer sections of Jerusalem. All the streets in Ramat Eshkol: Nahal Zin, Straits of Tiran Street, Mishmar Hagvul, Parran Road, Ramat HaGolan Road, Midbar Sinai Way, were named after the sites of Israeli victories in the 1967 fighting. No street names anywhere in the country commemorate the battles of the Yom Kippur War.

Ari mounted the stone steps at the base of the building and pushed the red button on the wall to his left. Immediately the dark corridors were bathed in light. He now had sixty seconds to reach his door before the lights automatically shut off. Energy was conserved here. Suddenly the sound of several of Jerusalem's ubiquitous alley cats rose from the basement, their hissing and shrieking reverberating through the narrow corridors of the building. Ignoring them, Ari climbed the stairs to the fifth floor, inserted a key in the door at the end of the hall, and pushed himself inside—as if he were accustomed to doing so daily.

Yael was asleep on the couch. A black and white test pattern shone from the television; a half-empty bottle of Carmel 777 cognac lay on its side on the floor. Ari stood motionless at the entrance to the living room, surprised at how old his wife looked. Streaks of gray ran through her once ash-brown hair, and deep lines dug into the soft flesh beneath her eyes. Ari moved into the room and shut off the television set. She stirred groggily. Though he had ceased to love his wife long ago, it pained him to see her like this.

"Yael," he whispered as she slipped back into the fog accompanying alcoholic sleep.

At the sound of her name she opened her eyes. "Ari," she half cried.

He bent down and stroked her tangled hair. At the touch of his hand she stiffened, and buried her head in the cushion. He reached across the couch and gently took hold of her shoulder.

"No." She pushed his hand away, squeezing it as she did.

"Yael . . ."

"Go away. Why did you have to come back now, after so long."

"They want me to stay in Israel—for awhile."

"What difference will that make?" She turned away and pushed herself deeper in the couch. "I don't feel well," she said, her words muffled by the upholstery.

"Let me make you something hot to drink."

He rose and went into the kitchen without waiting for her to answer. Rummaging through the refrigerator, he couldn't find a bottle of milk. About to close the door and look in the cupboard for a jar of instant coffee he suddenly realized the plastic bag, mounted in the white holder he'd shoved to the side, contained milk. He took it out, warmed some, removed the skin which she hated, and brought a steaming mug into the living room.

Yael lay passed out on the couch, clutching the open cognac bottle in her arms. Ari set the milk down and removed the 777 from her grip. She mumbled something incomprehensible. Lifting his wife's unresisting body in his arms, he carried her into her room, drew back the bed covers, and slipped her underneath them—noticing as he left that a handful of multicolored pills were scattered over the nightstand.

Restless, he opened the sliding glass door and stepped out onto the narrow balcony. The night air was cool. Ari looked into the distance and imagined he could make out the ring of lights that surround Jerusalem like satellites: to the east, Jerico; to the north, Ramallah; to the south, Bethlehem. Closer by, atop a high peak to the west, the tower of Nebi Samuel stood silhouetted in the bluish white moonlight. There the prophet who lent his name to the peak sat in judgment over the nation of Israel; followed nine hundred years later by the Maccabees, who fasted on the same spot before they swept down on the Romans occupying their city. Ari had hiked to Nebi Samuel many times. From there, staring across the Bab el Wad valley, Jerusalem looked like a metropolis cast randomly atop a series of desolate mountains, with no rivers, no sustaining fields, in fact no reason for existing, except the belief in men's minds.

Ari stood there for a long time thinking about what the Colonel had said, wondering how long it would be before he was given a new assignment. Finally he went inside and fell asleep on the couch.

Rising early the following morning, he left the apartment, drove to the Sanhedria Pension in the Bukharian quarter just outside Mea Shearim, and rented a room.

FOUR

MAY, JUNE, JULY

IN THE SUMMER of 1947, after being warned that the Zbrojovka Brno arms works in Prague would deal only with the authorized representative of a sovereign nation, a young, virtually untried Haganah intelligence lieutenant managed to acquire eight signed and sealed blank letterheads from the Paris legation of Ethiopia. The desperately ill-equipped provisional Jewish government in Palestine was immediately able to purchase ten thousand Model E-18 Mausers, one hundred MG-34 submachine guns, and several million accompanying cartridges. No one asked where the letterheads came from. Ari did not volunteer an explanation. Then a decade later a mysterious sabotage incident occurred at the outbreak of the Sinai Campaign. At dawn on October 29, 1956, a Soviet Ilyushin with half the Egyptian General Staff on board plunged into the Mediterranean somewhere off the coast of Lebanon. In its baggage compartment was a small chest bought by an Egyptian general as a gift for his wife. It had been purchased at a discount from a recently opened import-export firm, Hans Hoffmann Ltd.

And now—refresher courses.

After Ari was debriefed Yehuda Shamir gave him a

32

dog-eared Royal Canadian Air Force Exercise Manual, explaining that it was better than anything they had in Hebrew, and suggested he work out on his own. There had been a time when Ari daily did calisthenics before breakfast, but over the years, he couldn't remember exactly when, he'd replaced the knee bends with coffee and a cigarette. Following the Canadian system he exercised each morning for twenty minutes. After the fifth day he accidentally misplaced the manual. He didn't ask for another one.

On the pistol range Ari discovered, much to his surprise, that his aim was way off. He checked out a Llama Model VIII 9-mm automatic pistol, choosing the nine-shot .38 over the seven-shot .45, and began practicing an hour each afternoon. After a few days his accuracy improved considerably, but it never quite matched his old performance levels. His scores were still kept on file in the room on the second floor of the walled police compound directly across from the central post office on Yafo Road.

Ari was given some instruction in the new uses of explosives. The Colonel was particularly fond of tetryl, a high-power charge made from dimethylaniline and nitric acid, which when inserted in a tobacco pipe or ballpoint pen turned those implements into lethal weapons —but these lessons were occasional and brief. Ari spent most of his time in Operational Planning. Due to his familiarity with London he was asked to evaluate the feasibility of recruiting, as quasi-operatives, a number of the numerous East End Jewish taxicab drivers who regularly made the run to Heathrow Airport. Theoretically at least, he read from a file, it should be possible for them to queue in the ranks outside incoming Soviet and Arab flights, pick up specially targeted passengers, and rifle

33

their briefcases, which normally were placed in the empty space next to the driver, below the rear-riding customer's field of vision. Ari wrote a lengthy evaluation detailing the positive and negative aspects of the plan, including in it an additional section on the possible consequences to his country's relations with England should one of the cab drivers be caught and confess that he was working for the Israeli government. Ari was in favor of mounting the operation, but to protect Israel he strongly suggested the Mossad limit its contact to one carefully selected British Jew, who could then do the necessary recruiting under the auspices of a local fringe movement, possibly the Heirut party.

Ari wrote his report rapidly in the hope that the sooner he finished, the closer he would be to a field assignment. In actuality his superiors were so pleased at the speed and insight with which he completed his analysis of the projected operation that the case histories of three Egyptian agents, earmarked for study by the Colonel's administrative aides, were diverted to his desk.

The weeks bumped into each other. A month passed, followed by another, then another. The paperwork piled up. As soon as he completed one assignment another took its place. Ari began to drink, not a lot, but more than he had before. He firmly believed the solution to personal difficulties was rigorous self-discipline. Knowing exactly how much Scotch he could swallow before his intellectual capabilities diminished, he never exceeded that limit. But recently he'd been reaching it more often.

Several times Ari spoke to the Colonel, requesting reassignment to Europe. Cordial as always, the Colonel praised him lavishly for the work he'd done since returning to Israel, but said little else. Growing increasingly restless as he realized he was becoming more than a temporary pencil and paper pusher, Ari pressed for a date when he could plan on going abroad. The Colonel intimated that he didn't have one and didn't know when he would. In the meantime, he added, the Service must utilize each man where he was most needed. For once Ari fully understood him. Everyone in intelligence life paid homage to that sacrament.

Unknown to Ari there was quite a lot of whispering going on about him during his colleagues' coffee breaks and lunch hours. Everyone seemed to be speculating about the reason for his reassignment to Operational Planning, but nobody could get close enough to him to learn his side of the story. It was rumored he'd made a mistake on Cyprus, that somehow he was connected to the capture of Dov Elon in Damascus, and didn't even know it. No one was sure of the facts. All agreed, though, that in his time he'd been one of the best field agents the Mossad ever had. And probably still was, many thought.

From the Bukharian quarter Ari walked toward the center of town. The afternoon was warm and pleasant. Soon he passed the black and white sawhorses drawn across Yehezkel Street by the police at sundown every Friday night to keep vehicles out of Mea Shearim during the twenty-four-hour Sabbath observance. Inside the orthodox quarter young men in their white, open-throated shirts and girls in white Sabbath dresses laced with colored embroidery mixed comfortably with the bearded Jews wearing long black gabardines and their modestly dressed wives, many of whom were pushing baby carriages through the open streets.

Ari was hungry. Generally he took his meals at the Restaurant Stark on King George Road, but on Saturdays, when the Jewish restaurants in Jerusalem were closed, he walked into the Old City and patronized the Arabs.

Crossing toward the police barrier at the end of Straus Street that marked the southern boundary of Mea Shearim, Ari noticed a young woman, partially hidden in the shadow of the massive Histadrut building, pointing a camera with a telephoto lens at a bearded, black-garbed Jew seated on a stone step near the corner. Hurriedly he moved toward her.

"I wouldn't do that," he said in English. Her clothing and her expensive Nikon photographic equipment told him she was one of the numerous American tourists who invaded Israel in the summer.

"What?" she said, lowering her camera and revealing a striking face.

Ari pointed toward the old man. "He would consider it a personal affront and a desecration of the Sabbath."

"Oh, I'm sorry.. I didn't realize." Her cheeks reddened. "Thank you for telling me." The woman, tall, apparently in her late twenties, had blue-gray eyes shaded by dark lashes, and dimples that deepened when she talked. The front strands of her champagne-colored hair, parted down the middle, curled as they fell along the sides of her face. She wore a V-cut peasant blouse exposing a gold necklace and the upper curves of well-formed breasts. Her nails were long and clear; Ari immediately noticed that she used little makeup.

"Your accent." She hooked her camera strap over one shoulder. "Are you British?"

"Something like that," he said, anticipating the next series of questions and knowing his pride would prevent him from telling her he was a former spy put out to pasture to tend a flock of papers.

"That's encouraging. These Israelis have been driving

me crazy. They're all hands." She smiled, suddenly seeing his small blue eyes. They were attractive. "My name's Kim Johnson."

"Hans Hoffmann," he said, returning her smile. "And don't worry about the local men, if anyone becomes excessively aggressive just give him a curt *bli yadayim*. It means hands off. He'll get the message."

"Bli yadayim," she repeated out loud. "Thank you, I'll make use of that." She picked up the leather case at her feet. "You'll have to excuse me but I must be heading back to my hotel. I didn't realize the restaurants would be closed and I haven't eaten since this morning." She slipped her camera in the case and zipped the top closed. "Thanks again for the advice." She turned and started to walk toward Yafo Road.

He stood there for a moment. The last months had been unbearably lonely . . .

"Wait a second," he said, catching up with her. "I was just going to have an early dinner in the Old City. Would you like to join me?"

She hesitated.

"I know a great place, the Golden Arabesque Restaurant. It's got everything: ceiling-to-ceiling Oriental rugs, arched wooden porticos, hanging beads, camel saddles for seats."

"Does it have food too?"

"Of course. They serve the most exquisite Middle Eastern cuisine south of Beirut—tender mansaf, savory kebab, succulent chicken. So, are you coming?"

A smile etched her lips. "Sure, why not?"

As they walked toward the Old City Ari thought about how alone he was—then pushed the realization out of his mind.

Yafo Road, its shops shuttered, its sidewalks deserted, testified to Jerusalem's rigorous observance of the day of rest, differing from sections of the country, like heretical Haifa, where buses and some businesses operated seven days a week. Reaching the end of Yafo Road, they gazed upon the walls of the Old City, proud barriers imprisoning Old Jerusalem in a massive belt of stone. Hidden inside a maze of vaulted alleyways and dark passages were sixty thousand people: Jews, Moslems, Christians, and Armenians—each sealed by race and rite into separate quarters. Ari bypassed Yafo Gate, certain to be crowded with tourists and nonreligious Israelis, and they entered the Old City via Damascus Gate, across from the East Jerusalem bus station and the spires of St. Stephen's Church. Passing through the walls, they mounted a ceramic-tile staircase leading to the Golden Arabesque Restaurant.

Inside, rows of hanging beads divided the dimly lit dining room into semi-private cubicles. Bowing in welcome, the maître d' guided them to a low carved-legged table, surrounded by red pillows, and bearing a round brass tray for a top. An Oriental rug blanketed the floor. Lanterns hung from the ceiling. Wailing music, turned low, played in the background.

"What about the camel saddle seats?" Kim asked as they settled onto the soft cushions.

"If you would like one," the maître d' said. "At another of our tables . . ."

"No, that is quite all right." After the maître d' handed them menus and left, she turned to Ari. "You weren't kidding about the saddles, were you?"

"No." He glanced at the menu, then closed it. "Do you like lamb?"

She nodded, knocking the brass table with her knee as she shifted position.

"Good. It's the only thing to order in an Arab restaurant. Most of the beef in the Middle East comes from

38

Argentina. It loses something during the voyage."

He motioned to the waiter, who approached immediately. "We'll have mezza and kebab for two," he said. "And bring a bottle of Cabernet Sauvignon select, 1969 if you have it."

The waiter nodded and moved through the beads.

"They have French wine here," Kim said in surprise.

"Not exactly. The wine served in the Old City is Carmel, grown in Rishon le Zion. But the Cabernet Sauvignon select has an unusually delicate bouquet; it's as good as anything Barton and Guestier or Bouchard bottles."

"You seem very familiar with the country. I take it you live in Israel?"

"I do for varied periods of time," he explained. "I'm in the import-export business. I purchase merchandise in the Middle East and South America and sell it in Europe." He slipped back into his alter ego effortlessly; in many ways he was as much Hans Hoffmann as he was Ari Ben-Sion.

Just then the waiter arrived carrying a round copper tray bearing the Cabernet Sauvignon and the tiny dishes comprising the mezza. As he poured the wine and spread the small portions of dips, salads, meats, sauces, and vegetables on the table before them Kim looked at Ari in amazement.

"This is incredible. You'll have to tell me what all these things are."

He took a piece of flat pita bread and dabbed it into one of the dips. "I'll start you with tehina, but after that you experiment on your own." He brought the piece of bread to her mouth and she took a bite, then savored the taste for a moment.

"What is it?"

"Ground sesame seeds."

"I like it."

As she reached for the shakshouka, highly spiced vegetables sautéed in oil, Ari took a sip of the cool wine and looked up at her. "Are you here as a tourist?" he asked, wondering about her last name, which obviously wasn't Jewish.

She shook her head. "No, I'm in the Middle East for a combination of professional and personal reasons. I've been commissioned by *People* magazine to do a photographic essay on women whose husbands were killed in the 1973 War. The assignment will take me to Cairo when I finish in Jerusalem." She tore off a piece of the pita bread. "As for the personal reason—I'm running away from a bad marriage."

Ari nodded sympathetically. He liked her candor; it was refreshing.

"Something you prefer not to talk about?"

"Not really," she said. "I find the more open I am about my past the more readily people I'm with will share the details of theirs." She scooped a tiny mound of homous onto the pita and chewed it thoughtfully. "Ted and I met in college and thought we were perfect for each other. You know, same age, same background, same upper-middle-class upbringing, et cetera. He became an architect and I went into free-lance photography. Soon after the wedding I started selling my pictures but due to the recession in the United States none of the construction firms were hiring. I had to support both of us. He grew irritable and increasingly hostile every time I made a sale. Finally he took a job in a bookstore. Then came drugs. For four years I tried to make the marriage work, but I couldn't. In the end I walked out." She drained her glass. "It hurt, particularly the fear that my success had contributed to his suffering."

"I understand the feeling," he said softly.

Soon the kebab, chunks of grilled lamb marinated in finely cut onions, spices, and marjoram and arranged on hot metal plates, was set before them.

"You must travel a lot in your business," Kim said, spearing a piece of lamb with her fork.

"Yes, I do."

"Traveling can become terribly lonely. I mean living out of suitcases and hotels all the time, making friends, then having to leave. Do you enjoy it?"

His mouth momentarily full, he nodded. "If you make close friends they'll always be there regardless of how much time elapses between visits; and if the relationships are not the same when you return that means they weren't good friends in the first place, so you've lost nothing." His words left him uneasy; they were too logical, too sterile. He wondered if his recent malaise wasn't the result of more than being chained to a desk, if even reassignment to the field wouldn't leave him empty, alone.

"That's fine when you meet people who live in places you return to," she said, refilling her glass. "But what happens when you become close to someone there's little likelihood you'll see again once you move on?"

He pushed the rice pilaf around his plate. He had no answer to that.

After dinner they walked through the Christian quarter toward the New Gate, one of the seven portals allowing access to the Old City. The night was cool and comfortable. Sharp stars winked in the sky. As they neared the gate he took her hand and they mounted a narrow stone stairway alongside the wall. The ramparts, replete with crenellations and towers, continuously knocked down and reconstructed over the centuries, were most recently erected by Suleiman the Magnificent during the Ottoman period.

41

They walked side by side along the parapet until they reached a ledge projecting out of the stone. Sitting down, they gazed over the city in silence. The houses flowed into each other with almost no space between them. Their white stone roofs, domed so that the pressure from the winter snow would not collapse them, shimmered in the luminous night.

In the foreground the twin cupolas and the Romanesque belfry crowning the dark, incense-filled caverns of the Church of the Holy Sepulchre protruded from the hill at Golgotha, where it's presumed Jesus Christ was crucified. Farther away, rising from the plaza where the Temple of Solomon had stood, the golden-domed Mosque of Omar sat serenely at the center of its spacious esplanade, the smaller, silver-domed al-Aksa Mosque stationed off to the side. Looking beyond the Old City wall, past the Biblical Valley of Jehoshaphat, Ari followed the terraced graveyard covering the Mount of Olives to the wooded groves of Gethsemane. From there his eye shot upward to Mount Scopus and the buildings of the university, pale fingerlike structures silhouetted against the black sky.

"You know, it's funny," Kim said, parting the silence. "But I'm as mixed up religiously as this city is."

Ari waited for her to explain.

"My father was Protestant and my mother Jewish, so they compromised and brought me up nothing."

"Maybe you're better off," he said, pleased that she was legally Jewish and surprised that he cared.

"I don't think so. I would rather have been given one faith or the other. It's important to believe in something, particularly for children."

"Do you have any preference between the two?"

"Not really. But I guess I know more about Christianity than I do about Judaism. My parents are dead, but

42

when I was young, even though they agreed to ban religion from the house, sometimes my father would tell me stories about Jesus. I still remember them pretty well." She leaned back against his shoulder. "I think one of the reasons I took this assignment was because I hoped to learn more about Judaism while I was in Israel."

"There's no better place to do that than Jerusalem," he said, gazing out at the brightly floodlighted spot, below the Mosque of Omar, that marked the site of the Wailing Wall. There, even now, a handful of black-coated Jews, bobbing back and forth to the rhythmic chants of their ancient prayers, watched over the thousands of petitions to God, written on scraps of paper, and wedged into the cracks and crevices of the great stone blocks of the Wall.

Surrounded by the sounds of night they talked for a long time—rushing into an evening the type of unburdening that usually takes weeks. Strangers adrift, they tried to compress time, to cover their backgrounds in a burst. She shared at length the story of the souring of her marriage and he spoke about a wife who'd disintegrated into an alcoholic. She confessed to tremendous feelings of guilt and he admitted that he bore a similar burden. She talked about the important part a career plays in forming a person's self-image and he readily agreed. Finally it grew cold and they abandoned the walls and took a taxi to the New City.

After sundown Jewish Jerusalem burst back to life. Lights popped on, movie marquees lit up, restaurants and bars opened their doors, and by the hundreds the city's inhabitants swarmed into the downtown triangle formed by the intersection of King George, Ben Yehuda, and Yafo streets. The rich aroma of roasting coffee floated over the crowd as Jerusalemites wandered up and down Ben Yehuda drifting from café to café, invariably

43

bumping into friends they greeted with noisy shouts of recognition.

Kim and Ari waded through a throng of people and ducked into the stark and brilliantly lit Café Atara, where luckily they found an empty table on the second floor. Ordering espresso and pastry, they ate in silence, content to people-watch. Afterward he walked her to the Eden Hotel on Hillel Street. Retrieving her key from the desk clerk, they stepped into the elevator, both wondering what the other was thinking. Once inside her room she moved toward a cassette player on the dresser and snapped in a tape. The nordic tones of Edvard Grieg's *Peer Gynt Suite* floated through the air.

"I had a lovely evening," she said, turning to face him.

He crossed the room, sensing the softness of the body outlined under her cotton blouse. Placing one hand on her waist, he brought their mouths together. Her lips, warm and pliant, roamed over his. Her fingers circled the small of his back. He breathed in the musky fragrance of her perfume. As the *Morning Movement* ended they moved onto the bed.

FIVE

AUGUST

ARI SAT on the stone platform of the outdoor amphi-
theater atop Mount Scopus separating the segments of
a Jaffa orange. A few feet away Kim, the ends of the scarf
tied around her neck flapping in the breeze, stood at the
edge of the rear balustrade, peering out over the gorge
at the Wilderness of Judah. The barren hills, broken by
deep ravines winding down through the rocky slopes to
the Dead Sea, were a blazing brown. The sea itself shone
as the sun touched its water.

"Do you want some?" Ari asked, removing the white
pith from the orange.

She shook her head no.

He checked his watch, which read three-thirty. During
the summer, in order to eat their major meal of the day
and hide from the heat, most Jerusalemites went home
between one and four, then returned to their jobs and
worked until seven. Ari would have to leave soon if he
wanted to be back at the Ministry in half an hour. But he
was in no hurry to do so. He'd been with Kim for close
to three weeks; he knew when something was on her
mind, and he knew she'd tell him when she was ready. He
would wait.

A few minutes later she sat down, took a segment of

45

orange off the brown bag in front of him, and tossed it in her hand.

"I have to be going soon."

"You taking more pictures this afternoon?"

"No, I'm finished with that." She looked at the cliffs rising on the Jordanian side of the Dead Sea. "You don't understand. I meant leaving Israel."

He peered past her toward the Arava, where the Hills of Judea broke off and the desert began.

"I can't very well photograph Egyptian war widows from here," she explained. "Originally I wanted to be in Cairo more than a week ago."

A sadness started to press down on him but he said nothing. She leaned over and kissed his cheek.

"When?" he asked.

"I don't know. I want to stretch it out as long as possible. Maybe another ten days." She tossed the piece of orange back on the bag, brought her hands to his shoulders and kneaded his flesh. "Let's not discuss it now. I had a long morning in Jericho; I'm too tired to talk. Besides, you said you had a meeting at the Trade Ministry at four—you don't want to be late."

He nodded and began picking up the scraps remaining from their lunch.

"Can we have dinner?" she asked.

For the first time since she started speaking he smiled. "Of course, I'll meet you at the hotel at seven-thirty." He rose, took her hand, and helped her up.

They walked back through the rows of vacant seats in silence.

Ari sat at his desk not even pretending to work; the depression he fought consciously now, deepening. A side of him long dead had burst alive in the past three weeks. He could not, would not, let her go. Though he

46

knew quite well that a relationship with a woman was not enough to sustain him, he'd realized recently that its absence was part of what was wrong with his life. Somehow he'd figure out a way to stay with her. It had to be possible. But an entire afternoon's agitated thought brought no solution to his dilemma.

A little before seven Ari, staring blankly into the corridor, heard the sound of approaching footsteps. As the Colonel hurried by he looked in and for a long second their eyes met. The Colonel's forward momentum carried him past the door but he turned back and entered the cubicle where Ari worked.

The bare-walled, windowless office contained a formica desk and a gray steel filing cabinet. There was no room for an additional chair, but at least Ari had the privacy he'd requested.

"How are you doing?" the Colonel asked.

"I hate what I'm doing," Ari said, taking a paper clip off his desk and reshaping the wire into a line. "I'm bored, restless, and anxious to get out of here."

The Colonel nodded. "I understand, but do be patient. We'll have something for you eventually." He took a Dunhill Montecruz from his inside coat pocket and screwed the cap off the aluminum tube. "Actually I've got something now, but I don't think it's quite your type of assignment."

"What is it?"

The Colonel lit his cigar and waved the match out in the air. "Several days ago I received a message from the Chief Rabbi and the Headmaster of the Alliance Israélite Universelle school in Damascus. They're worried about the safety of their families. An American news program called 'Sixty Minutes' recently broadcast a second report showing that Jews in Syria are not suffering under the Baath regime. As a result the Syrian government, feeling

47

free now to do what it wants, has begun cracking down on the leaders of the Jewish community, blaming them for the initial bad publicity. The Chief Rabbi and the Headmaster of the Alliance school have asked us to take their children out of the ghetto so they can't be used against them." The Colonel chewed on the end of his cigar, drawing the hot smoke into his mouth. "But an assignment to cope with the repercussions of an American television program isn't important enough for you. I'm going to send Shaul Barkai and another junior officer." He glanced at his watch and yawned. "You must excuse me, it's nearly seven and I still have a pile of paperwork to wade through before I can get out of here." He moved toward the door, then turned back. "Don't be too concerned, Ari—eventually something appropriate for you will come up. It's just a matter of time."

As he left Ari began doodling on the corner of a classified report. While the Colonel was talking it had struck him that he could volunteer for the mission. But this assignment wasn't at all what he was accustomed to—this Operation Breastfeed, this Operation Nursemaid. His field was military intelligence. He'd spent his life concerned with matters critical to the survival of Israel. How could he volunteer for . . .

He lit a cigarette and thought about Cyprus. He shouldn't have been away from his receiver. The Colonel had been angry. Maybe . . . by going to Syria, by saving the lives of a handful of children he could atone for his carelessness. More than even the score.

"Shit," he mumbled to himself. "Come on, Ari, this kind of sentimental crap is exactly the stuff the characters say in those lousy plays at the Habima Theater in Tel Aviv. Besides, the Colonel's right. This assignment isn't important enough."

Abruptly he ground out his cigarette and headed for

the hallway. Any field work was a hell of a lot better than what he was doing at the moment.

The Colonel had just finished a cup of coffee and was about to go over the most recent transmission from the Gideon network in Egypt when he heard a sharp knock on his door.

"Come in," he said, looking up in surprise as Ari entered. "Did I forget something in your office?" he asked.

"No." Ari noticed that there was a new Matisse reproduction hanging on the wall behind the Colonel's desk. "I was just thinking about what you said."

"Yes." The seams and wrinkles around his eyes tightened, demanding further explanation.

"It's about taking those kids out of Damascus. I'd like to do it."

The Colonel closed the file in front of him and pushed it to the side. "Ari, this is not the type of mission I'm inclined to send you on. First of all, to be quite honest, it's not exactly top drawer and second and more importantly, I'm looking for an agent who can pass as an Arab. That's why I want Shaul Barkai."

"But you said you needed two agents. What about Hans Hoffmann?"

The Colonel rubbed the back of his neck. "I really don't think it's a good idea."

"Why not? As a wealthy businessman anxious to purchase large quantities of furniture and textiles he would be able to move freely inside Syria."

A long silence followed.

Slowly the Colonel got up and walked around the room, searching for an ashtray. He found one, put it by his chair, then ignored it. His thoughts were elsewhere.

"Well, what do you think?" Ari asked finally.

Pacing behind his desk, the Colonel began mumbling out loud. "Hans Hoffmann could gain access to the German colony in Damascus. And from there, yes, if he had a good cover story . . . possibly as an ex-SS officer . . . and you do know Dachau well." He stopped and looked directly at Ari. "It could work. But are you sure you . . ."

"I'm sure," Ari said forcefully, drowning out the rest of his sentence.

"It just might be a good idea at that." The Colonel settled back into his soft chair. "All right, I'll send you to Syria. Pack a suitcase and take the bus down to Kibbutz Revivim the day after tomorrow. Report to Yosef Tsur. I'll tell him to be expecting you."

Ari nodded.

"Okay, that's all. Now leave me alone so I can work out the details."

Buoyed by a sense of hope Ari thanked him and left. He'd never been to Revivim but he knew about the kibbutz, located thirty-five miles southwest of Beersheva. There on a desolate stretch of the Negev desert, behind the hills outside the settlement, the Mossad had constructed a walk-through scale model of Damascus.

Throughout the evening Kim suspected that something had happened that afternoon; after they made love she was sure of it. It was as if a heavy weight had been knocked off his shoulders and he could charge into every activity with renewed relish. Kim wondered how long the change would last. Several times she asked if anything special had occurred that day. Each time he brushed aside her queries with a kiss and a terse no. She knew better than to press him; like most successful women she'd learned that was not the way to get what she wanted.

As they lay entwined in the soft afterglow of sex she ran her fingers from his buttocks up his spine to the nape of his neck then back again. After a few minutes he took her hand in his, brought it to his lips, and brushed the knuckles with a kiss.

"I want to ask you something," he said, turning to face her.

She looked at him, her blue-gray eyes bright in the darkness.

"I just had an idea. The way things have worked out I find I'm going to be flying to Damascus to purchase a rather large quantity of Arab textiles and furniture. I may be there for several weeks or longer. I don't know yet. The point is, you could do the other half of your photographic essay from Syria instead of Egypt. It shouldn't make much difference which of Israel's major adversaries you cover." A note of expectancy edged his voice. "We could meet in Damascus."

Silence filled the room.

"Kim . . ."

No response.

"Do you want to?"

"I don't know," she said, restlessly shifting position under the covers. "What about *my* plans?"

"It seems silly for you to be in Cairo while I'm in Damascus."

"Couldn't you buy similar merchandise in Egypt?"

"No."

She propped a pillow against the headboard and leaned back against it. As he moved near, touching his mouth to her thigh, she outlined his nose with her forefinger. "I do want to stay with you. I guess I could cable my editor. I don't think he'd mind if I . . ."

He pulled her down to him and covered the rest of her sentence with his lips. She snuggled against his chest. Her skin felt warm where it met his. Her scent was familiar, comforting.

Gradually they came together trying to freeze the

51

sweep of time, to hold onto the moment, to keep it from receding into the past. Breathing audibly, they rocked back and forth; Ari surging into a rolling climax, followed seconds later by Kim. Afterward they both drifted asleep.

Ari arrived at Kibbutz Revivim Tuesday afternoon, at the peak of the sun's arc across the heavens. The fiery ball, consuming an entire quadrant of the sky, sucked all moisture from the air. The kibbutz, set in the midst of rolling hills of rock and arid earth, survived on water piped down from the north. Walking along a row of white stucco cottages surrounded by patches of grass and leafy palms, he asked directions to the communal dining room and was taken there by a brown-skinned girl wearing shorts and sandals. Yosef Tsur, a slight, thin-faced man with a pencil moustache, was waiting for him inside.

After lunch, Tsur, a Syrian Jew who had escaped from Damascus in 1961, took Ari to his cottage, a one-room house on the fringes of the kibbutz with a window facing the desert. The walls of the cottage, bare now, would soon be covered with aerial photographs of Damascus. Ari was told to rest. Avraham Mendelssohn, an expert in the history and internal workings of the Waffen SS, would be in to see him at five.

For the next eight days Ari's time was split between Tsur and Mendelssohn. Up at five-thirty to escape the summer sun, which was unbearable by eleven; each morning Tsur drove him by jeep to the mile-long scale model where a host of Israeli agents had first familiarized themselves with the Syrian capital. Over and over again Tsur walked him through the streets of Damascus, spending a large chunk of time in the southeast sector of the inner city—the Haret al Yahoud, the guarded ghetto where Damascus's three thousand Jews were imprisoned.

In the evenings and nights, Mendelssohn drilled Ari on everything he needed to know to pass as an SS officer. He reviewed the titles, modes of address, collar insignias and the types of uniforms worn at various occasions, quickly—for they were already etched on Ari's mind. He remembered them from Dachau. Next Mendelssohn rushed him through the ideological course he would have received had he been trained at the SS police school near Rabka in the Carpathian Mountains. Then came the marching songs, drinking songs, and various unit songs. In the past Mendelssohn had always spent a minimum of several weeks turning former German Jews into SS officers, but the Colonel had ordered him to take only eight days this time. Ari was expected to move socially among the Nazis, not penetrate their organization. Consequently, he need not be letter perfect. Though Mendelssohn thought his instructions a bit unusual, he didn't question them.

The following Wednesday Ari took the bus back to Jerusalem, where the Colonel outlined the steps he and Lieutenant Barkai were to take to bring Chief Rabbi Sassoon's and Headmaster Kimche's seven children safely to Israel. For security reasons, from this point on, the mission was to be referred to only as Operation Goshen: the Biblical name of the land the Hebrew slaves inhabited before Moses led them out of Egypt.

When the particulars of the briefing had been laid out and all questions answered the Colonel stacked the papers scattered in front of him and turned to Ari.

"Now, if and only if something of a desperate urgency arises you can contact our permanently placed agent in Syria, Operative Sixty-six."

Surprised, Ari looked up at the Colonel. "There've

always been rumors. For years I've heard we've had somebody high up in the Baath Party but it's never been confirmed. How did . . ."

"Don't ask any questions," the Colonel said, cutting him off. "Operative Sixty-six is a member of the Syrian Parliament. He was a sleeper agent for twelve years. You needn't know more than that. As the last of the last resorts here's how you reach him . . ."

After he'd gone over the procedure for contacting Operative 66 Ari rose to leave. But the Colonel halted him with a sweep of his hand.

"Just one more thing. While you're with the Nazis, if you could find out how much they know about Dov Elon and how much he's told his interrogators it would be most helpful."

Ari nodded and continued toward the door, aware from a lifelong association with the Colonel that his casual, last-minute orders were invariably crucial—occasionally, they even superseded the primacy of the original assignment. He took the Mossad chief's request and filed it in the back of his mind. The Colonel's offhand tone betrayed the importance of his words; Ari would not forget either.

After spending a final night with Kim and arranging to meet her at the New Ommayad Hotel in Damascus, he flew to Frankfurt.

SIX

SEPTEMBER 4

GUY LAVALLE sat in his room in the Ledra Palace Hotel staring out the window. Across Marcos Drakos Avenue stood the ancient Venetian wall which still surrounded the old city of Nicosia. At the base of the wall, near United Nations Square, someone had painted the word ENOSIS—the name of the nationalist movement, active intermittently since 1878, that favored the union of Cyprus with Greece. Beyond the arrow-shaped battlements that topped the enormous ramparts Lavalle could see the twin minarets spiraling above the skyline from the Turkish section of the old city. They belonged to St. Sophia's, once a magnificent crusader cathedral, now the equally splendid Selimiye Mosque.

Moving across the room, Lavalle picked up the phone on the nightstand and dialed. If all went well he would be back on the Continent in the morning. The phone rang for a long time. Just as he was about to hang up someone answered.

"Hello." The female voice sounded half asleep.

"Michelle Giroux?"

"Yes."

"I think I have some information you might be interested in."

"Who is this?" she asked suspiciously, pushing away the covers.

"My name is of little importance. I could give you any one of a dozen, but you may call me Guy if you like."

Michelle sat on the edge of the bed and ran her fingers against her hair. It was nine A.M. She was not her best until after lunch. "What kind of information?"

"It's about a mutual friend, or should I say adversary."

Michelle lit a cigarette and inhaled slowly. "What are you selling and how much do you want?"

Lavalle laughed into the receiver. "I see then that we understand each other."

"What are you selling?" she repeated coldly. Like most agents Michelle approached the informer with contempt, particularly when he possessed quality information; for the better the information the greater the fear that lurking among one's own colleagues was a malcontent, anxious to buttress his deflated ego by selling you out.

"Do you know a Hans Hoffmann?" Lavalle asked, slowly reeling out the bait.

"If I didn't, there wouldn't be much point to this call, would there?" Michelle decided to play his game; she was excited. Hans Hoffmann had been her biggest assignment before he'd gone back to Europe and disappeared. It had taken her months of standing in line at the Ottoman Bank before she'd been able to lure him into initiating a conversation. Her superiors would reward her appreciably for additional information about the Israeli.

"Then you're interested?"

"That depends on the extent of your information and the price." Michelle ground out her cigarette and nervously lit another one.

"Would you be interested in knowing where he is right now?"

"How much?"

"Five thousand French francs."

"How will I know you're telling the truth?"

Lavalle tugged at his short, dark beard. "You won't."

"Where can we meet?" Michelle asked.

"Have the money this afternoon. I'll be outside Salim's Oriental Bazaar in the Turkish quarter at two o'clock."

"How will I recognize you?"

"I'll recognize you."

He hung up. Satisfied with the arrangements, Lavalle went downstairs and had a leisurely breakfast.

He watched her from the shop across Asmalti Street, just off Ataturk Square. She wore a white blouse and a brown plaid skirt. Her black hair was pulled back and tied with a ribbon, exposing a quite lovely face. She was petite, yet perfectly proportioned. Lavalle suspected that more than a few men fell for her.

Michelle seemed comfortable in the bazaar, arguing with the Turkish storekeeper over the price of a ring with experienced intractability. After a few minutes she placed the stone on the counter with affected disinterest and started to leave. The merchant swore to himself, muttered an oath in praise of Allah, and gave in to her price, making her promise not to tell anyone how little she paid for the turquoise gem. Michelle slipped the ring on her finger, remembering he'd said the same thing to her the last time she had made a purchase there.

Lavalle waited until ten after two before crossing the street. Michelle was looking at some long embroidered dresses hanging in the open air when he drew near.

"That one's very nice," he said, as she fingered a black dress with gold stitching. Michelle turned to find a tall, lean man with dark hair and a short beard looking over her shoulder. He was about thirty, younger than she had expected. "Shall we walk?" he suggested.

She nodded. They headed deeper into the bazaar, past leather shops and displays of suitcases spilling into the street, past clothing stores and innumerable merchants who bid them enter just to look: "No charge for looking." Finally they stopped across from a candy factory, heavy with the aroma of sticky honey.

"Who are you?" she asked, speaking first.

He smiled. "A friend."

"That's not enough, my superiors will want to know more."

"Then tell them we have something in common, a mutual dislike for Hoffmann and the rest of the Zionist swine."

"They will want to know who you represent."

Lavalle turned abruptly. "Do you want to ask questions or do you want the information?"

"The money is in my purse. Now where is Hans Hoffmann and what is he doing?"

Ignoring her, he began to walk along Beuyum Hamam Street toward the Saray Onou Mosque, noticing that due to recent hostilities on the island the bazaar was almost devoid of tourists. She hurried to catch up, rushing past a bus sign that gave the mileage to Kyrenia: twenty-seven or forty-two kilometers, depending if one is a Turkish or Greek Cypriot. Greek buses are not allowed to pass through the Turkish sectors of Cyprus; consequently, the distances they must travel are greatly increased. But the sign was an old one. In 1974 invading forces from Turkey seized a third of the island, occupying everything north of a line running from Famagusta through Nicosia to Kokina. Greek buses no longer travel to Kyrenia.

Lavalle soon stopped, but this time he looked at her without speaking. Understanding the message his eyes conveyed, she withdrew an envelope from her purse and handed it to him. Without bothering to check the sum, he slipped the money into his coat pocket.

"Tomorrow Hans Hoffmann will fly from Frankfurt to Damascus. What he is doing there should not be very hard for the Syrian Second Bureau to determine for itself." With that he turned and hurried away.

SEVEN

SEPTEMBER 5

FIFTEEN THOUSAND feet up and descending, the wings of the Lufthansa 707 seemed to shiver as the plane rolled in a pocket of turbulent air. Ari looked out the window at the desolate Syrian plain, broken by thorny shrubs and thistles. Although Damascus is less than fifty miles from the sea, the Lebanon and Anti-Lebanon mountain ranges cut off the moisture-laden winds and allow only a few inches of rain to fall on the Syrian capital each year.

Below him the Barada River, winding down from the mountain grottoes east of Beirut, cut a channel through the barren soil. Entering Damascus, the river separated into six main arteries and fanned out into al-Ghutah, an oasis of more than a hundred square miles. Beyond stretched al-Sahra, the desert; then five hundred miles away, Bagdad, where the Barada dies. For centuries Damascus maintained contact with the outside world solely by means of camel-driven caravans which plodded across the sands. She is the oldest continuously inhabited city on earth; her sisters, Nineveh and Babylon, expired long ago. As the airliner began its final approach into the wind Ari fastened his seatbelt and looked down at the ancient metropolis, taking in the narrow streets, minarets, mosques, mausoleums, and generally colorless skyline.

The plane banged down on the tarmac, bounced, then slid into the desert runway. Ari felt his breast pocket; his passport, the letters, cards, and documentary paraphernalia of a German national were all there. The Israeli Secret Service was meticulous, especially with the most minor details. His clothes, down to his underwear and socks, were of European manufacture, and his suits reflected the style and quality fitting a German commercial traveler in the import-export business. In the false bottom of his toiletry case the Mossad had installed a miniature transmitter; a long-range antenna, wired into the cord of his electric shaver, would allow him to communicate directly with Jerusalem.

As the passengers began to disembark Ari rose and stretched. The last ten days would have been hell if they had not served to inject meaning into a life devoid of purpose. He reveled in the night-long briefings, in memorizing the twists and turns of Damascus's underground sewer system, in walking through the scale model of the city with Tsur. He knew every building in the Haret al Yahoud, the Jewish quarter, as well as the names and backgrounds of scores of its inhabitants. Getting into the *haret* without arousing suspicion posed a problem—but one the Mossad had anticipated and solved. The Colonel had activated Hans Hoffmann for one more mission, but Ari was determined not to make it his last.

As he came down the steep steps from the plane the hot wind kicked the sand up from the runway and sent it sailing toward the terminal. Ari reached the ground and hurried past the olive-uniformed corporal who held a Kalashnikov AK-47 assault rifle at his side, right forefinger wrapped around the trigger. Parked along the edge of the field were five MIG-21s. Beyond them Ari caught the glint of Russian RPG-7 missile launchers. Damascus International Airport was used by both civil airlines and the Syrian Air Force.

Ari cleared customs without delay, the Syrian Embassy in Bonn having stamped his worn passport with a three-month visa. When the ambassador was informed of Herr Hoffmann's intent to import large quantities of Damascene furniture and textiles, he had insisted on seeing Ari personally, and providing him with letters to smooth his entry. The ambassador assured him that he would have no trouble communicating in French. Assigned the mandate over Syria at San Remo in 1920, France retained control over the area until May, 1945, when after a final armed clash and the threat of British intervention, the Gaullists withdrew and the Arabs proclaimed an independent state. But French influence remained strong, pervading the organization of Syria's institutions as well as providing the country with an official second language.

Making his way into the crowded arrival lounge, Ari allowed an Arab boy to pile his bags on a cart, watching as he placed the vital toiletry case on top of his other two suitcases.

"Get me a taxi," he said.

The ragged youngster nodded and pushed the cart ahead of Ari, whistling merrily, apparently in his mind already spending the generous tip this wealthy businessman would surely give him. The boy rolled the cart outside, then as the door swung closed behind him and in front of Ari, he abruptly grabbed the small toiletry case and ran. Ari bolted out the door and chased him down the sidewalk, brushing past businessmen in styleless suits and tarbooshed sheiks. But the years had taken their toll on Ben-Sion. Despite the extra weight of the case the boy gained easily and Ari, frustrated and panting, was forced to stop. In disbelief he watched him disappear into a group of blue-coveralled workers. Breathing heavily, Ari turned back, hoping the boy would be satisfied with the shaving cream and the variety of soaps and scents and not search further and find the transmitter. Even if he did it would be unlikely he'd take it to the police and admit to having stolen the case from an arriving passenger.

Sweat rolling from his forehead and armpits, Ari slowly made his way toward the baggage carrier, cursing under his breath, for by chance the boy had chosen his most important piece of luggage. Contact with Jerusalem was now cut off. He was on his own.

Moving past rows of sandbags piled against the concrete terminal, Ari headed toward the taxi drivers calling for customers with a loud *Shaam . . . yallah as-Shaam!* Immediately four surrounded him, shouting in Arabic and French, arguing among themselves, each swearing he'd seen the tourist first. Ari pointed to a moustached man whose black and white checkered keffiyeh fell over his shoulders, and he grabbed the suitcases off the cart. Following the Arab to his taxi, Ari wiped his forehead with his sleeve, then stepped into the cab. Resting his arm on the ledge of the window, he quickly jerked it up. The metal was too hot; the heat burned through his shirt. As the taxi driver screeched away from the curb Ari closed his eyes. The smell of gasoline clung to his nostrils.

Passing rows of yellow stone houses with red tile roofs, they approached the city from the south, via Khalid ibn Walid Street. At the intersection of El Nasr Boulevard the traffic stalled. Villagers riding mules, boys leading donkeys, and elderly men on bicycles with nargilehs strapped to their backs wove in between the horn-blow-

63

ing Fiats, Peugeots, Czech Skodas, and early-model Chevrolets. Drivers leaned out their windows and shouted curses up ahead. On the sidewalks peasant women in full-length festan, their foreheads circled in gold coins, countrymen in dark blue *cheroual* pantaloons, Yizidis in loose-fitting trousers with brocade sashes, and businessmen in dark suits all went about their business, oblivious to the pandemonium in the street. To the left, through the square in front of the Hejaz Railroad Station, Ari saw the two pencil minarets and the domed prayer room of the Suleiman Tekkiyeh, a convent for the Whirling Dervishes, built by Suleiman the Magnificent in 1554. As he leaned forward to take a better look the back of his shirt, wet, clung to the vinyl seat. Returning his head to the upholstery, he waited for the honking to die down and the taxi to start up again. It was cooler when the car moved.

The New Ommayad Hotel was located at the corner of Brazil and Maysaloun streets on a little hill overlooking the Barada River. Ari paid the driver, who anxiously accepted his deutschemarks, and walked up the stone steps to the hotel. Inside he handed the clerk his passport and reservation voucher and in turn received a *fiche de police*, a questionnaire required of all foreigners. A red-coated and -capped bellboy brought his luggage to the fifth-floor suite.

The rooms, a large bedroom and a smaller adjoining one, were white plaster with matching blue patterned rugs and draperies. The bellboy flipped a switch on the wall and the black blades of the overhead fan sliced slowly through the air. Ari gave him a handful of the piasters he'd received downstairs in exchange for his hard currency and ushered the boy out the door. After unpacking he took a long, cold shower. Then he phoned the Government Trade Bureau and spoke to the director, Amin al-Husseini, who'd received a cable from the Syrian Embassy in Bonn and had been expecting his call. Al-Husseini said he was free and would be happy to welcome him in his office in half an hour if that was convenient. Ari thanked him and hung up. Gathering his papers together, he went downstairs and decided to walk the short distance along the river to the central government offices located off Marjeh Square. When he reached the street he was already sweaty.

Standing inside the square that connected the decaying Surujiye Suq with the modern, bustling center of town, Ari stared up at the monument commemorating the completion of the Hejaz telegraph line to Mecca. The fifty-foot, soot-covered obelisk, erected in 1911, was surrounded by a large area of grass, burnished brown by the long summer. At its base, Ari watched a juice seller crush a mound of carrots under a vise, working the lever back and forth until the liquid dribbled into the glass.

The fronts of office buildings—five, six stories high, with neon signs protruding from their roofs—faced the square on all four sides. Their once creamy white façades were darkened by the exhaust and dirt of the city. It was from these windows, Ari remembered angrily, that inflamed Damascenes threw refuse at the dangling body of Eli Cohen, the Israeli spy hung publicly on May 18, 1965. More than ten thousand Syrians had crowded into Marjeh Square, pushing and shoving in order to secure the best possible view. Ari dipped his head in deference to the memory of his colleague, then moved toward the Trade Ministry, uneasy as he pictured himself suspended from the same gallows.

"Salâm 'alêkum," greeted al-Husseini as Ari was led

into his office. "It is my great pleasure to welcome you to Damascus," he continued in French, the language they had spoken on the phone. "Please have a seat." He pointed to a wooden chair across from his desk. Al-Husseini, though of average height, was slight of frame. His face was thin and would have been considered plain if not for his eyes; they were deeply recessed and shaded by thick brows. He wore a French tailored business suit without a tie.

Ari settled into the chair offered him and looked around the room. Al-Husseini's office was sparsely furnished. Cheap, assembly-line-produced tapestries hugged the walls. A series of cracks spread across the ceiling.

"Your accommodations are satisfactory? If not I could . . ."

"That will be unnecessary. I have a very comfortable suite."

"Good." Al-Husseini smiled. "Let me ring for some light refreshment." He spoke into the phone in rapid Arabic. "I think you mentioned a letter when we spoke earlier," he said, returning the receiver to its place.

Ari reached into his breast pocket and produced the letter the ambassador had given him in Bonn.

"You will be here for some time?" the Trade Bureau director asked, unfolding the letter and slipping on a pair of reading glasses.

"At least several weeks, possibly longer."

Al-Husseini scanned the page rapidly. "This is very impressive. So you think there might be a large market for Syrian textiles and furniture in Europe?"

"That depends on the price. Inflation is spiraling in the capitalist world, with it inevitably comes a jump in the cost of labor. If I buy quality goods here inexpensively, I can sell them all over the Continent at prices European manufacturers won't be able to compete with. We should be able to operate at a substantial profit both for me and for your Syrian merchants."

"I can show you whatever is of interest," he said, removing his glasses. "If you wish I will have a man with a car at your disposal in the morning."

There was a knock at the door and a young boy entered carrying a silver tray. He placed it on the desk in front of al-Husseini and left hurriedly. On the tray was a flowered pot and a pile of little porcelain cups without handles, stacked one inside the other. The Trade Bureau director filled one with coffee and passed it to Ari.

"Some people prefer more sugar, but this is *mazbout*. It's medium sweet, flavored with cardamon seeds. It pleases most tastes."

Ari held the hot cup with the tips of his fingers. As he sipped the coffee the ginger aroma of the cardamon drifted up from the surface of the liquid. "I like it," he said.

Al-Husseini smiled. "Good, we are off to a pleasant start. Now, tell me, what would you like to see first?"

Ari set the coffee on the edge of the desk. "At the moment I'm most interested in hand-carved backgammon sets; recently the game has become an international craze."

Al-Husseini laughed. "In this part of the world we have been playing shesh-besh, what you call backgammon, for nearly three thousand years. Damascus's olive wood sets are the most delicately crafted in existence. You shall see some tomorrow as well as brocade woven from the finest silks. My personal assistant, Mustafa Suidani, will accompany you both to the shops and to the factories in the outlying districts. He will be at your hotel whenever it is convenient for you."

67

"I'd like to start early. Could he pick me up at 8:00 A.M.?" Ari asked, wanting to leave the impression that he was a serious businessman.

"If that is the hour you wish, he will be there. I think it best we leave any discussion of quantities and money until after you've had the opportunity to examine our merchandise for yourself. But as the average per capita income for all Syrians is less than ten dollars per week I think you'll find our prices quite reasonable." Al-Husseini glanced at his watch and grimaced. "I must apologize for the abruptness of this meeting," he said, rising. "But there are pressing matters I must attend to now. However, if you have no other plans for this evening, I'd like to invite you to dine with me."

Ari stood. "Thank you, I would be delighted to do so."

"Excellent. Then I will meet you at the New Ommayad Hotel . . . say at seven o'clock."

"Your hospitality is most gracious. Seven o'clock will be fine." He turned and moved toward the door.

"If there is anything else I might do to make your stay more pleasant, please do not refrain from asking."

Ari stopped and looked back at him. "Possibly there is one thing."

"Yes."

"Arabs and people of my background have shared an important concern ever since the Zionists moved into the Middle East. It is known that there are Germans of the old order living in Damascus. It can grow quite lonely in a foreign land without the company of one's countrymen. If you could arrange something, it would be quite enjoyable to spend an evening with those with whom one has something in common."

"I understand fully," al-Husseini said. "I'll see what I can do."

Ari thanked the Trade Bureau director and left.

Outside, he decided to walk; in a crisis, familiarity with his immediate surroundings could prove crucial.

Proceeding down Sa'ad Zaghloul Street, across from the Palace of Justice, he passed into Old Damascus without being aware of it. The houses were piled so thick against and on top of one another, they were indistinguishable from the walls surrounding the inner city. The narrow street, flanked by open shops overhung with clothes, twisted and curved, leading finally into the Suq Hamidieh, the broad, high, central marketplace. Overhead, the sun beat against the arched corrugated iron roof, slanting through stone and bullet holes, sending streams of light against the windows of the shops. Ari wove his way through crowds of bearded Druze, deeply tanned Bedouin, village women wearing long embroidered dresses, and dark-eyed, miniskirted Damascene girls. Hamidieh Street, criss-crossed by alleys, was lined with fruit and vegetable sellers sitting on stools next to stands piled high with tomatoes, sticky raisins, cabbage, eggplant, and *sabbara* pears. One old man, his keffiyeh flowing down his back, stood rearranging a small hill of watermelons, in the midst of which a number of broken red samples were haphazardly exhibited.

Ari studied the area carefully. Kibbutz Revivim's scale model had provided him with an accurate layout of the city's streets and alleys; but the positions of the people and stalls, the best avenues for quick maneuver, could be determined only in person.

Farther on, flies buzzed around chunks of raw meat hanging from iron hooks inside a series of butcher shops. Ragged beggars sitting on the ground stretched out their hands pleading for baksheesh. Boys from unseen restaurants carried trays laden with soup and stuffed peppers to customers in the lanes. Children, barefoot and dirty, played in the water that trickled along the edge of the sidewalk. Peddlers' cries reverberated off the high vaulted roof, punctuated by the rat-a-tat-tat of the three-wheeled motorized carts that moved goods from shop to shop through the masses of pedestrians. Along the façades of the buildings electric lights blazed, as only patches of sunlight managed to pierce through the frayed awning overhead.

The stench of the food market was overwhelming. Ari hurried forward, breathing through his mouth. Two hundred yards into the suq he reached the nargileh shops, displaying a seemingly infinite size and variety of waterpipes on carpets spread across the sidewalk. In the dark shoe-sellers' bazaar walls of footwear descended from frames on all sides, the smell of leather hanging heavily in the air. In the darkness the wooden sandals, Moroccan slippers, and bobbled tartan boots all glittered with cut-glass ornamentation. Ottoman daggers, vases etched with birds of paradise, and cheap opaline ware from China lined the shelves of the antique shops. Peddlers thrust garments at Ari and tried to press wooden boxes inlaid with camel-bone and mother-of-pearl into his hands. But it was not until he reached the silk bazaar that he stopped.

Inside Tony Stephen's shop the bright-eyed Christian-Arab merchant let rolls of colorful damask tumble over the counters. Ari fingered the lustrous fabric, breaking off a thread and putting a match to it. Instead of burning, like polyesters, rayons, and other synthetic fibers would, it curled. The shopkeeper smiled, pleased that his customer knew the test for pure silk.

Just then the high-pitched, plaintive call of the muezzin, beckoning believers to the third of the day's five appointed times of prayer, rose above the din outside. First came the long, drawn-out musical wail *Allah akbar* from the Great Ommayad Mosque, and the muffled an-

70

swer *Ashhad an la ilah illa llah* from the at-Tawba. Then in rapid succession voices chimed in from all over the city, rising in splinters of sad refrain, falling tremulously away.

On the sidewalk some people spread out prayer rugs where they were, knelt to the ground, and faced Mecca —most unaware that in the first years of Islam, hoping to draw Jews to the new religion, Muhammad had prayed toward Jerusalem. Others, Ari among them, hurried over the short distance to where the marketplace opened into the courtyard of the Ommayad Mosque.

Inside the 145-yard-long prayer hall a thousand bodies knelt in unison, foreheads touching the carpets. The imam of the mosque, dressed in white robes, stared up at the blue-domed roof and cried, *"Allah akbar!"* and the congregation repeated after him, "God is great!"

Ari peered in through the ornately inlaid porticos, then looked up and followed the flight of chirping sparrows, who darted among the eaves and Roman capitals, around Byzantine cupolas and the mausoleum that reputedly holds the severed head of John the Baptist. Above the courtyard, with its variegated marble panels and double arcade of columns, glittered twenty thousand square feet of mosaic, the finest in Islam.

Suddenly, listening to the singsong chant echoing off the walls of the long prayer hall, sweat broke out on Ari's brow. Instantly he knew why. The fear was back. The terrible fear of discovery, the all-pervasive awareness that the slightest mistake, the most minute miscalculation, would bring the secret police crashing down on him. Pain would follow, excruciating pain, and then if he was lucky, a quick death. But spies, Ari knew from experience, rarely bumped into luck.

After a few minutes the fear passed, leaving in its wake an emptiness that clung to him. Slowly he left the mosque and headed for the Bab al-Farraj Gate, where he could hail a shared sheirut taxi, distinguishable from private cabs by their special red and white number plates.

At seven o'clock al-Husseini had picked Ari up at the New Ommayad and driven to the Caves du Roi Club, where they sat waiting for a third party, someone al-Husseini wanted him to meet. The restaurant was designed to approximate the atmosphere of an underground cavern. The walls and floor were of rough stone. A sheet of red cloth covered the ceiling and the same colored shades circled the dimmed hanging lamps. The tables and chairs were of unadorned wood. Soft music rippled through the background.

"There he is now," al-Husseini said, setting down his glass of arak and pointing to a tall, elderly man who despite his age moved hurriedly in their direction. He had fair skin and gray hair. The Trade Bureau director slipped off his seat and stood as the man approached. "Herr Hoffmann, I would like to introduce Sabri ibn Mahmud."

Ibn Mahmud bowed slightly and extended his right hand. "My pleasure," he said in French, though everything about him was German, from his appearance down to his manners and the abruptness of his body movement.

As they moved to a table in the far corner of the small room Ari turned to Ibn Mahmud. "You are German?" he asked in that language.

"That depends on who is asking."

"Herr Hoffmann can be trusted," al-Husseini interjected. "He is a friend of the Syrian ambassador in Bonn. He carries a personal letter of introduction."

Ibn Mahmud nodded. "My real name is Franz Ludin.

I was formerly first officer in the Propaganda Ministry of Dr. Josef Goebbels."

A smile spread over Ari's face. "This is indeed a great honor. So few of Germany's true sons are still alive. We meet all too rarely these days. Herr Ludin, if you will allow me I would like to propose a toast." Ari lifted his glass and raised it toward the ceiling. *"To those that died and to those forced to scatter over the globe, seig heil."*

"Seig heil," Ludin exclaimed, emptying his glass. Then pouring another round of arak, he looked over at Ari. "You were a member of the National Socialistische Arbeiterpartei?"

"Waffen SS," he said proudly.

Ludin added water to his arak and the clear grape alcohol turned a milky opaque. "Where were you trained?"

"At the police school in the woods near Rabka. That's in the Carpathian mountains not far from . . ."

"The Polish ski resort of Zakopane," Ludin finished his sentence for him. "I knew the school well, it was run by SS Oberscharführer Oskar Walke."

"I'm afraid you are mistaken, Herr Ludin. The school commandant was SS Obersturmführer Wilhelm Höfle of Hamburg."

Ludin smiled and took another sip from his glass. "I apologize, Herr Hoffmann, for attempting to trick you, but the Jews are everywhere, one cannot be too careful."

"One can never be careful enough," Ari agreed.

"Where were you stationed during the war?"

"Dachau concentration camp," Ari said, looking down at his plate. "I was only a minor functionary, an Untersturmführer in charge of organizing the productive work of the prisoners in the labor kommando. No war crime charges were filed against me."

Ludin stared across the table at the man more than a

73

dozen years his junior. "You seem almost embarrassed that no one is hunting you."

Ari nodded weakly. "Somehow I feel I could not have served the Führer to the utmost if . . ."

"Don't be naïve, Untersturmführer Hoffmann. You had your task to perform, others had theirs. By chance you were not chosen to assist directly in the extermination of the Jews. If you had been you would have complied without hesitation. And nobody would have tried to stop you. Why do you think Allied bombers leveled Munich, but left Dachau, a mere eleven miles to the northwest, untouched? Because the Americans knew if they rescued the Jews, they would have had to absorb them in their borders, and they wanted them as little as we did."

"Herr Ludin donates his services as an expert on the Jewish Question to the Syrian Ministry of Orientation," al-Husseini said.

"There are Jews in Syria?" Ari asked, acting puzzled.

"A mere four and a half thousand," al-Husseini explained.

"Dealing with them is like asking the designer of the Aswan Dam to teach a child how to block the water draining down the side of a street," Ludin said.

Ari nodded understandingly.

As al-Husseini had taken it upon himself to order for his guests, soon steaming plates of Kharouf Mechout, stuffed roast lamb, were brought to the table. With their meal the waiter suggested a bottle of Domaine de Tourelle, a popular Lebanese rosé. Ludin nodded his approval and the waiter hurried after the wine.

The three men ate with relish. The minutes fell away as they alternated arguing Middle East politics with telling war stories. Ari played his role with the polish of the professional. He wanted to appear ingenuous, a bit naïve. He felt he could win over the aging Nazi by playing on his vanity, on their common past. Ludin could be of invaluable service if manipulated skillfully from the outset.

As baklava and coffee were served Ari yawned. "Pardon me," he said, looking at his watch. "It's later than I realized. I've had a long day." Though genuinely tired, he was anxious to return to the hotel for a quite different reason.

Al-Husseini lifted his cup to his lips and drained the contents.

"Don't hurry yourself on my account," Ari said. "I don't mind taking a taxi."

"In that case please feel no obligation to stay," al-Husseini said, lowering his coffee to the table. "Besides, the two of us have some business to discuss that I'm sure would only bore you."

"Then I think I shall avail myself of some much-needed sleep. It was indeed a pleasure meeting you, Herr Ludin," Ari said, rising. "As I know virtually no one in Damascus I hope I can take the liberty of calling on you at your convenience."

"No need to be so formal, my friend. First of all, you must call me Franz. Second, all government offices are shut on Friday, the Moslem holy day. Why don't we spend the afternoon and evening together and take in a few sights?"

"That's kind of you, I'd enjoy that very much."

"Good, then I shall pick you up at three, the day after tomorrow."

"I'll be looking forward to it." He shook hands with both men and left the restaurant.

Back at the hotel, Ari went immediately to the front desk, where the night clerk informed him that a Kim Johnson had registered two hours earlier and could be found in room 204. Even though the second floor was only one flight up he took the elevator. Moving down the hallway, he knocked on her door, waited, then pounded harder; but to his surprise no one answered. Wondering where she had gone at such a late hour, he wrote her a note, slipped it under the wood, and took the elevator up to his suite.

Kicking off his shoes, he sat on the edge of the bed, then stretched out and tried to push the tiredness from his limbs. He'd put the loss of the transmitter out of his mind all day, but now the impact of what had happened began to hit him. The Colonel, assuming he was too experienced an agent to misplace the toiletry case, had not arranged an alternate method of communication. If any more unexpected problems arose there would be no way to contact Jerusalem. He was cut off—on his own until he met Lieutenant Shaul Barkai in the Christian quarter of Damascus on the twelfth.

Ari yawned out loud and let his thoughts drift elsewhere. A large part of him resented that he was in Damascus, resented the fact that he'd volunteered, almost begged for assignment to a mission intended for two less experienced agents. Sure, he wasn't a hundred percent as sharp as he used to be; he began to realize that on Cyprus, but certainly he still had a number of good years left. Years that could be spent . . .

Just then he heard a light tapping at his door. With a smile on his lips he moved across the room and opened it. Kim was standing in the hallway. For a long second he just looked at her. He kept forgetting the strong physical impact she had on him until they met after an absence and it struck him again. Dressed in a short skirt, her legs in cloth boots laced to the knees, her blue-gray eyes softly shaded and sparkling, she seemed more the creation of a long-suppressed dream than a woman he'd grown to know intimately.

"Well, are you going to let me in?" she asked, bringing her hands to her waist in mock anger.

"I think I could be talked into it."

She entered the room and he drew her into his arms, comforted by the familiarity of her touch and the musky fragrance of her perfume. She kissed him, letting her lips linger over his, then moved toward the chair next to the dresser.

"I'm exhausted," she said, sitting down. "I wanted to see the city. I've been walking for . . . I don't know . . . hours."

He sat on the bed near her and looked at the open door leading to the balcony. "Don't you think it's dangerous for a woman to be out alone here at night?"

"No," she said, the edge of irritation cutting through her voice.

Even before she answered he was sorry he'd asked the question. He really wasn't worried about her safety; that's not what had prompted his supposed concern.

"How was your flight?" he asked quickly, changing the subject.

"Fine. I'm glad you convinced me to go through Greece instead of Cyprus. I really enjoyed myself in Athens."

Even if one had the foresight, as Kim had, to request her Israeli visa be stamped on a removable piece of paper, flying from Nicosia to Damascus was tantamount to advertising the traveler had begun his journey in Tel Aviv. Once in Syria all passengers arriving on flights from Cyprus were closely watched—a pointless policy since no one attempting anything subversive was foolish enough to enter a Moslem state from the island country so near to Israel's coastline.

Kim fingered the long strands of her champagne-colored hair, trying to draw the static electricity out of it. "Did you complete the necessary business transactions with your partners in Frankfurt?"

He nodded, hating to lie to her.

She looked up at him. "Is anything the matter?"

"No. Why do you ask?" It made him uneasy that she could immediately sense when something was on his mind; then again, her ability to reach into him was a great part of what made her so attractive.

"I don't know. You seem a little tense."

"I'm sorry. I'm probably just tired." He massaged the back of his neck with his hand. "It's been a long day."

"Here, let me do that," she said, moving onto the bed. She worked the flesh in his shoulders and neck, kneading the tightness out of his muscles.

"You're going to put me to sleep," he said as a liquid warmth flowed under his skin.

She stopped and circled her hands around his chest. "Actually I wouldn't mind that. I'm absolutely worn out."

He turned and kissed her on the forehead. "Let's go to bed."

They undressed, slipped under the covers, and entwined in each others arms, drifted from the world of conscious thought.

EIGHT

SEPTEMBER 5

AFTER MEETING Michelle, Guy Lavalle drove directly to Larnaca Airport and boarded a CypAir flight for Paris. He spent a day roaming the banks of the Seine, visiting art museums and viewing his favorite paintings. He was especially fond of Manet's *Le Déjeuner sur l'Herbe* and Pissarro's *The Orchard,* hanging in the Jeu de Paume at the edge of the Tuileries between the Louvre and the Place de la Concorde. Both Manet's bold plains of color and Pissarro's splashes of light depicted the outdoors with extraordinary feeling. Lavalle appreciated their artistic innovations. Finally, certain that he wasn't being followed, he met his contact and switched passports. Resuming his real identity, Lieutenant Shaul Barkai, member of the Mossad since 1968, youngest agent ever to be awarded the Ot Haoz medal, a man on his way to a very promising career in Israeli intelligence, flew back to Tel Aviv.

The Colonel stood at his window, waiting for Barkai to be brought in from the airport. Below, in President's Park next to the Knesseth, he watched a group of children playing war. One intrepid boy climbed a tree, waiting until two unsuspecting comrades crossed under him;

then he jumped and quickly stabbed both of them in the back with a rubber dagger. The two boys fell to the ground in mock death throes. Seconds later they got up and began arguing about who would play the paratrooper next and who would have to be the Arabs. Though their game saddened him, the Colonel felt a vague sense of well-being—at least in this generation the Jews would fight back.

The sight of the children made him think about Rabbi Sassoon's and Nissim Kimche's offspring. It was not beyond the Syrians to induce parents to cooperate by threatening to torture their children; they'd done so before, most recently on the eve of the American newscameramen's arrival in Damascus. The Colonel reached into his pocket for a cigar, then changed his mind. For weeks he'd wondered if it was worth risking two and possibly three agents to save seven children. He knew why, in the end, he'd decided it was. The potential propaganda value of the kids was enormous. For why would the leaders of a community voluntarily send away their children knowing if they did that they would never see them again? The international news media had to draw the correct conclusion: the plight of Syria's Jews was that bad.

The Colonel closed his eyes and tried to rest for a moment. Lately he had been burdened by a growing sense of national insecurity—a feeling that Israel was alone among the nations, a thorn sticking in the massive flank of the world, a state whose existence irritates even her friends. The pressure grew increasingly harder for him to shoulder after the expulsion from UNESCO, as Israel was pushed still farther from the family of nations. Sometimes he wondered if the world wasn't right. Maybe the Jews were committing some fundamental, perhaps catastrophic error, which if not rectified, would doom the Israelis and Arabs to Semitic suicide.

"Excuse me, Colonel," Lieutenant Barkai said from the open doorway.

The Colonel slowly turned back from the window. "Please shut the door and sit down."

Barkai complied immediately. "I wasn't interrupting you, was I?"

"No," the Colonel said, falling heavily into his chair. "I was waiting for you. How did it go on Cyprus?"

"Satisfactory, sir. By now the Syrian Second Bureau should be on to Ari."

The Colonel nodded and lit a Montecruz. "Do you think there's any chance she suspected you were an Israeli?"

"No, from her point of view I could be from any one of a dozen intelligence services. Besides, looking at it from the other side, why would we be setting up our own man? If we wanted to get rid of him surely there would be more direct methods."

The Colonel looked hard at the Syrian-born lieutenant. "You spoke to Ben-Sion before he left for Damascus. What did you think of him?"

"Well," Barkai stalled. "I don't think he's quite as sharp as he once was. Apparently he never realized you maneuvered him into volunteering for the mission."

"Beyond that?"

"I'd rather not say, sir. I really don't know him well enough."

The Colonel blew a puff of smoke into the air. "You didn't like this assignment much, did you?"

"It's not a question of like or dislike," Barkai snapped. "I followed your orders."

The Colonel nodded, pleased that Barkai understood the moral code of field agents. "Lieutenant, intelligence work has one law: it's justified by results. At times you may be asked to do things that will seem immoral to you. Indeed, in the Biblical classroom, in the everyday world, they are immoral; but not to the Service. Results, not morality, save lives, and the business we're in is saving Jewish lives." He snuffed out his cigar. "That's what Ari went to Syria to do."

NINE

SEPTEMBER 6

IN THE MORNING Kim took the stairs to the second floor. Though Ari would have liked her to stay, the plan developed in Jerusalem demanded his bed be available. After she left he went down to the lobby and waited for Mustafa Suidani, al-Husseini's assistant. The next few hours proved to be commercially productive. Ari bought a hundred and fifty backgammon sets and ordered them shipped to his company in Frankfurt. If anyone cared to check, the firm, Transworld Enterprises, was a legitimate one. When he left the factory he took one of the sets with him, explaining that he would send it ahead as a sample. He would mail it to Frankfurt, but not until he had coded a message about the lost transmitter and hidden the slip of paper in the board game. Richtman, certain to find the arrival of the small package unusual, would search it carefully.

After Suidani dropped him back at the hotel, Ari went to the desk and arranged for two picnic lunches to be made up. He phoned Kim's room, and a half-hour later they were speeding in a rented car toward Mount Kassioun, intent on escaping from the heat that hung over the city. Driving out Farouk El Awal Boulevard, they entered the orchards of al-Ghutah. On both sides of the road trees pushed up through the dry earth, their branches laden with apples, plums, figs, and mandarins. Irrigation channels flowed everywhere, fighting a constant battle with the sun. Farther north, on the outskirts of the Mohajirine district, women, holding their pantaloons above their knees, crushed apricots in stone troughs, while children picked the kernels from the gruel. At the base of the rolling foothills of Mount Kassioun, the road ended.

They climbed through the trees, the air cooling as they wound upward along a path cut by the hoofs of sheep and goats. Finally Ari plopped down on a grassy knoll. Kim collapsed at his side, somehow panting and laughing at the same time.

"It's beautiful," she exclaimed.

He nodded, following her gaze up to Jabel al-Sheik, Biblical Mount Hermon, where Nimrod the hunter had dwelt, and near which the tribe of Dan had settled after fleeing from the Philistines. For a long time he stared at the snow-capped peak, beyond whose summit stretched the land he loved, but between whose borders he was not content to live. An ironic paradox.

A long way to the west poplar trees surged up the Anti-Lebanon Mountains. On a further slope the Jordan River, beginning as a bubbling spring, trickled toward the Dead Sea. To the east the orchards pushed back the desert, drawing around Damascus like protecting soldiers. Beyond the outskirts of the city rose the barren mounds of el-Aswad and Mania; behind them the sand continued until it joined the sky.

"Do you ever laugh?" Kim asked, leaning against his back.

"That's a strange question."

"Do you?"

"Of course I laugh."

"I just wondered." She reached for the bag that contained the chicken sandwiches the hotel had made, and handed one to him. "You know, a relationship between an older man and a younger woman never works."

He bit into the dark bread. "Then why are you here?"

"I don't know, maybe you remind me of my father," she said jokingly, hoping he would smile. But he didn't. Suddenly the warm wind rose, rustling through the olive and walnut trees surrounding the glen where they sat. Kim gazed down into the valley, following a flock of sheep with her eyes. "I'm a little afraid of you," she said.

"Afraid of what?"

"I'm not sure. I just sense there's a whole part of you that's hidden, that I can't get to. Sometimes I reach out but instead of feeling flesh, I touch a wall. It's as if there's something important I don't know. Every time I get close to discovering whatever it is, you become vague and evasive. Maybe that's what frightens me." Kim stroked his hand. "Do you understand what I'm saying?"

"Not really."

She turned away in frustration. A long silence followed, broken finally by Kim. "What do you believe in?"

"Results," he said without hesitation.

"What do you mean, results?"

"Winning."

She sensed he was not talking about business, about closing the big deal, beating out the competition. "You mean like in a war, defeating the other side."

"That, or crushing the enemy within yourself."

"What enemy? What is it you're fighting?"

"What makes you think I'm fighting anything?"

"I can feel it. It's like there's a bunch of people locked in combat inside you, with none of them able to emerge victorious. Everything seems so contradictory. Sometimes I almost think *you* don't know who you are."

Then for the first time since they met he laughed, a low bellow that seemed to burst from deep within him. "You've been reading too much Freud," he said mockingly.

He hurt her; it showed in her eyes. She had tried to open an entrance into understanding him, only to have the door slammed shut in her face. She could not have known she'd trod on a raw nerve, that he'd laughed only to protect himself from her painful probing. It bothered him that she'd been so accurate, that she sensed so much in so short a time. It was disarming, as well as potentially dangerous.

Later, as they walked in the tall grass toward the Tomb of Abel, a small boy sitting among the rocks held out a bunch of pink grapes and stuck his hand in his pocket signifying he wanted money for the fruit. Ari shook his head no and to his surprise the boy did not run after them to pursue his offer. Instead he started eating the grapes himself. Kim watched him, a smile on her face.

Reaching a small secluded meadow, they lay down, deciding to rest for a while. The tall blades of grass rippling in the wind enclosed their bodies in a sea of green. A staccato chant rose from the minaret in the valley below, calling the Moslems to prayer. Kim unbuttoned her blouse exposing bare breasts, and brought his head to them. He lay there for a long time feeling the warmth of her chest on his cheek.

"I suppose traveling around so much you make love to quite a number of women."

"Does it matter?"

"I guess not," she said.

He turned and looked at her. "I've been to bed with a lot of women but made love to few."

A smile flicked the corners of her mouth, then it disappeared. "You had a bad dream last night. You were

86

mumbling in your sleep—something about barking dogs, an oven, and the smell. I couldn't make any sense out of it."

She watched his body stiffen. "Is anything the matter?"

"No," he said, pulling her on top of him. "I'm sure it was nothing."

TEN

SEPTEMBER 7

THE BAZAARS of Damascus, thin, crooked streets, flanked by open shops and overhung with clothes, seem to cry out in shame. Not because the beauties of the past have vanished, but because they've degenerated. For decades advancement has meant the ebb of artistry; changelessness, a slavish cleaving to the past. At best the work of the old masters is carefully copied. The crafts themselves, once proudly utilitarian, now service the tasteless tourists. The heavily inlaid trays, copper veined with silver or brass, seem clumsy, anachronistic. Where once an old man took fifteen days to pound out the black designs painted on the metal surface of a small plate, now a series of young boys work on an assembly line, each specializing in a specific part of the design. Rarely is a piece wrought that even resembles the old excellence.

"I'm afraid you may be disappointed," Franz Ludin said to Ari as they walked under the vaulted roof of rusty, corrugated tin that covered the Street Called Straight. "The garments in the Suq el-Bzouriye are mostly woven from synthetic fabrics."

Shops pushing in from both sides of the street left only a narrow, noisy passageway between them. The air, trapped under the roof, was thick and hot. Somewhere near here, Ari remembered, the disciple Ananais received a vision from the Lord commanding him to go unto the house of Judas on the Street Called Straight and inquire after a man named Saul. Cured of his blindness and converted by Ananais, Saul of Tarsus, renowned as the scourge of Christians in Jerusalem, became Paul the Apostle.

Ludin stretched out his hand, waving it at the donkey carts and motorized rickshas loaded with an array of fresh vegetables, rolls of damask, and electrical appliances. "At one time this was a mile-long, hundred-foot-wide thoroughfare known as Doconomos. Under its arches regal Roman processions passed. Now the Doconomos is fifteen feet below us and only one of the seven great Roman gates of Damascus still stands."

Ari smiled to himself, thinking Ludin, if not fated to be born in the century of Nazism, would have wanted to spend his years as a Roman.

"Ahmud Azziz, a young merchant I know, sells hand-loomed dresses of the purest silk," Ludin continued as they skirted around a mound of dung left recently by one of the donkeys. "Maybe he can direct you to quality merchandise selling at a reasonable price."

"I hope so," Ari said. "It is certainly worth speaking to him about it."

They passed into a narrow cobbled alley shot through with patches of sunlight streaming down from the holes in the roof overhead. The scent of crushed rose petals freshened the air. "There's a perfume factory nearby, Damascus rosewater," Ludin explained, as they moved through an entrance in the stone alley leading to a courtyard. Ludin circled a blue-tiled fountain overgrown with crawling ivy, took the heavy brass knocker that hung on the door, and pounded the wood several times. "Azziz doesn't have a phone so I couldn't call him, but he's usually home Friday afternoons." There was no discernible sound of movement within, so Ludin rapped sharply on the door again. Still no response. "It seems Azziz is not in," he said, turning to Ari. "I'm afraid I've wasted your time."

"Nonsense. I enjoy the opportunity to just walk around Damascus and talk to you. Besides, visiting these merchants and haggling over prices become tiring after a while. I think I'm ready for some diversion."

"Tell me, what can I show you? Damascus is overflowing with exotic sights: the tomb of Saladin, the minaret of Hisham, the Tekkiyeh of Suleiman, the Madrassa Selimiya."

"Excuse me, Herr Ludin. Your offer is most gracious. But after one has been sightseeing all over the world, visiting even the most magnificent structures becomes tedious."

"My friend, if there is something you would like to do instead—the baths, a woman. Please, just ask."

"Well, when we dined with al-Husseini you did mention something about Jews in Syria. I was quite intrigued. Do you think it would be possible for me to witness your methods of dealing with them?"

Ludin smiled in self-contentment at his continuing role in the drama of the destruction of the Jews. For a second Ari lost himself; he wanted to pounce on the former German propagandist, kick that smile off his face, crush it under his foot. He knew that murdering Ludin would make him no better than the animal the Nazi was, but that didn't matter. It didn't matter at all.

"I like you," Ludin said, wrapping his arm around Ari's shoulder and leading him back toward Straight Street, past a bakery with a yellow pyramid of stale berazlik biscuits stacked in the window and slabs of makrouk bread, still pulpy and steaming, spread over the stone

90

floor. "Germany is getting weak, effeminate. The young are falling over themselves trying to imitate American dress and music. They ignore their Aryan heritage. Goethe, Schopenhauer, Nietzsche are abandoned for the likes of Günter Grass, a blubbering schoolboy who peddles the myth of German guilt for profit. Fools, all of them! They're blinded by self-righteous sentimentality. For the time being we must abandon Germany, our work lies here in the Middle East. Before we can return we must slash the arteries of Israel and drown the Zionists in their own blood."

"And the Jews of Syria?"

"We practice on them. Come, I'll show you."

"In 1947 there were twenty-five thousand Jews in Damascus and over forty thousand in the entire country," Ludin said as they parked the car on El Amine Street on the fringes of the Jewish quarter. "Today a little over four thousand remain, and soon . . ." He lifted his hands in the air and let the rest of his sentence drift into suggestion. They got out of the car and began to walk. A bus, brown with Iraqi dust, rumbled by, spewing dark exhaust into the air. "Now only a few streets still belong to the Jews," Ludin continued.

Ari knew the history of the Jews of Damascus well; Tsur had drilled the details into him. The Christians have sliced into the Haret al Yahoud from the north, the Moslems from the west and south. The streets where the Jews live are quiet. The doors of sunken courtyards are edged open and slammed shut to receive children from school. The walls are broken and crumbling. A subdued flow of Arabic parts the silence from various windows, the words often sounding like prayers. The use of Hebrew is met by beatings. Palestinians roam the streets at will; rape is not uncommon. Residents of the quarter have been known to leave their apartments to walk across the street, only to return months later. Some don't return at all. Or as two of the girls Tsur had described, they are sent back in separate pieces.

Ludin approached the two soldiers lounging on the corner of El Amine and El Hadjara streets. He uttered a phrase in Arabic and presented a card to the elder of the two privates. Immediately they grabbed their lightweight, Japanese-built Armalite rifles, bolted up from the sidewalk and stood rigidly to attention. Ludin swore at them in a German they couldn't possibly understand and headed up El Hadjara Street with Ari. Far off in the west the sun had dipped beneath the mountains of Lebanon, spraying clouds of bright orange through the evening sky. The snowcapped peak of Hermon stood silhouetted in the orange mist, slowly fading from view with the descending of night.

"We have plans to significantly reduce the size of the Jewish population here," Ludin said, his lips curving into a smile. "But we must retain a small number whose position can be exploited for internal consumption. In the eventuality of a setback at the front, the populace must be allowed to vent their frustration on someone. Such release is healthy."

"What are the chances of any of the Jews actually having contact with Israel?"

Ludin laughed. "The word *Musawi*, follower of Moses, is stamped in red on their identification cards. They can't visit abroad or emigrate; a government ordinance requires they obtain written permission before leaving the city; soldiers are posted at all entrances to the quarter; Palestinians are housed everywhere among them—they hardly talk to each other. Contact with Israel is impossible."

92

"I see. What about a synagogue? I assume there once was one in the ghetto."

"What do you mean, once. There are two main synagogues, the Al-Frange and the old Jawbar synagogue. You wouldn't want the American politicians protesting about religious intolerance in Syria, would you?" Ludin laughed and Ari forced himself to join in. "Come on, I'll show you the Jawbar; the Al-Frange is where we take the tourists and newspaper reporters."

"But I didn't bring my skull cap," Ari said, trying to be flippant.

Ludin laughed even louder. "I think they might be persuaded to allow us to enter anyway."

The stone synagogue was dark. Fifteen, maybe twenty old men sat on divans against the walls, all, it seemed, muttering different prayers. The couches were of a faded red, ragged and torn. No one stood on the raised platform in the center of the room to lead the congregation in prayer. One door of the ark was missing and the other swung loosely on its hinges. It hardly mattered, for there were no Torah scrolls for the doors to protect. The floor of the synagogue was mosaic and the walls covered with aged tapestries. Though rows of candelabras hung from the ceiling only one light, directly over the dais, was lit. Nobody looked up or whispered when they entered. The old Jews just continued to pray, as their ancestors had for centuries.

"They huddle here and wait for their messiah to come," Ludin said. "They're insufferably stubborn. We managed to kill off six million of them, and they learn nothing. With the smell of burning bodies in the air they marched to the gas chambers, praying. Clearly a pathological people. But then you were at Dachau, this is not new to you."

Ari nodded. Haunting Hebrew melodies droned in the background beneath their loudly spoken German. "As a whole I find them wretched creatures," Ari said. "That is, with one small exception."

"What is that?"

"Herr Ludin, I don't dare tell you. I'm afraid you will look upon me with disgust."

"Nonsense. You are a German, a former SS officer."

"But in front of you I'm embarrassed to talk about my weakness."

"We all have weaknesses. Besides, I'm an expert on the Jewish Question. I may be able to be of assistance."

Ari bit his lower lip. "I need a drink. Is there someplace we can go?"

Ludin nodded. "I know a clean restaurant that serves liquor. It's just outside the walls."

As Ari followed him out of the synagogue he cast a final glance back at the old men.

They moved along winding streets, then passed through the Bab Kaysan, a huge Ottoman gate that opened onto the spacious Ibn Assaker Boulevard. The restaurant was only a short distance away. Inside, they sat at a table with a red and white checkered tablecloth and ordered a bottle of arak. The room, brightly illuminated, was long and narrow, with copper plates dotting the yellow walls.

After the arak was set before them Ludin rolled his glass between his hands. "Now tell me, what is it that's troubling you?"

Ari drank off half his glass and looked down at the floor. "It began at Dachau. Some of the officers . . . well, it would get lonely . . . months on end without female company. There were no women around; that is, there were Jewesses, but no real women. So a few of us decided since in the end we were going to kill them anyway, there really wouldn't be any harm in taking a female in for the night, as long as we were careful not to allow any of them to live long enough to bear our children. Some of the officers bribed them with food. There was always a large number of the animals who would do anything for a few scraps of meat, but they didn't seem to do anything for me. Those girls always licked your ass and begged to come back the next night. But one day a dark little Jewess named Rachael was assigned to one of my labor details. She couldn't have been more than eighteen or nineteen. When I asked her if she'd like to come to my quarters she spit in my face. I had two enlisted men carry her to my room on the spot and then, well, I availed myself of her." Nervously he gulped down the rest of the arak.

"How was this Rachael?" Ludin asked, his tone flat.

"Exhilarating, absolutely beyond description. I'd previously experienced nothing causing comparable excitement. After she was gassed there were others, all defiant, resentful, angry, and young. Since the war I've slept with many women." He filled his glass and took a long drink. "But it has never been the same."

Ludin stared silently across the table. Ari looked away from him; it was essential that Ludin make the next move. "You have surprised me," the Nazi said, withdrawing a pack of cigarettes from his coat pocket. "Would you care for one?" He held the pack outstretched in his arm. Ari took a cigarette and lit it. Ludin had to react sympathetically, the entire mission depended on it. He drew a mouthful of warm smoke deep into his lungs.

Ludin slowly removed a cigarette, but left it dangling between his fingers. "I've heard of other cases like this, of German officers who got a thrill from raping Jewish women. We shall not speak around the issue, you did rape them." Ari took a long drag off the cigarette, agree-

95

ing with Ludin by his silence. "The question remains as to why only Jewish women. Possibly your attraction is a manifestation of a hatred of women. Or a projection of some self-hatred. Or a misplaced fear that sleeping with a decent German woman bridges over to a violation of your mother. We would have to spend a long time together before I could uncover the source of your abnormality and be of any assistance."

Forcing his hand to shake, Ari reached for his glass and brought the licorice-tasting liquid to his mouth. It wasn't going right. Ludin was reacting like a psychiatrist outlining future therapy options for a patient. "But I can see why you led me to the point where I conveniently dragged the story out of you," Ludin continued. "You are looking for another Jew-bitch sex goddess right here in Damascus."

Ari nodded, blowing smoke into the air.

"Maybe you'd like a nineteen-year-old, small, dark and defiant—another Rachael."

Ari crushed out his cigarette. It was important that he gain this Nazi's respect; it might be crucial later. "Listen, I'm not asking you for anything," he said, almost angrily. "If you want to do me a favor, fine, I'll accept it. But I won't bend down and kiss your feet in gratitude."

Ludin touched him gently on the arm. "Do not get defensive, my friend. We are both Germans of the old order. There are not so many of us left that we can afford the luxury of dissension among ourselves. Go back to the hotel, have dinner and wait. I'll deliver someone to your room in a couple of hours."

Ari smiled faintly and hurried out of the restaurant.

Close to three and a half hours elapsed before there was a knock on his door. When he opened it two uni-

96

formed policemen shoved a young girl into the room. She was short, dark, and had small brown eyes that darted quickly around the hotel suite. Ari didn't need to be told that she hated her captors. The girl tried to squirm free from the arm one of the policemen held tightly around her waist.

"If she doesn't stop that throw her on the floor," Ari said. At the sound of his voice the girl went rigid. "You may let her go." The policeman dropped his hand and the girl, suddenly with no one to fight, remained still.

"We were instructed to deliver this woman and to leave a number where we can be reached. You may phone us when you want her returned," the officer who had held the girl said, holding out a slip of paper.

Ari nodded and took it from him. "You two may go now, thank you."

The officers turned and left.

"What did they tell you?" Ari asked, gazing at the young Jewess.

"They said that if I didn't come and please you my father and mother would be beaten." She spat out the words and began unbuttoning her blouse.

"Have you ever slept with a man before?"

"I've been raped twice," she said coldly. "Once by a Palestinian and once by the policeman I reported the crime to."

"Your name is Rachael Khatib, isn't it? You have a brother named Yair who lives with his wife and two children on Haroe Street in Haifa. Your favorite color is yellow and you have a scar on your upper right thigh from a pot of boiling water that Yair accidentally spilled on you."

In fabricating the story of his sexual transgressions at Dachau he had described Rachael as the type of Jewess he desired, mentioning her name in the hope Ludin would send her and not another girl. The plan was not as tenuous as it first seemed, for Rachael was the only young Jewess left in Damascus with the fire to fight. Ludin would know that.

Ari slipped a ring with a small turquoise stone off his finger and held it out to her.

She took it hesitantly, staring at the ring and then back at him, fear frozen on her face. "How did you get Yair's ring? How do you know about me?"

"I'm an Israeli," he said.

She stared at him in utter disbelief. "But the police . . ."

"They think I'm a former Nazi. You needn't concern yourself with the details. I've come to take Rabbi Sassoon's and Nissim Kimche's children to Israel. We're worried they're going to be used to pressure their parents into cooperating with the authorities. Success will depend on how quickly we move and how quietly. I don't want you to speak to anyone except Nissim Kimche about what I'm going to tell you. Everyone else is to think you were raped. Is that clear?"

She nodded. "What do you want me to do?"

"First of all," he got up from the edge of the bed and brought a chair over, "I think you will be more comfortable sitting down." She smiled and took a seat near him. He was amazed at her calm, at the tears she had not shed when confronted with her brother's ring. Ari now knew why the Colonel had insisted he contact her—she was controlled and unusually strong. "Now," he said, trying to comfort her with a smile, "I want you to arrange it so that two weeks from today on the twenty-second . . ."

Just then there was a knock at the door. "Quick, on the bed," Ari whispered. Understanding, she kicked off her shoes, loosened her blouse, and dropped onto the mattress. He pulled his shirt off and ran his fingers through his hair, mussing it. When he opened the door Kim was standing in the hall wearing a short skirt and a tight-fitting body blouse, cut well below the neck. She smiled at him and stepped into the room; then she saw the girl lying on the bed. For an instant she stood immobile, unable to speak, her eyes attached to his naked chest.

"Kim."

"I should have called, but I didn't think . . ."

"No, it's not what it looks like." A heaviness pressed down on him. It was happening again; his job was encroaching on his private life, threatening to destroy it, the way it destroyed Yael.

"It couldn't possibly be what it looks like," she said sarcastically. "You're just having a business meeting. She's quoting you the latest figures on Damascene furniture."

"Come outside." He grabbed her hand and pulled her into the hall, closing the door behind them.

"I know I'm young, but shouldn't that girl be home doing her schoolwork."

"Stop it," he said roughly. "I can't explain, but there's nothing between me and that girl."

"I can see that—you're half undressed."

"Kim, no," he half demanded, half pleaded.

"If there's nothing going on why is she lying on your bed and why can't you explain?"

The hall was empty, quiet. "Because if I explained your life would be in danger." As soon as the words left his mouth he regretted speaking them.

A shadow of fear crossed her face, darkening her eyes. "What is it? Who is that girl? What's she doing in your room? What are you doing in Damascus?"

"I can't tell you!" he said, frustration breaking off the edges of his words.

She clutched onto his arm. "Let's get out of here, out of this hotel and out of Damascus. I'll go with you anywhere you say. We can take a plane in the morning. I'll finish my pictures later. I'm frightened. You're involved in something dangerous. I know it. Please, let's leave now, forget whatever it is you're doing."

He drew her close and kissed her. For a second she seemed to fight him, but only for a second.

Dropping her head to his shoulder, she looked up at his small eyes. "Please let's leave. It can't be that important."

"It is. Trust me." Gently he pushed her away from him. "I have to go inside now. I'll call you tomorrow."

With that he turned and went back to Rachael and the Service.

ELEVEN

SEPTEMBER 8

IN THE MORNING Ari picked up the scrap of paper lying next to the phone, dialed, and arranged for the officers to come for Rachael. As she emerged from the other room he suddenly thought about Dov Elon. This girl would have been perfect for him. He could just picture them romping through the fields on Dov's kibbutz, wringing the sweetness out of life the way one squeezed the juice from an orange. Abruptly he turned and looked away from the girl. What was the use? For all practical purposes, Dov was dead.

He crossed the room and stared out the window at the harsh sunlight already glinting off the tiled roofs of the city. Ari wondered about his colleague. Strangely enough, though one of the things he was supposed to find out was how much Dov had told his interrogators, he didn't even know what the young intelligence officer had been doing in Damascus. When he'd asked, the Colonel had hedged, explaining that the knowledge would be an unnecessary burden in the event he was captured and interrogated. Such secrecy bothered Ari. In the old days the Colonel had never withheld information from him.

After Rachael had been taken away Ari sat on the edge

of the bed and looked at the bottle of arak resting on the nightstand. The liquid was clear with a slight green-black tint to it. He'd been drinking a bit too much recently and he knew it. Reaching over a pillow, he poured a glass half full and gulped the liquor quickly, as if by throwing the contents down his throat he could faster forget his drinking it.

Remembering the unmade bed in the next room, he slowly got up. Details are of paramount importance, he repeated to himself. The whole mission could be foiled by a cleaning lady finding underwear bearing a suspicious label, or the extra bed slept in when the gentleman had brought a young woman to his suite for the express purpose of sexual liaison.

He tugged at the sheets and blankets on the bed where Rachael had slept, trying to smooth the wrinkles out of them. But whenever he pulled on one end of the blanket, inevitably a new crease appeared someplace else. Angrily he moved to the head of the bed and drew the blanket taut, stuffing the edges underneath the mattress. When the bedspread was in place he moved back into the main room, noting, to his dismay, that his breathing was labored and his forehead damp.

He was slipping and although the realization was painful, he no longer could avoid admitting it to himself. First there was the untimely affair with Michelle on Cyprus, then in Damascus Airport he let that stupid kid take the transmitter from under his nose. But an incident that occurred in Jerusalem, right after the Colonel's final briefing, worried him most of all.

Late in the afternoon he had been walking past the construction site at Kiryat Wolfson when a terrific explosion rocked the earth. Instinctively he dove to the ground. He lay there huddled against himself for a long time—his hands shaking, his heart beating wildly. Finally he realized the blast had been caused by construction workers dynamiting foundations through the stony crust of the city. An hour later his hands were still trembling.

The Colonel would call it a sign.

Ari wiped the sweat from his brow and reached for the phone. When the receptionist came on he asked for Kim's room. The phone rang for a long time before she answered.

"Did I wake you?" he asked.

"No, I was in the shower." She sounded distant, detached.

"Can we have breakfast together?"

"What about your friend? Isn't she hungry?"

"She's gone."

"Already. What's the matter, wasn't she very good?"

"Kim!"

"Okay, okay. I'm sorry." She paused and then spoke softly, "I'm sorry."

"What about breakfast?"

"I can't. I'm going out to take some pictures this morning. The Foreign Ministry phoned a little while ago; the Israelis bombed the refugee camp at Khan esh Shih just after sunrise, killing a lot of civilians. The Ministry offered to provide a car and driver if I was interested in photographing the damage. I'm being picked up in twenty minutes."

"I see."

There was a long silence parted by Kim. "Can we have dinner instead?"

"I guess so."

"What time?" she asked.

"How about seven, here in the hotel?"

"Fine," she said. "I'll call you when I'm ready."

Kim slowly returned the receiver to its place and relaxed the grip on the towel wrapped around her body.

It fell to the floor exposing her full breasts and flat stomach. She looked at herself with satisfaction. It pleased Kim that he wanted her.

Ari wandered aimlessly through the Suq el-Bzouriye, thinking about the mission. He would meet Rachael one more time, pass the information to Lieutenant Barkai, then fly out of Damascus. In less than two weeks the children would be in Jerusalem. Ari wondered where he would be.

He turned a corner into a dark and deserted passageway. Muddy water trickled down the alley, flanked by jewelers working in tiny, glass-fronted shops. Their wares—turquoise-studded bracelets, agate rings, and heavy brooches—were all oppressively alike. Farther on an old man sitting on a stool in the dirt, smoking his nargileh, looked up at Ari.

"English. You speak English?" he asked, the lines criss-crossing his face dancing as he talked.

Ari smiled and stopped.

"An American tourist?"

"Something like that," he said.

The old man pulled a wooden box from under his stool and lifted the lid, exposing a jumbled array of glass vials. He reached in, grabbed a handful, and motioned his potential customer nearer. "Perfumes, the sweet blossoms of Damascus." He studied the labelless vials for a long moment, finally choosing an amber-colored one. Uncorking it, he dabbed Ari's wrist with the top. The smell of sandalwood rose from his skin.

"It's very nice," Ari said, bringing his hand close to his nose.

The old man grinned, exposing a set of rotting teeth. Quickly he dabbed Ari's arm with the tangled aromas of musk, violet, jasmine, and chypre.

104

"Enough," Ari said, as the scent of orange blossoms was rubbed near his elbow. "How much?"

The old man studied his customer's face, trying to decide how tough a bargainer this foreigner was. "One for four pounds or five for fifteen pounds," he said after a minute.

Ari smiled. "Surely you are not serious. The bottles are tiny. I'll give you ten pounds for five of them."

"Ya-allah! That is half price. It's impossible. I cannot." He started to put the vials away, then stopped. "Ten for twenty-five pounds. Think of your woman. Give her my perfume and she will make love to you fifty, a hundred times more passionately."

Ari smiled. "Five for twelve pounds."

"I cannot possibly go lower than fourteen."

"Not even to thirteen?"

"No. It's too cheap. You are stealing food off my table. My grandchildren will starve."

"Well, then I guess we cannot agree on a price." He shrugged and started to walk away.

"Thirteen pounds fifty piasters is my final offer," the old man called after him.

Ari turned and took out his wallet. Hunting through the thick wad of currency, he found a twenty-pound note, handed it to the old man, and received his change and the bottles in return. The merchant smiled; he'd made a healthy profit.

As Ari continued down the deserted alley he realized suddenly that someone was following him. He glanced up ahead. Wood doors leading to cramped apartments lined both sides of the passageway. Quickening his pace, he listened. There were two, no, three pairs of feet that also increased their gait. Caught in an alley with no avenue of escape, he cursed himself for not bothering with extra precautions.

105

The footsteps were approaching rapidly. He searched the ground for a stick, a sharp stone, a piece of glass. There was nothing. But there's always something: a watch, an ashtray, a business card—anything that can gouge or cut becomes a weapon in trained hands. He reached into his pocket, pulled out a ball-point pen, and as the alley curved, broke into a run. The footsteps chased after him. Ari glanced back. Three young Arabs. No chance of escape. He spun around and crouched, clutching the pen like a dagger. He was quite calm.

The Arabs stopped and approached slowly. Two carried clublike sticks. The third held a length of pipe menacingly in front of him. Ari backed up against the wall. Give them less of a target, he told himself.

"We want your wallet," the one with the pipe said. "You're going to give your dollars to the Palestinians for a change."

They must have watched him buying the perfume. "I'm not an American," he said. "I'm a German, a friend of the Arabs."

"Liar."

The young man lifted his pipe and moved closer, his eyes scorched with hate.

"Wait!" Ari shouted, reaching for his back pocket. "Here." He tossed his wallet and pen at the man's feet. As the Arab looked toward the ground Ari rushed forward. He grabbed the arm holding the pipe and pulled it down hard against his knee. The pipe flew out of the man's grasp and bounced noisily on the floor of the alley. Then with a powerful cutting blow he drove the side of his hand into the man's neck, pulled him up again by the shirt, and hit him in the face with an upward thrust of his open fist. As he slumped to the pavement the other two charged.

Ari bent his left shoulder low to the ground and lashed

out with his right foot, catching one Arab in the small of the stomach and propelling him against the wall. The other swung the stick at his head. Ari managed to throw up his arm. The blow glanced off it and harmlessly hit his shoulder. With a cutting chop he struck the man's wrist, knocking the club to the ground, then quickly drove a knee hard into his groin. As the man cried out and fell backward Ari heard the sound of the first Arab coming up behind him. He turned around just as the blow came. It seemed to part his skull. The alley spun. He felt a warm, tingling sensation. Then nothing. As he lost consciousness he thought he heard voices and the sounds of a scuffle around him.

He woke, surprised to find he was propped against the wall of the alley. He'd been struck somewhere in the middle of the narrow street; he must have fallen to the ground there. Who could have moved him? On a hunch, he felt his back pocket. His wallet was in place. He pulled it out and found, as he expected, that nothing was missing. Not even the Syrian currency.

As he stood up a wave of pain rolled through his head. He touched the back of his skull. There was no blood. He wasn't hurt badly. He took a few steps in the direction he'd originally come from then bent to the ground. Something had caught his eye. A series of weaving lines parted the thin layer of dust and dirt covering the pavement. There were six of them. It was as if three men had been dragged away by the shoulders, the heels of their shoes leaving these tracks.

Slowly Ari walked back toward the Street Called Straight, trying to sort out what had happened. If the muggers were irate Palestinians, and even that was uncertain—then who had attacked them, returned his wallet, and fled rather than reveal their identities? He saw

107

only two possibilities. Lieutenant Barkai, following him for some unknown reason, could have rushed to his aid the moment he was in physical danger. But he dismissed that idea immediately. Barkai was due in the country on the twelfth, four days from now. He wouldn't have arrived early, even as a precautionary measure, not unless he was involved in something much bigger than the escape of seven children. And that was impossible—Ari would have known.

The other possibility, the Syrian police, was equally implausible. For if the police rescued a foreign businessman lying unconscious in an alley, certainly they would take him to a hospital. On the other hand, they might not have called a doctor if they knew who he really was, but if that was the case they wouldn't have bothered protecting him in the first place. The whole incident just made no sense. He realized the best thing to do now was to put the dilemma out of his mind—to let his subconscious work on the problem in its own way. The answer would come to him in due time.

Back at the New Ommayad Ari took three aspirin and climbed into the shower. He had a nasty bump on his head but the swelling would go away in a few days. He'd phone room service and have some ice sent up as soon as he was dry. The jets of hot water streamed against his body, the steam clouding the tiled bathroom. The oppressive heat of Damascus drained him. He decided he would try and rest for a few hours before meeting Kim for dinner.

"It was horrible," Kim said, after they had been seated in the hotel dining room. "Screaming women, crying children unable to find their parents, bleeding bodies strewn in the rubble. I took a picture of one young man sitting on the steps of a wooden shack, the tears rolling down his face. He held his dead son in his arms."

"Do you know why the refugee camp was bombed?"

"Kol Yisrael Radio is claiming a commando group that infiltrated the Golan Heights and attacked a school there was trained in Khan esh Shih."

Ari picked up the menu and stared blankly at the Arabic and French lettering. He wondered if the Israeli retaliatory raid accomplished anything, if it edged the Middle East closer to peace, if attacking a refugee camp brought any measure of comfort to the families of those slain in the Golan. He shook his head in sadness. He accepted the raid for what it was: the Israelis' attempt to mask a pervasive sense of helplessness with an excessive show of strength. Retaliation produced nothing; it merely spurred the cycle of violence. Ari belonged to that school of men who believed war should be fought exclusively by soldiers.

"What are you going to do with the pictures?" he asked, putting the menu down and sipping the water.

"I've already sent them to my editor. I think they illustrate graphically the senselessness of these killings. I hope they'll be printed and given wide circulation, with or without my name."

"Why? What possible good will it do to show the absurdity of raids and retaliation? Everybody already knows killing is senseless. Can your pictures ground the war planes or silence the shelling? Will a photograph splashed across the cover of *Newsweek* save one life?"

"Maybe not, but at least the world will see what's really happening here. People are deadened by the sterile recital of statistics; so many casualties this week in Middle East fighting, so many planes lost, so much money spent. But one picture, one sensitive layout can move millions of readers."

"So what if they're moved," he said angrily. "What

109

difference does it make? Are they going to cease digging graves in Khan esh Shih or the Golan Heights because people are moved?"

"Well at least it's a place to start."

He wanted to say, "Yes, the wrong place," but he stopped himself. He realized suddenly that his anger was misdirected; he was venting *his* frustration on her. The afternoon's events and his inability to understand them had set him on edge.

A long silence held. She toyed with her silverware as if she was pondering what to say next. Finally she studied his face and spoke:

"Who was that girl in your room last night?"

"I can't tell you, Kim."

"Why not?"

"It's best that you don't know." His voice was soft, contrite.

"That sounds like an excuse."

"I want you to trust me."

"How can I? You ask me to change my travel plans, to meet you in Damascus. I do, and *you* jump into bed with another girl, state that you can't explain because my life would be in danger, and after all that you expect me to simply keep quiet and trust you?"

He said nothing. It was becoming increasingly difficult to play the role of Hans Hoffmann in her presence.

"Who are you?" she asked, her voice starting to quake. "Nothing makes any sense. What were you doing in Israel? Why did you suddenly decide to come to Syria? Who was that girl? What was she doing in your room last night? This import-export business is some sort of front, I know it. What are you *really* doing in the Middle East?"

"Kim, don't ask any more questions."

"Why the hell not?"

Ari felt the shadow of the Service creeping behind

110

him. As soon as he'd changed passports in Frankfurt he had become Hans Hoffmann, import-export magnate, ex-Nazi. He was obligated to play that role with everyone, regardless of personal considerations. But he was finding it nearly impossible to continue doing so with her.

"I lied to you when I was in Israel," he said. The rest of his sentence stuck in his throat; he had to force the words out. "I didn't tell you everything about me."

"I know that."

He thought about the three Palestinians and his mysterious rescue. There was a chance that somehow the Syrians had broken his cover; if so, she might be in real danger. He had to protect both of them.

"I'm not exactly who I appear to be."

She stared silently into his eyes, waiting.

"Telling the truth now is difficult." He hesitated, uncertain if he did have to tell her.

"Go on," she said.

He nodded. "During World War II I was an SS Lieutenant at Dachau concentration camp."

She looked at him in horror. "Oh no," she mumbled. "No, not that." She hesitated for a moment, then bolted up, knocking over her water glass. "How could you? I can't..." Shaking, she ran toward the exit, bumping into the maître d' as she fled the room.

Ari sat there, numb. He expected her to be alarmed, upset, a little afraid; but the intensity of her reaction startled him. She was an American. She couldn't even have been born until after the war was over. He stared toward the exit sign, wondering if she had become so emotional because she was half-Jewish. The irony of that possibility paralyzed him. He wanted to get up and chase after her, tell her the truth; but he knew he couldn't, not while they were in Syria.

111

TWELVE

SEPTEMBER 11

NEAR THE JORDANIAN BORDER the narrow highway turned into the twisting main street of Der'a. Proceeding toward the olive wood factory across town, Mustafa Suidani drove the dust-covered Peugeot 404 through a maze of crooked alleys. Entering the poorer quarter of the village, Ari quickly rolled up the window—he preferred the heat to the stench. The corridorlike, shabby streets were strewn with refuse and human waste. Housewives used them as a garbage dump, indiscriminately casting potfuls of water and the remains of food out their windows. Hoards of undernourished children with sick eyes and running noses, wearing only underwear or nightgowns, played among the refuse. Dogs, chickens, camels, and horses wandered around unbridled; swarms of green-black flies buzzed over dung heaped in the street. As Suidani navigated a sharp curve he narrowly averted a barefoot man, standing calf-deep in mud, washing his jackass. The donkey brayed plaintively as the car accelerated by.

The unpleasant physical surroundings notwithstanding, shopping for merchandise to export to Germany became an enjoyable diversion for Ari. At first he'd dreaded the day-long trips with Suidani, for they expended much time and produced little. But soon he found that it was on these excursions that he could really relax into the role of Hans Hoffmann. He argued with manufacturers, demanded pieces be custom crafted to rigid specifications, and stomped out of shops in mock outrage, only to be called back and have the price lowered, a deal agreed upon, and sweet mint tea served amidst much handshaking and smiling. Ari gained a genuine satisfaction from striking a successful deal, as if he really were a German businessman who would reap succulent profits from his bargaining. As the years bumped into each other, then brushed away, a sense of accomplishment, any accomplishment, was all Ari had left to cling to.

Kim was gone. She had departed on a three-day visit to Aleppo without saying good-bye. The desk clerk assured him that the American lady, taking only a small suitcase with her, had not checked out of the hotel. Ari was relieved. He could wait.

Aleppo had once been a thriving Jewish community, he remembered from one of the texts Yosef Tsur had given him to read. Then in December, 1947—a few months before the partition of Palestine—anti-Jewish rioters attacked the *haret,* destroying one hundred and fifty Jewish homes, fifty shops, ten synagogues, five Jewish schools, one orphanage, and one youth club. Afterward the angry mob burned one hundred and sixty Torah scrolls in a public bonfire. No accurate estimate of the number dead could be taken, for thousands of Aleppo's Jews fled the city and sought refuge in Lebanon, making it impossible to determine if those missing had escaped or been killed. The Syrian Internal Security Service tried to halt this exodus unsuccessfully—that is, until they ordered frontier guards to shoot any Jew attempting to cross the border illegally. Emigration ceased; those left

113

behind huddled together waiting for the outbreak of war, hoping for an Israeli victory, yet knowing such a success would be brutally blamed on them. When cholera broke out in Syria in early 1948 a rumor spread that the Jews had poisoned the water. Mobs swept through the ghettos in Aleppo and Damascus—the killing and looting began again. Like a ceaseless drumbeat in a night without end, the Jews recited the haunting mourner's prayer and buried their dead. Upon "request" they contributed forty thousand Syrian pounds in support of the Arab defense of Palestine.

In the years following the 1948 war, with the help of vast sums of money and agents working inside Syria, large numbers of Jews passed illegally into Israel, most of them via Mardjayun, Metulla, and Bint Jubayl. When the Syrian government finally discovered this route and sealed off its southern border, arresting scores of its own citizens on the charge of helping emigrants enter Palestine, Israeli agents opened a corridor from Syria to Lebanon, from whose shores the Jews traveled to Israel by motorboat. Not all arrived safely; hundreds were caught and imprisoned. Others were not so fortunate. In November, 1950, a band of Arab seamen smuggled thirty Syrian Jews out of Damascus, promising to take them to Israel. Halfway between Beirut and Haifa the Arabs turned on their passengers, took their valuables, and murdered them. Twenty bodies were washed ashore and buried in Haifa.

The trickle of escaping emigrants continued to flow until the Six Day War. Immediately after Israeli troops captured the Golan Heights the humiliated Syrians locked a stranglehold on the few thousand Jews left inside the country, imprisoning them in guarded ghettos —as if afraid that the Jewish community would vanish, depriving the populace of someone to blame for their

114

country's military defeats. Air Force Commander Hafez Assad, taking control of the government in 1971, eased the restrictions on Syria's Jews somewhat, but still only a handful had managed to escape since 'sixty-seven.

When Ari returned to the hotel from the olive wood factory at Der'a he found a message tucked in his mailbox. He unfolded the yellow piece of paper, hoping the note was from Kim, only to discover that Franz Ludin had called and requested Ari telephone him at his earliest convenience. Disappointed, he moved across the faded red carpet to a house phone in a corner of the lobby and asked the operator to connect him.

"Well, how has the buying been going?" Ludin asked, after they had exchanged greetings.

"Not bad. I was in a village in the south today. Vile place, but I found some handcarved olive wood bookends and chests inlaid with camel-bone that I think might sell well in Europe."

"And the price?"

"After an hour of haggling I threatened to find another factory, and the proprietor hastily agreed to a fifty percent reduction."

"Which means he's still making twenty-five percent."

"At least," Ari agreed.

Ludin laughed. "Listen, I'm having a few friends over for dinner on the sixteenth, some people I think you'd be interested in meeting. Are you free?"

"If not, I would immediately become so."

"Good, let's say about seven-thirty. I'll have a car and driver pick you up."

"Excellent. I'll look forward to seeing you again and meeting your guests."

"I think you will enjoy yourself. I'm trying to arrange to have someone you should know join us, Hauptsturm-führer Rudolf Heinneman. He was also at Dachau. But

115

he's not well. It's uncertain if he will be able to come."

Ari's mouth went dry. The Colonel had not foreseen any of the old SS officers from Dachau being in residence in Damascus. Heinneman would spot him as a fraud!

"I don't seem to remember a Hauptsturmführer Heinneman," he stalled, trying to think of an excuse for not knowing the infamous Nazi. "But then there were quite a number of officers at Dachau in 'forty-four, 'forty-five."

"That seems strange. I was sure you two would have worked together. You were in charge of the productive labor of the prisoners and Hauptsturmführer Heinneman was responsible for the Sonderkommandos. Your workers must have been transferred to him after they were no longer strong enough to be of use to you."

The Sonderkommandos ran the gas chambers. Ari realized he'd better change his story. "Of course. I remember the Hauptsturmführer now. We called him 'The Kosher Butcher.' I'd forgotten his real name, hardly anybody used it." He hesitated for a moment, then continued. "We talked on occasion but actually our jobs were quite distinct; we almost never came into contact." He knew his explanation was inadequate.

"A pity. In any event you should have plenty of old times to talk about."

Sweat formed where Ari held the receiver. "If not, we shall create some stories that never happened," he said, laughing the way men do when they're recounting some sexual exploit that is drawn from their imagination rather than their past. He switched the receiver to the other side and wiped his hand on his pants. Somehow he would have to convince Heinneman that he really was an officer at Dachau. He had one thing in his favor—he knew Heinneman well. As a young man Ari had peered

116

through the barbed concentration camp wire and watched the bald, monocled Nazi strut around the compound. Even after so many years Ari could picture him clearly: a tall, thin man with an aquiline nose and narrow lips that always held a cigarette. Heinneman's most distinctive feature, though, was a raised vein, running along his forehead and part of his cranium, that pulsated when he was angry. Ari was not surprised to hear he was ill; the Butcher of Dachau had to be seventy or more. Yes, he remembered him—a young man does not forget the face of the person who burned two hundred and fifty thousand Jews.

"My driver will come for you at seven-fifteen," Ludin said, snapping Ari back into the present.

"I'll be waiting in the lobby."

"Good, then until Sunday . . ."

"Oh, one more thing before you hang up. If it is not too much of an inconvenience, Herr Ludin, that Jewess you sent me. I wouldn't mind . . ."

"What time do you want her?" Ludin asked impatiently.

"After dinner. I see no reason to waste good money on feeding her."

"She shall be there. Now, you must excuse me."

"Yes, of course. We will talk Sunday evening."

Ludin said good-bye and hung up. But instead of doing so himself, Ari turned around and faced the center of the lobby, affecting a continued conversation. Sitting in a leather chair on the far side of the room was a small, squat Arab, dressed in a dark business suit. Ari wanted to take a better look at him, for he had caught the Arab glancing up from his book several times while he was speaking to Ludin. At this point Ari was not ready to jump to any hasty conclusions; he just memorized the

117

reader's face. Satisfied that the Arab's physiognomy was permanently etched in his memory, he hung up and walked to the front desk.

Approaching the bell captain, he took a ten-pound note out of his wallet. "The American, Miss Johnson. When she returns to the hotel I would consider it a favor if you called me." Ari slid the bill across the desk.

"As the Monsieur wishes." The bell captain took the money and slipped it into his pants pocket.

"I'd prefer that Miss Johnson did not know about this discussion."

"Of course."

Ari nodded and went into the bar, thinking about the incident in the alley and the man with the book, trying to create a connection. If somehow the Syrian Second Bureau had penetrated his cover, to protect him until they learned why he came to Damascus, they might have attacked the muggers. If so, that would explain the man in the lobby: a team of agents would be watching him. He took out a fifty-piaster coin and spun it on the counter. But the Syrians could not have found out he was an Israeli, not so quickly. It was impossible. And the Arab by the phone—in all likelihood he was exactly who he appeared to be, a man choosing to read in a cool place rather than venture out in the afternoon heat. Ari ordered an Al Chark beer and reached into the bowl of salted pistachio nuts the bartender slid in front of him. When the beer arrived he took a long drink. The cold liquid felt good as it rolled down his throat. He nursed the rest of the Al Chark, sipping it slowly. But an hour later he was still stuck with the same conclusion: only the Mossad and the Second Bureau had sufficient reason to rescue him from the Palestinians.

118

As he left the bar he wondered if any Israeli agents he knew nothing about had recently entered the country.

Later, he stood on the balcony waiting for Rachael to be delivered to his room. He had asked to see her almost as an afterthought, being careful not to appear overly anxious. Ludin hadn't seemed suspicious.

Moving inside, Ari opened the dresser drawer and removed a bottle of Chivas Regal. The Scotch, with a stiff eighty percent import tax added on, had cost him a lot of money; but it was worth it. He was sick of the licorice taste of arak. Besides, his expense account was designed to enable him to purchase unforeseen necessities, and good Scotch was definitely a necessity. Next to the bottle lay a stack of Villars Larme de Crème chocolate bars. He had wanted to buy Rachael something. Never very good at selecting presents, he settled for the candy after rejecting a dozen more personal items.

Sprawled on the bed thumbing through a day-old edition of *Le Monde,* he was sipping his second glass of Chivas Regal when the sounds of a scuffle in the hallway interrupted his reading. He went to the door, pulled it open, and the same two police officers shoved a girl into the room. "Oh no," he whispered to himself. It wasn't Rachael! This girl was tall, thin, and at least ten years Rachael's senior.

"What about the other girl?" he asked, trying to keep his face from registering any alarm.

"She's been arrested. We brought you this one instead."

"There's not much difference between them," the other officer added.

The girl looked down at the floor, trembling.

"Call us when you're done." The officers turned toward the hallway.

"Just one more thing," Ari said, his words halting them in place. "Why was the first girl arrested?"

The taller of the two looked back. "Because she's a Jew."

Before Ari could ask if there was any connection between Rachael's visit to the hotel and her arrest, they were gone. As the door slammed shut behind them, tears burst from the girl's eyes.

"Please don't cry, I'm not going to hurt you," Ari said. He went to the dresser, poured two glasses of Scotch, and extended one toward her. She vigorously shook her head no. He pointed to a chair in the corner of the room. "Sit down," he said. She stood pressed against the wall, riveted in place. He pushed his own glass away; he didn't want it either. "You won't be harmed, please sit." She darted toward the chair and fell into it, clasping her arms across her chest, trying to keep them from shaking. Ari took a chair from next to the bed and sat across from her. "What's your name?"

"Saliha Maaruf."

The name was not familiar. Tsur, who had briefed him in detail on the inhabitants of the ghetto, had not mentioned a Maaruf family. Ari thought about the man he had seen in the lobby and the sudden arrest of Rachael; there had to be some connection. Her arrest on the heels of her visit to the hotel was too much of a coincidence. Some extra sense inside him warned of a trap.

"What happened to Rachael Khatib?" he asked.

The girl drew her legs tight together and seemed to collapse into herself.

"What happened to Rachael?" he repeated.

"She was arrested."

"I know that. When and why?"

Saliha hesitated, then spoke rapidly with nervous inflections. "The morning after she came here to the hotel,

120

the soldiers took her and her father away. They don't tell you why, when they're coming back, if they're coming back." The girl broke into tears again.

Ari took a handkerchief from his pocket and handed it to her. He wanted to believe this girl was legitimate, that she was a Jewess randomly selected to serve as Rachael's substitute; but he held back. If he gave the details of Operation Goshen to a Second Bureau agent he would soon find himself dangling from a rope in Marjeh Square. "How do you know Rachael came to this hotel?" he asked.

Saliha dried her eyes. "Everybody in the *haret* knew it. Jewish women, alone, never venture far from their apartments. Rachael was taken to spend the night in a fancy hotel with a German, then she was arrested. It is not the type of thing that remains a secret."

Ari got up, retrieved a glass of Scotch from the dresser, and drank half of it in a gulp. "What did she say about the night she spent here?"

"Nothing."

"What did she say?" he repeated roughly.

"That you yelled, beat her, and made her . . ." The rest of her sentence dissolved into a torrent of tears.

If this girl is working for the Syrians she's a damn good actress, he thought to himself.

"We assumed she didn't please you," Saliha continued between choked sobs. "And that's why you had her arrested."

Ari drained his glass and reached for the bottle, his hand shaking noticeably. Each question drove more strength out of him. He gripped the edge of the dresser to steady himself. He believed this girl was telling the truth—he wanted to believe it. Her anguish was too pervasive, the fear in her eyes, stark naked, real. She was terrified that she was next, that she would be

121

beaten, raped, and thrown into a prison cell.

"I did not have Rachael arrested," he said softly.

A puzzled look of uncertainty clouded her face; she stopped crying.

"Do you know Yakov Dahman?" he asked quickly, mentioning the name of the recent escapee who had come to Kibbutz Revivim to speak with him.

She started to answer, then stopped and lowered her eyes. "No, I never heard of him," she said after a moment.

He sensed that she was lying, that she was afraid to talk about a Jew who had escaped. Or, he asked himself, was that just what he wanted to believe? Maybe she really was a Syrian agent who had never heard of Dahman; that would explain why neither he nor Tsur had mentioned the Maaruf family—they didn't exist. Ari could not ignore the possibility that Rachael had been arrested to get her out of the way, so that the Second Bureau could plant this informer near him. He had to decide immediately: either he risked trusting her or he aborted Operation Goshen. There could be no delaying his decision. If he did not sleep with her and she really was a Jewess, he would lose the trust of the Jewish community, who at the moment already blamed him for the arrest of Rachael and her father.

"Tell me about Ibrahim Sassoon," Ari demanded, searching for some way to determine if she came from the Jewish quarter or the Second Bureau.

"The Rabbi?"

Ari nodded. "What happened to him during the Yom Kippur War?"

She looked down at the floor. "He was tied to the gate of the Al-Frange Synagogue, arms spread out like a cross. Then he was beaten with palm branches."

"What about Rachael's brother? What do you know about him?"

"He doesn't live in Damascus any more."

"Where does he live?"

"Israel," she said.

"What city?"

She mumbled something.

"What city does he live in?" Ari asked angrily.

She cleared her throat. "Haifa, he lives in Haifa."

"And his name?"

"Yair."

"And Eli Dahman, where does he live?" Ari shouted.

"In Israel," she whimpered. "Don't ask me what city. We just heard that he was smuggled across the Lebanese border. That's all I know."

Ari paced the room. "Why did you lie to me before when I asked you if you knew him?"

"I was afraid," she cried out, bursting into tears again. "It's illegal for Jews to leave Syria. I could be put in jail just for knowing he's in Israel."

"Recite the first paragraph of Israel's Confession of Faith," he demanded.

She stared at him, a puzzled look of bewilderment on her face.

"Don't you know the Shema?" he asked accusingly.

"Va'ahavta et adonai eloheha b'chol l'vavcha . . ."

"Enough," he said. "That's enough." He went to the dresser and refilled his glass. The bottle was half empty. He knew that all he had succeeded in proving was that she was either a Jewess or a highly trained agent. And if the Second Bureau had sent somebody after him, it would not be a sloppily arranged affair.

He touched the Chivas Regal to his lips, then stopped.

He had surpassed his limit and he knew it. He set the Scotch down.

"Why are you asking me all these questions?" she asked, sitting back in the chair, pushing herself as far away from him as possible.

He stared at her for a long time, hoping that something in her eyes would tip him in either direction. "Because I'm an Israeli," he said finally, wondering if he had just pronounced his death sentence.

She looked at him in disbelief. "But Rachael said that you . . ."

"She really could not go around broadcasting that she had met with a representative of the Israeli government," Ari interrupted her.

"But the arrest?"

"I didn't know anything about it until tonight."

Suddenly a look of terror crossed her face. "You're lying. You're trying to trick me. I'm going to be beaten and put in jail like Rachael."

He went to the dresser drawer, took out the chocolate bars, and handed them to her. They were soft; the heat had melted them. "As a former Nazi and an Arab sympathizer I don't have to trick you, I can take whatever I want. I have nothing to gain by pretending to be an Israeli."

She stared at him for a long time, the fear in her eyes fading. "Why are you here? What does Rachael have to do with it?"

"We'll talk in a few minutes. First, eat the chocolate; it's imported from Switzerland."

Ari moved out onto the narrow balcony and stared down at the noisy, neon-lit city—at the muddy Barada River with its concrete banks, at the dark windows of the Tajhiz Secondary School directly across from the hotel. A warm, sandy breeze blew across Damascus from the El

Hamad Desert. The wailing refrains of Fairuz, Syria's favorite singer, rolled from a transistor radio on the balcony above him. Feeling the fear of isolation, Ari turned and went back inside.

The chocolates still lay on the girl's lap; she hadn't touched them. Lowering himself to the edge of the bed, he smiled at her. "Do you know Nissim Kimche?"

"Yes," she said. "He's the Headmaster of the Alliance school. He lives on Tel el Hadjara Street near the old Dahdah Palace."

As she began to calm down he noticed her brown eyes, no longer fearful, were large and sad. He touched her hand. "You can eat the candy, there's nothing in it."

She nodded and carefully began unwrapping the foil cover on one of the bars.

He waited until she had bit off a piece of the cream-filled chocolate and swallowed it.

"Rachael was going to contact Headmaster Kimche and relay a message to him. I have no idea if she had time to do so. For now I have to assume that she did not." The girl stared at him, silently chewing the chocolate. "I want you to take her place. Do you think you could tell the Headmaster something for me without anyone else overhearing?"

"I don't know." She fingered the candy bars nervously and looked away. "I'm afraid."

"I understand, but it's important, otherwise I wouldn't ask. You might be saving the lives of some of your friends. And I promise, it won't be dangerous." He held her hand in his. "Will you do it?"

A hard silence. Finally she nodded. "All right."

"Good. The message is short: just tell Nissim Kimche to arrange for his and Rabbi Sassoon's children to be in the basement of the Alliance school precisely at 7:00 P.M. on the twenty-second, that's eleven days from now. You

125

needn't be concerned about anything else."

"But what should I say if he asks why?"

"Don't worry, he won't." Her question made him uneasy; details were the first thing a Syrian agent would want.

"Is that all?" She had expected something much more complicated.

"Yes, except you are not to let anyone but Kimche know you met an Israeli agent; everyone else is to think you were sexually molested."

She nodded, exhaling tensely. She looked worn out.

"Are you tired?"

"Very."

"All right," he said, rising. "We'll continue this in the morning." His steps unsteady, he crossed the room and bolted the front door. He wanted no uninvited intruders. "I'll sleep in the small bed. You can stay here."

"Thank you," she said, as he closed the adjoining room door behind him.

Kicking off his shoes, he sat on the edge of the narrow bed, then stretched out. The tiredness seemed to explode within him. The thoughts inside his head were jumbled, confused. He knew he had to work things out, grapple with his uncertainties, decide what to do next. But the ability to fit a pattern over the last days' events eluded him. Suddenly he wondered if Karl Richtman hadn't been right in Frankfurt; maybe he was too tired. He closed his eyes and the Scotch spun inside his head. He fell asleep wondering if Saliha worked for Sarraj, hoping she was legitimate, and that a fate similar to Rachael's did not await her departure from the hotel.

There was a knocking on the bedroom door. Ari opened one eye just enough to discern that it was morning, then let himself sink deeper into the mattress. The knocking grew louder. He strained to wake up, sweating in his sleep. The last weeks had exhausted him, but he'd be fine as soon as he was out of bed and functioning. Finally, he forced himself into full consciousness. Realizing to his dismay that he was fully clothed, he wiped his forehead on the pillow case and unbuttoned his shirt, allowing the air to flow against his damp collar. The tapping on his door continued. He slipped on his shoes and thought about the girl who was trying to rouse him, hoping he had done the right thing in trusting her.

He opened the door.

"The phone was ringing and I thought it might be important," she said self-consciously. "But it's stopped now."

Ari affected a smile in an attempt to calm her.

"What do you want me to do?"

Ari looked at her bed; the covers were tangled and draped half over the floor. She hadn't spent a peaceful night either. "If you don't mind, you could make the bed in the small room," he said. "I'm going to take a shower. I'll be right back."

"I'll do both of them," she volunteered.

"No, just do the one." She nodded and hurried past him into the adjacent bedroom. He moved toward the window. Taking the Chivas Regal from the dresser, he held it up to the morning light and looked through the amber bottle. The dark convexity of the glass shone out of its lip. There was something warm and comforting about the color amber. Scotch fills the meek with courage, provides the lonely with a friend, and helps the bored bide time. Ari shook the bottle vigorously, watching the bubbles form on the liquid's surface, then disappear a second later. Scotch also distorts one's judgment, destroys the body, and drowns reality in a false sense of well-being. People who drink because they can't cope

127

with life soon find they can't cope with alcohol. He shook the bottle again, trying to keep the bubbles from disappearing, but he couldn't, the same way he couldn't seem to keep his world from disintegrating around him. Slowly he turned from the window and made his way to the bathroom, still clutching the Scotch.

He looked into the mirror, not liking what he saw. His hair was matted against his skull, crease lines ringed his eyes, and he needed a shave. He screwed the cap off the Chivas Regal, brought the lip of the bottle to his nose, and inhaled. The odor stung the inside of his nostrils. He hesitated for a moment, then poured the Scotch down the drain.

Ari emerged from the shower with a fresh sense of vigor and determination. He dressed quickly and crossed into the main room, where Saliha sat waiting in the same chair she had occupied the night before.

"Did you sleep well?" he asked.

She shook her head. "I was up most of the night."

"I'm sorry." He moved to the phone on the nightstand and smiled at her. "Don't worry. Everything's all right. You'll be home in a little while."

He picked up the receiver and dialed the five-digit police number, assuming he was not delivering their agent back to them.

THIRTEEN

SEPTEMBER 12

A<small>RI</small> <small>LAY</small> on the bed, tangled in thought when the phone rang.

"Monsieur Hoffmann, this is the bell captain. Your friend the American photographer has just arrived in the hotel."

Ari sat up excitedly and ground his cigarette into the bedside ashtray. "Is Miss Johnson in her room now?"

"She just stepped into the elevator."

"Thank you very much." Ari hung up and hurried toward the door. When he reached her room he entered without knocking.

"You," she said, turning back from the window where she stood staring out at the city. "How did you know I was back?" Irritation was evident in her voice.

"Either I come down here every hour or I bribed the bell captain."

"What did it cost you?"

"Ten pounds."

"You could have gotten a decent whore for that price," she said caustically.

"Kim."

"You shouldn't have wasted your money, because you're finished climbing into my bed. Go back to your friend the bell captain. I'm sure for another ten pounds he can find you a consenting female. Maybe you can get somebody else right here in the hotel, since you're used to not having to go too far."

"Why did you leave for Aleppo without saying anything?" he asked, ignoring her sarcasm.

"I had to get away from you."

"Because I'm a former Nazi?"

She turned and moved toward the window without answering.

"As an American you find Nazis utterly despicable?"

"Yes," she said, facing him. "As an American and as a Jew."

"I'm still the same man you met before you knew."

"What difference does that make?"

"What if I tell you I was in charge of organizing work useful for the war effort, that I didn't have anything to do with the killings?"

"But what did you do to stop them? You were right there and you did nothing—that's even worse." She took a pack of cigarettes off the end table and nervously lit one. "You're a murderer by virtue of your silence."

Feeling her slipping away, he groped in the nothingness. There had to be a way without telling her the truth.

But he found none.

"Kim," he pleaded, at a loss for words. "Stay."

"Why? What am I? A balm to assuage your guilty conscience? The token Jew who's somehow different from the vermin you exterminated? Why do you want me? I thought Nazis believed they would be polluted if they slept with anyone with Jewish blood." Anger cut through her voice. "Didn't Hitler enact some law to protect you from the poison secreted by our genitals?"

"To me you're a person, not a Jew."

"In other words, a Jew's not a person."

130

He stood there numb, as if he were some clay object she was sticking her thumbs into, but on closer inspection he saw the thumbprints were his own.

"I don't hate Jews," he said.

Nervously she knocked the ash from the tip of her cigarette. "I don't understand. How can a Nazi not hate Jews? It's impossible. It doesn't make sense." She paused for a moment. "That is, unless . . . your behavior . . . I told you my mother was Jewish that first night in Jerusalem. It didn't matter. You still continued to see me." She crushed out her cigarette and looked at him. "You're not really a Nazi, are you?"

Ari's cheeks whitened. He was making a mistake and he knew it; but something in his subconscious told him he could trust her, that if need be he could tell her everything. Two intruders in a hostile land, their fates were intertwined, dependent on each other. But to protect himself, to protect her, he had to remain anonymous.

"I can't tell you who I am," he said, dropping into the chair by the bed. "Anything I say would only endanger you."

"How? I don't understand. You said that before—it scares me."

"Kim, just be patient. In a little while I'll be able to leave here, then I'll explain everything."

"Why can't you at least tell me who you are and what you're doing in Damascus?"

"I just can't!" he shouted. Angry at himself he moved onto the bed next to her and spoke in a gentle voice. "I'll be finished here in ten days. Trust me until then, please, it'll be the best for both of us."

She kicked at the fringes hanging from the edges of the bedspread. "I want to, but . . ."

"All I'm asking you to do is wait for a week and a half."

131

She hesitated.

"Please."

She stared out the open window, then dropped her gaze to the floor. "I went to Aleppo to work you out of my system, but I couldn't. I shot ten rolls of film but every time I looked through the viewfinder I kept seeing your face." She smiled. "Even when the lens cap was on. I didn't want to believe you were a Nazi. I tried to block it out of my mind, to convince myself that the concentration camps were a long time ago, that you could not have been part of . . ."

He kissed her, toppling the two of them over. Half-heartedly she struggled against him, pushing his hand away as he reached for the buttons on her blouse.

"Don't. It's the middle of the afternoon."

"I noticed."

She laughed and let him pull the soft material away from her body.

Afterward he lay back, thinking about the mission. Everything would work out, he told himself. Turning on his side, he rested his head against her shoulder.

"Is Hans Hoffmann your real name?" she asked, breaking the stillness.

"No," he said.

"What is it?"

Silence.

"I won't tell anybody. You can trust me."

"I know that."

"Why are you in Damascus?"

"I can't tell you."

"Why not?" she said, suddenly angry. "Is screwing me all you care about?"

"If a body was all I wanted I would pay for it."

"Well, what do you expect me to do; just jump into

bed with you on demand, not knowing who you are or even what your name is—and then talk about the weather afterward?"

"When my work's finished here . . ."

"What work? What are you? Some underworld figure? A smuggler? A dope dealer? An assassin?" She hesitated. "A spy?"

"Does it matter if I'm any of those things—or all of them?"

"Yes, no. I don't know. Oh God, why can't we just get out of here." She kicked at the blankets. "So don't tell me, don't tell me anything." She slammed her head into the pillow.

He moved toward the side of the bed and stepped on the floor. "Just be patient. After the twenty-second I'll be able to tell you everything."

She stretched her hand toward him. "Don't leave yet."

"I have to."

"More secret business?"

"Yes," he nodded, dressing quickly.

"Will you be back early?"

"I don't know, maybe. I'll call you." He stretched across the bed to kiss her good-bye but as he came near she turned away.

After Moslem troops wrestled control of Damascus from the Byzantine Empire in 635, the Jews and Christians were pressed into those parts of the city farthest from the west winds and fresh waters of Lebanon. Ari thought about this as he squeezed through a crowd of veiled women and sweaty men on the Street Called Straight. Heading east toward the Bab Touma, the Christian quarter, he turned the corner and neared a sherbet seller. Wearing red and white striped robes, with brass ewers strapped to his chest and bowls clicking, the man approached, urging him to "eat the sweet fruits of Damascus and make love five times a day." Ari shook his head no, and increased his gait, skirting around two dogs fighting over a mutton bone in the narrow street.

The Bab Touma, crushed and confused, its streets wrapped in sudden belts of din and silence, struck Ari as being medieval. The few new houses he spotted seemed to be wedged in against the jumbled architecture of other generations. Decorated coffee tables, shesh-besh boards, mother-of-pearl inlaid boxes, and polygonal stools called *kursi* spilled onto the sidewalk from open shops. Soon he passed the khan of Suleiman Pasha, a Turkish warehouse, once filled with bales of Chinese and Indian silk. Now, empty oil drums lined its crumbling walls.

As he proceeded north up Dja Afar Street in the direction of the Church of Saint Ananias the lane twisted and narrowed, winding past closed doors. From around a curve in the alley a group of ragged boys emerged, their pajamalike shirts dirty and torn. Realizing from his dress and coloring that Ari was a foreigner, they clustered around him chanting: "Anania! Anania!" in unison. He shook his head, indicating that he was not interested in visiting the church. But they insisted, their cry reminiscent of the bleating of sheep. Ari dug into his pocket, withdrew a handful of coins, and flung them back behind him. The gleeful boys scurried after the money, squealing and shouting as they fought each other for the piasters. Ari hurried out of the alley and through the ancient Roman arch from whose base Azaryeh Street began—certain now that he wasn't being followed.

Reaching his destination, he walked down a flight of stairs to the dark Café Shaam. Since Ottoman rule the *kahwa* has been an accepted meeting place for student groups, conspiring merchants, army officers, and gov-

134

ernment officials. In fact the city's coffee houses are so closely linked with political factions, according to the affiliations of their customers, that the police and Internal Security Service mapped and classified them, invariably asking suspects which ones they patronized.

Ari stood at the entrance for a while waiting for his eyes to adjust to the lack of light. Kibbutz Revivim's scale model of Damascus was exact; Ari had found the café without difficulty. Stepping inside, he glanced at the luminous dial on his watch. It read 5:30; he was half an hour early. As his eyes grew accustomed to the darkness he made out the shadowy figures of men seated at low tables, playing shesh-besh, and sucking on glowing nargilehs. The heavy aromas of tobacco and hashish hung in the air. Ari moved across the room and sat on a straw stool at a vacant table. In the center of the table was a nargileh. He removed the cover and dumped a small quantity of French Gitanes Blend into the metal bowl at the top of the pipe. Soon a special waiter approached and placed a chunk of burning coal over the tobacco. After snapping the lid back on Ari brought the long snakelike tube to his mouth and inhaled. The water in the glass jar at the base of the nargileh bubbled as the smoke was drawn through it, cooled, and sucked into his mouth.

After a while a different waiter moved near and asked if he would like something to eat. Ari ordered salted olives, red peppers, a tray of sweetmeats, and a pot of mint tea. In the event Lieutenant Barkai was late, he would wait. Ari assumed that Barkai had crossed safely into Syria. He was supposed to have arrived early today. Carrying a forged Moroccan passport, the French- and Arabic-speaking lieutenant should have had no trouble entering the country.

While he waited Ari nibbled the sweetmeats and occasionally sucked on the nargileh. He let the tea steep.

135

Waiting was the fundamental task of intelligence agents. Anyone could be trained to kill or blow up buildings. But the ability to wait for hours, days, or weeks if need be, without becoming tense, without betraying that you indeed were engaged in an assignment—such patience could not be taught. It had to exist in a person.

Ari allowed the thoughts to ripple through him. Noticing the total absence of women in the café, he mused about the anomalies of Moslem Syria. Fifty years ago polygamy and concubines had flourished in Damascus and a generation before that a woman appearing on the streets unveiled was automatically assumed to be a prostitute and could have been slain by any male passerby without fear of retribution. Even now many women would not talk to a man openly, or dare meet him; for such behavior could easily taint their reputations. A woman who has been touched by another man is often considered unacceptable by prospective suitors. On the eve of Druze weddings the bride hands her husband a knife and asks him to stab her should she not prove a virgin. Even after marriage most Syrian women are relegated to a lowly status. They cannot leave their homes without their husband's permission and rarely speak with his friends, or for that matter, converse with their own spouses in public. Syrian men never talk about their wives and consider it an insult to be asked about them. Because of the distance they must keep from women, many males find release from otherwise unsatisfiable pressures in homosexuality. In the far corner of the room two young men sat close together, one's hands reaching under the other's loose robes.

Behind the counter of the coffee house the radio blared the high-pitched songs of Om Kalthoum, the beloved Egyptian singer whose funeral in Cairo in 1975 drew crowds as large as, and causing as much damage as, the mourners who rampaged through the Egyptian capital following the interment of Nasser five years earlier. After a while Ari's thoughts drifted to Kim. He wondered whether his life still had to revolve solely around the Service. In any event, he swore that he would not let this assignment ruin his relationship with her. Sweeping the room with his eyes, he checked to make sure that Barkai was not seated at one of the low tables. Then he asked the waiter for a shesh-besh set and began playing against himself.

The blacks were ahead of the whites three games to one when Ari poured out the last of the tea. He slowly took one sip from the small porcelain cup at a time. The liquid left an unpleasant aftertaste in his mouth. It was lukewarm and poorly strained.

The hours ground into each other then blew away. Two men at a neighboring table, who wore styleless black suits and flowing keffiyehs tied with gold ropes, offered Ari some hashish to mix with his tobacco. He smiled at them, graciously declined, then looked at his watch and followed the second hand around the dial. The calender date read the twelfth, the day the Colonel had set for the first meeting between the two halves of Operation Goshen. After ordering another pot of tea Ari took up the small dice and rolled, beginning game five of the blacks against the whites. A double six came up and the blacks surged out ahead again. He wondered if the results of the game weren't somehow symbolic.

It was a little after nine when Ari first allowed himself to realize that Barkai probably wasn't coming. By ten-thirty he was sure of it. But there was always a chance the lieutenant had been delayed and would still show. So Ari tossed the dice, relit the pipe, and waited. The water at the bottom of the nargileh was warm now, and it did little to cool the harsh tobacco. Ari let the tube drop from his

137

mouth and focused his concentration on the game. When the music blaring through the café was interrupted for the last and final news report of the night at midnight, he stood slowly, stretched, and headed for the door.

Outside he leaned against the stone wall of the building, hoping that if he lingered an additional minute Barkai might miraculously appear. The minute turned into two, then five. Ari walked up the steps to the street and stopped, listening hard to what he thought was the sound of approaching footsteps—but in reality was the creation of his own imagination.

He started to walk under the moonless sky. The combination of the darkness of the streets, the arches over them, and the narrowness between the walls was a bit unnerving. From a nearby passageway he heard the howl of a wolf-dog, followed by rasping and swishing sounds as the animal dragged refuse along the gutter. Wild dogs, long-muzzled like wolves, slept in the fields and ruins during the day, then glided into the old city at night, after the town was silent. Suddenly a pack of them, snarling and yelping, rushed up and attacked the first dog. The barking, echoing down the dark alleys, sent a shiver through Ari. He saw nothing. He only heard the noise: the horrible howling, the snapping, the snarling. The attacked animal cried out in a long, high-pitched wail. Then its throat was ripped open and silenced.

Ari hurried through the night, the sounds of the dogs fading behind him. A fall-back meeting with Barkai had been arranged for the eighteenth at noon. If he was not contacted at the hotel he would have to wait until then.

FOURTEEN

SEPTEMBER 16

FRANZ LUDIN'S DRIVER picked Ari up at the New Ommayad and drove toward the western edge of the city, over the Nabek Bridge and into the fashionable Jisr district. Turning into Ibrahim Mansour Street, they passed the honey-colored minaret of the Raoudah Mosque spiraling into the sky directly across from the walled Italian Embassy, which had handled diplomatic relations with the United States until President Assad reestablished ties with America in 1974. Soon the Czech Skoda stopped in front of a white stone villa at 14 Ataa el-Aiyouby Street, between the Banque de Syrie d'Outre-Mer and a florist shop. Ari got out and passed through a fountain courtyard into an arcade with vines climbing through the latticework. Hearing his approaching footsteps, Ludin swung the front door open and welcomed his guest in.

Ari bowed with Prussian correctness. "I've been looking forward to this evening." *With trepidation,* he might have added. For if Rudolf Heinneman was well enough to attend the party, and his suspicions were roused by not remembering an Untersturmführer Hans Hoffmann, Operation Goshen would meet an abrupt end—and Ari's life with it. Ludin led him through the classically Syrian house whose rooms, opening into two courtyards, were

139

not linked together. As they stepped outside into the iwan the three men standing there stopped talking. A quick glance informed Ari that though they were all German émigrés, Heinneman was not among them.

"Kameraden, I would like to introduce SS Untersturmführer Hans Hoffmann."

Ari smacked his heels together and remained at attention as the three men approached.

"Herr Hoffmann, may I introduce Colonel Ludwig Streicher, former instructor in military tactics at the Berlin War Academy, presently adviser to the Syrian army; my associate from Goebbels's propaganda ministry, Gunther Brunner; and Adolf Eichmann's aide, Heinrich Wolff." The three men knocked the leather of their shoes together, each bowing stiffly as he was introduced.

Following the war these Nazis, along with an estimated one hundred former Reich officials still living in Damascus, were actively recruited as military advisers by the Arab Wehrmacht Lieutenant Colonel Akhram Tabassa. Some, contacted in Germany and Austria by former Nazis carrying Syrian passports, underwent a crash course in Arabic, then proceeded to Rome and Geneva where clandestine processing stations set up in the Syrian legations supplied them with the papers necessary for travel to the Middle East. Others, fugitives contracted by the French and Spanish foreign legions to fight in Indochina, were sold to the Syrians for $500 apiece, smuggled through the French zone in Germany under the guise of legionnaires, and delivered for embarkation to ports in Italy and Turkey. The higher-ranking German officers, watched over by the paternal eye of SS Hauptsturmführer Rostal, who was in charge of the ODESSA's European branch, gathered in Augsburg where they were given forged passports. From there they were driven across the border in newspaper delivery trucks

140

to Lindau on Lake Constance, where Austrian women and children, hired to pose as their relatives, accompanied them to St. Gall in Switzerland. Major Gunther von Hardenberg, stationed in Beirut, met each plane from Geneva. His association for Christian German War Refugees assigned the Nazis to units in the Syrian army and helped them on their last lap to Damascus. Ludin, Streicher, Wolff, and Brunner had all been passengers on Hauptsturmführer Rostal's underground railroad.

As Ludin poured a round of drinks Ludwig Streicher approached Ari, glass in hand. "When we get together like this it reminds me how much I miss Germany. Where did you serve during the war?"

"Dachau."

Streicher turned to their host. "It's a pity Heinneman couldn't be here. I'm sure he would have enjoyed speaking to Herr Hoffmann."

Ari began to relax—he had escaped the Butcher of Dachau, again. Now, with the threat to his cover eliminated, he could concentrate on other matters. Accidentally he had struck a gold mine of high-ranking Nazi officers. He decided that upon returning to the hotel he would hide a coded request for further instructions in one of the backgammon sets and send it to Frankfurt. Maybe the Colonel would give him permission to liquidate Ludin and the others, if he could figure out a way to do it without jeopardizing his principal assignment. That is, if he heard from the Colonel. Though he had tried to put it out of his mind, the fact that Barkai had not shown up worried him—it worried him a lot.

"Heinneman has not been feeling well," Ludin said. "But he promised to try and join us for a little while later in the evening."

The muscles inside Ari's stomach tightened. He was not out of danger yet.

"Splendid," Eichmann's thin, balding aide, Heinrich Wolff, said. "Now let's get our guest a drink and have him tell us about the new, democratic, wet-nursing German republic." They all laughed. Wolff took Ari by the arm and led him to a low, mother-of-pearl table serving as an outdoor bar. "The Israelis and West Germans look for me everywhere," he said. "They accuse me, quite wrongly, of having killed Jews during the war. Fortunately, I'm comparatively undisturbed in Damascus and allowed to earn a respectable living here."

Ari took the Scoresby Scotch the well-known fugitive offered him. A member of Eichmann's staff in Bureau IVB 4a, Heinrich Wolff had been responsible for the deportation of Jews from Greece, France, Slovakia, and Austria to extermination camps in Poland.

"Why did you say *comparatively* undisturbed?"

Wolff glanced at Streicher and sipped his drink. "Earlier this year we caught an Israeli spy masquerading as a Syrian banker with connections to the Krupp arms fortune in Germany. He turned out to be an Iraqi Jew. Spoke Arabic with a perfect Syrian accent, I'm told. Ludwig knew him."

"What happened?"

"The Second Bureau spotted an irregularity in his cover story, did some checking, and discovered he was a fraud," Wolff said.

"And they arrested him?"

"Yes. Lucky thing too. He would have escaped, but evidently his people didn't show at the rendezvous point. They left him stranded."

"It was very strange," Brunner added. "Some heads must have rolled in Tel Aviv over that one. We're certain he sent a distress signal to Cyprus with the transmitter we found destroyed in his apartment. The Israeli's liaison officer must have been away from his post."

142

Ari staggered back, fighting to keep his composure. Dov must have signaled for help the weekend he was in Kyrenia with Michelle. He was responsible for the ordeal the boy was undergoing. Nobody had told him!

"You've suddenly turned white," Brunner said. "What's wrong?"

"Nothing, nothing," Ari answered quickly, understanding now why the Colonel had brought him home. He forced a cough and set his Scotch down. "A piece of ice got caught in my throat. It's passed. I'm fine now." He picked up his glass, took a long drink, then looked at Brunner. "Is this Israeli spy still alive?"

"We don't know. The Second Bureau chief, Suleiman Sarraj, has kept the details surrounding his interrogation very quiet."

"Has he made him talk?"

"We have no idea. As I said, Sarraj has been tight-lipped about the whole thing."

Ari frowned and turned toward the tall, powerfully built Streicher. "This could have been dangerous for all of us. Heinrich said you spoke to him. Were you able to find out what the Israeli was doing here?"

"No."

"But he must have said something that gave you a clue to the purpose of his mission."

"I'd rather not discuss the incident," Streicher said.

Ludin stepped between his two guests. "Excuse me for interrupting, gentlemen, but dinner is about ready." He took Ari by the arm. "And let us discuss more pleasant matters inside. Come, I want to show you the case of Weingut Erath Liebfraumilch that just arrived from Mai-kammer. Select a bottle for us to drink with our food."

As they settled into the den after the meal Ari glanced

at his watch. He felt that after half an hour or so he could claim he wasn't feeling well, make his apologies, then scurry back to the hotel without focusing suspicion on himself or insulting his host. He should leave as soon as possible, lest Heinneman show up and betray him as an imposter. Fate and Heinneman's health had given him a temporary reprieve, but now it was up to Ari to avail himself of it. He'd press Ludin for details about Dov's capture and interrogation at a later date.

Just then the doorbell rang. The sound flushed fear into his bloodstream. A few moments later Ludin's Arab servant led an elderly man into the room. Ari felt something tighten in his throat as if a noose had been placed around his neck.

It was Heinneman.

Ari would have recognized him anywhere, at any time. Though he was bent now and he used a cane to steady himself, the man was the same. The eyes hadn't changed, the monocle was still there, and so was the vein that stretched across his forehead.

"Rudolf, come sit down and let me reacquaint you with an old *komerad.* Herr Heinneman, SS Untersturmführer Hans Hoffmann of Dachau Camp."

Ari leapt to his feet and saluted Heinneman, shouting, "Jawohl, Herr Hauptsturmführer."

"You were at Dachau?" Heinneman asked, lowering himself slowly to the couch.

"Yes," Ari said.

"Hoffmann, Hoffmann. I don't seem to remember the name."

"We only met once or twice."

As Ari sat on the couch, Heinneman squinted, and peered at him through his monocle. "Your face looks vaguely familiar—but an Untersturmführer Hoffmann. I remember no such officer."

"That's strange," Wehrmacht Colonel Streicher said. "How long were you at Dachau, Herr Hoffmann?"

Ari fought an inner battle, struggling against the tendency to simply allow himself to be taken, to end it all: the masquerade, the game, the isolation.

"Two years," he said.

"It seems very odd that Rudolf does not remember you."

Ari turned toward Heinneman. He could not understand why he and the other inmates had never pounced on this animal and beaten the life out of him with a rock, a board, or a shovel. There had been more than ample opportunity. Suddenly Ari wanted to do it now, before Streicher closed in on him. He looked at Heinneman's neck; he was certain he could snap it and be out the front door before Streicher, Ludin, and the other two recovered from the shock. There would be no possibility of escape, but at least . . .

"I was under Hauptsturmführer Frederick Gerhard's command," Ari said, facing Heinneman. "My detachment was responsible for the organization of the camp labor kommando. Since I was of insignificant rank possibly you did not notice me, but I definitely remember you. You were a model of excellence that we younger men attempted to imitate. There was no officer so well liked, so respected at Dachau. Your ruthless handling of the prisoners in punishment block number 11 was spoken of throughout the camp. When you passed the pathetic creatures shivered in fear. I remember one particular incident when a Jew was lying in the dirt and wouldn't get up as you ordered; you pointed a pistol at his head and made him polish your boots by licking them and then wiping the spittle off with his beard. When he finished you emptied your gun into his temple, splattering his head over the ground. Then you made two young Jews carry the body to the crematorium."

Heinneman smiled at the recollection. "Of course, I remember the day clearly. It was in the winter of 1944; Bitta, my German shepherd, had come down with a cold and I was concerned about her. The Jew had interrupted my thoughts. Funny you should remind me of that morning—I haven't thought about Bitta in years." Heinneman drifted back to the memory of his dog, then slowly forced his way into the present. "What made you recall that incident?"

"I was standing behind the barracks, laughing. The Jew rubbing your boot with his chin just struck me as being very funny. I've always remembered it."

Ari remembered that particular killing not because he'd stood to the side laughing, but because he had been one of the two boys ordered to carry the corpse to the ovens. While holding the frail body by the shoulders, the Jew's brains had dripped over his hands and onto his clothes.

"In which part of the camp did you live?" Heinneman asked.

"I was in barracks three near the little bridge and flower garden."

"A lovely spot. I used to like to walk there after a long, tiring day."

Streicher lit a cigarette, and blew the match out as he exhaled. He held the cigarette from underneath with the tips of his thumb and index finger, the way Germans do.

"Rudolf, do you remember Herr Hoffmann now?" Streicher asked.

Heinneman tapped his cane impatiently on the floor. Though technically Colonel Streicher held a higher rank than the ailing Hauptsturmführer, the SS officer privately held all Wehrmacht officers in contempt, blaming them for the demise of the Third Reich. "I'm an old man," he said, letting his monocle fall from his eye. "And not so foolish as to believe that my memory does not fail me. Just because I cannot remember one of the *komeraden* after more than a quarter of a century, there is no reason to suspect anything beyond the simple fact that I am becoming senile." He took his cane and lightly struck Streicher on the knee. "I suspect you too do not have the memory you had when the Führer was with us."

Ludin laughed, trying to chip away at the tension that blanketed the room. Ari and the other Nazis joined him. Whether Streicher was satisfied enough not to press his inquiries further, Ari didn't know. But the rest of the evening passed in trivial conversation. If Streicher was still suspicious of him, he kept it to himself.

Back in his room in the hotel, Ari locked and bolted the door, then collapsed on the bed, shaking.

FIFTEEN

SEPTEMBER 18

IN THE MORNING, several hours before his second scheduled attempt to contact Lieutenant Barkai, Ari plodded through the marketplace on the Street Called Straight, stepping around puddles of mud covered over, unsuccessfully, by newspaper. The vegetable bazaar was cluttered with stalls piled high with tomatoes, peppers, onions, cabbages, and eggplants. Women from the al-Ghutah orchards, dressed in black and ultramarine cotton, their hair and necks veiled, their eyes outlined with kohl in emulation of the gazelle, crowded between the stands offering to trade fruit for the vegetables. They were easily distinguished from the women of the desert region near Hijaneh who wore bright yellows and pinks, their foreheads circled by a series of gold discs. Passing a man sitting on a straw stool eating stuffed vine leaves sunk in goat's milk, Ari increased his gait, trying to escape the stench of rotting food trapped in the market by the corrugated iron roof overhead. Soon he reached the Roman arch on Bab Sharki Street just outside the Haret al Yahoud.

He skirted around the soldiers lounging on the corner of el-Amine and Tel el-Hadjara streets, casting a casual glance in their direction. If a person acts at ease in a given place, those observing him will probably assume he belongs there. Anyway it seemed everyone was allowed free passage in and out of the *haret*. Ari wiped the sweat off his brow with his shirt sleeve. Though it was the middle of September the eastern winds continued to blow in from the desert, daily depositing a thin layer of sand over the city, relentlessly pushing the afternoon temperature up over 100 degrees. The mornings and nights weren't much cooler.

Ari moved toward Rachael's apartment—if anyone became suspicious he could always explain his presence there with lascivious innuendoes. An uneasiness had plagued him ever since Saliha's unexpected appearance in his room. Rachael's being arrested immediately after spending the night in his hotel was too much of a coincidence; and if there was one thing his years in the Service had taught him, it was that most coincidences were humanly engineered. If so, Ari wanted to know by whom, and why.

The sound of a boy screaming invaded his thoughts, breaking them off fractured, incomplete. The cry for help came from an alley just ahead of him, growing in intensity as it cut through the still Jewish ghetto. At the sound of the screaming, wooden shutters on both sides of the street slammed shut. Trembling, the Jews attempted to ignore the pained plea forcing itself into their homes from the street below. But yanking the shutters closed offered no escape. The screaming flowed through the cracks in the broken wood, streaming into the hearts of whole families who sat numb, silent—wondering who would be next. Weeks, months, years ago, there had been a few who tried to fight back. They were now dead, along with their families, friends, and sometimes even their neighbors.

Ari hurried toward the source of the screaming, trying

not to run, not to appear too concerned. Turning into the alley, he stopped abruptly. The stench of burned flesh struck his nostrils. His mouth went dry and his eyes misted. Instinctively he turned away, the shrieking ricocheting inside his head. A young boy maybe sixteen or seventeen approached him, speaking in Arabic. Ari spun around and stared back to where a group of youths held a lean, scrawny-looking boy to the ground. A trash fire burned in the middle of the alley. One of the boys held a pointed stick over the glowing embers, the tip a fiery red. Blood and singed membrane dripped down the pinned child's face. His right eye had been gouged out. Now the youthful band, mercifully deciding to spare the other eye, was busy burning a Star of David into the screaming victim's chest. But the lines were jagged—the little Jew had squirmed, refusing to be held still. His brown skin was charred black and bloody, his chest burned repeatedly in an attempt to straighten out the lines of the six-pointed figure.

Though Ari didn't respond, the boy who approached him kept talking. The flow of Arabic fell unintelligibly on his ears, that is except for the repeated use of the word *Yahoud.*

"I don't speak Arabic," Ari said, gaining control of the anger churning inside him. He easily could have slammed into the crowd of boys, picked up the little Jew, and taken him to a nearby apartment building. But he dared not move or show any interest at all.

"He's a Jew," the young Arab said, switching to French. "We caught him stealing food from the apartment of a Palestinian. Not only do they seize our land, but they enter our homes and take the bread off our tables." The boy spat on the ground.

Ari hoped they would not adhere to the Koranic injunction, followed literally in Saudi Arabia and Libya,

150

that demanded a thief's hand be chopped off as punishment for stealing. Suddenly the child's screaming stopped. He had passed out. The boys let go of him and dropped their sticks; evidently it was no fun poking at an unconscious body.

Ari looked at the young Arab and spoke softly. "He's been taught a lesson. The Jew will not be so foolish as to attempt to take your food again."

The boy smiled, baring white teeth. Ari turned and walked back to the street, the smell of burned flesh lingering in his nostrils.

The *haret* was deserted and quiet. While Jews in other parts of the world gathered to protest their persecution, here there was only waiting, a treading on time; not life, but merely the absence of death. Ari walked up the dark stairs inside a building at 21 El Boustana Street. He held onto the rail because the wood underneath his feet swayed with his every step. As he slowly inched his way toward the third floor, the stairwell grew darker. There were no windows, no light. "Ouch," he said suddenly. A splinter from the rough railing had jabbed his fingers. He pulled it out and sucked at the tiny wound. In the dark he couldn't see if he had gotten the sliver all out or not.

The third-floor corridor carpet was faded and worn. The hallway itself was dark, musky, and heavy with the odor of stale air. It brought a chill to his bones, despite the heat. Ari knocked lightly on number seventeen and waited. There was no answer. He banged harder. Nobody came to the door, but he thought he made out a faint noise inside the apartment. He turned the handle and pushed. It wouldn't budge—the door was locked. Ari hammered at the wood until his knuckles hurt. Finally he heard the sounds of approaching footsteps.

A matronly woman opened the door. She was short

151

and wrinkled, with mousy brown hair pinned back in a braided bun.

"Madame Khatib?"

She nodded feebly, too tired to use words.

"I just want to ask about Rachael."

She slammed the door shut; but Ari caught his foot at the base, wedged it there, and forced his way inside.

Hate lodged in her small eyes. "Haven't you done enough? You've taken my husband away and destroyed my daughter. Can't you leave her alone. What can you possibly want with her now?" She shot a glance toward the closed door in the far corner of the room. Ari followed her gaze and moved across the apartment.

"No!" she shouted, clutching at his sleeve. "Don't take her away again. Don't do this to me." A stream of tears ran down her cheeks.

Ari stopped. "I'm a friend of Rachael's," he said, trying to reassure Madame Khatib. "I'm not going to hurt her or take her away. I haven't touched her. I wouldn't touch her. You must believe me."

She stood there: frail, vulnerable, confused. The tears continued to roll down her cheeks.

Ari opened the door to the tiny bedroom. Rachael sat looking out the window, her back facing him. She didn't move when he entered.

"Rachael," he whispered softly.

No response.

Ari stood in place. "Rachael," he called louder. His voice echoed hollowly off the walls.

Her mother pushed past him, grabbed the chair and turned it around. Rachael stared through them, offering no sign of recognition.

Ari bent near her. "Rachael, can you hear me?"

She didn't blink.

He rose, a look of horror impressed on his face. The

152

fury cutting through him was matched only by his anguish.

"How long has she been like this?"

"Ever since they brought her back."

"When was that?"

"Two days ago."

"What do the doctors say?"

"They can't find anything physically wrong with her. It's her mind. She's been . . ." Her voice broke; she couldn't go on.

"What did they do to her?" he shouted, venting his misplaced anger on Madame Khatib.

"I don't know. A neighbor found her wandering in the street. He brought her up. She hasn't spoken a word since."

Rachael continued to stare at them, a glazed look of catatonia in her eyes. Ari took the girl's head and held it against his chest. It was like touching a mannequin; she didn't respond, she just allowed herself to be moved. He stroked her dark hair, and looked out the window, wanting to cry and not wanting to cry at the same time. Her visit to his hotel room had not caused this, it couldn't have. Bending down, he looked into her vacant eyes, then brought his lips to her cheek. It was dangerous for him to be here, to have anything to do with her when it was obvious he could no longer claim his intentions toward this girl were purely carnal.

"I have to go," he said, turning to Madame Khatib. "If anyone asks, I came here intending to rape your daughter. That's important. Do you understand?" He drilled a hard glare at her.

She nodded. Though confused, she decided if questioned she would comply with his request. The way this foreigner held Rachael convinced her to trust him.

Abruptly Ari hurried into the main room. He couldn't

153

bear to be near the girl; every second in her presence was a reminder that she'd probably been arrested because of him.

Mrs. Khatib followed.

"Will she get better?" she asked tearfully, begging for a comforting reply.

"I don't know."

He moved toward the door and stopped. "Remember, if anyone asks, I came to rape her."

She nodded.

He placed his hand on the doorknob, hesitated, then turned back. "Do you know Saliha Maaruf? She says she's a friend of Rachael's."

"Saliha Maaruf." She paused for a moment, then shook her head. "I don't remember Rachael ever mentioning her."

"Are you sure?"

Madame Khatib nodded.

Ari arrived at the Café Teyrouzi in the northern Chouhada district, across from the Syrian Parliament, forty-five minutes early. Standing in the entranceway, he pushed his shoulder against the wood casing, trying to support what little energy he had left. The incident in the alley, the man in the lobby, and the arrest of Rachael all suggested that the Syrians were onto him. And now there was the possibility that Saliha was a Second Bureau agent, that he'd blown Operation Goshen. His mouth was dry. He felt the beating of his heart. Sweat clung to his clothes.

After glancing around the room, he settled into a corner table to wait for Lieutenant Barkai. The café was located in a better area of town than the one in which the two Israelis had first attempted to rendezvous; it was essential that Ari move around, that no pattern be ascribed to his activities. The Colonel had chosen Teyrouzi for no reason other than it had little in common with Café Shaam in the Christian quarter. Teyrouzi, large and well illuminated, with formica tables and white plaster walls lined with photographs of famous Arab personalities, was a particular favorite of Damascus's intellectual elite.

Ari ordered sweet coffee and a plate of shakshouka, vegetables fried in spiced tomato sauce. When the food arrived he ate slowly, occasionally glancing around the room. Barkai would show this time, Ari told himself as he chewed on a piece of makrouk bread. He was sure of it. If not, the Mossad would send somebody else or somehow get in touch with him. By now they'd received the message about his losing the transmitter, sent in the specially packaged backgammon set.

Without radio communication all he could do was wait for the Colonel's next move. He was sure it would be made this afternoon. It had to be—time was running out. The children were to be lowered into Damascus's sewer system in four days. There could be no delay: either Operation Goshen was executed according to the preset timetable or the children had to be abandoned. Those were his orders.

Soon Ari ordered a second cup of thick Turkish coffee. Barkai was late again. Ari looked at his watch—the second hand crawled unceasingly across the white dial. He flipped the band so that the face pointed away from him and he couldn't see what time it was. A simple crutch, but an effective one.

The minutes slowly fell away. Ari was not a particularly philosophical man and he resisted the opportunity to pass the time by pondering such abstract notions as man's fate and the reasons for the suffering he'd seen. Instead, he replayed the events of the last three weeks

155

over and over in his mind, searching for something he could not put his finger on—the answer to a question he was yet unable to formulate.

If Barkai didn't turn up he didn't know what he would do. Getting the children out of the ghetto was futile if the lieutenant was not prepared to transfer the youngsters to the boat that would take them to Israel. Ari could not carry out the entire operation alone, not with the Syrians on his back. Barkai had to show.

Just then he felt the need to urinate. "Too much coffee," he mumbled to himself as he rose and shuffled toward the rear of the room.

When he returned from the bathroom, he saw a man looking out from the front doorway, his back facing the café. Ari's heart skipped a beat. It was Barkai. Finally. As the adrenalin rushed through his veins he moved toward the lieutenant. Before he had crossed half the café, Shaul Barkai turned and gazed around the room. The taut hope inside Ari snapped. His eyes had been playing tricks on him. It wasn't Barkai! The man standing in the doorway was about the same height and build as Barkai but the resemblance ended there.

Ari stopped in the middle of the room and forcibly tried to calm himself. He was slipping farther than he'd realized. He went back to the table, fighting an internal war of nerves he had fought before and lost. He ordered a bottle of arak. When it came he gingerly unscrewed the cap, poured himself a glass of the clear liquid, and drank it quickly.

There was an unwrapped toothpick lying on the table. Ari hesitated for a moment, thinking that it might have been used, then laughed at himself. He took the thin piece of wood and began working his back teeth. It seemed silly to worry about other people's germs when he chose lovers so haphazardly, without any concern for

156

hygiene. He supposed everybody at times, unable to wait, made urgent love to a partner whose health was questionable. He remembered that when he was sixteen he and a German girl named Anna spent an entire summer with head colds. They were infatuated with each other and kept passing the cold back and forth. They couldn't refrain from kissing long enough for both of them to get well. Angrily Ari spat the toothpick on the floor, poured himself a glass of arak, drank it, then poured another. Why was he thinking about that German girl now?

He directed his thoughts elsewhere, concentrating on a still lake in the Bavarian Forest outside Regensburg that always soothed him when he walked along its shores. He could almost smell the scent of the pine trees climbing the nearby hills. Suddenly Rachael's face appeared on the surface of the water. She stared up at him without a sign of recognition. He closed his eyes. The image held in his mind for a moment, then dissolved into blackness.

Barkai never showed.

Before returning to the New Ommayad Ari stopped at a falafel stand across the street from the hotel. For fifty piasters he received a sandwich consisting of a round of pita bread, slit, and filled with discs of ground chick peas and pieces of tomatoes, pickles, and cabbage. He ordered his without the usual yogurt sauce. Eating the falafel as he walked, he hurried into the hotel and up to Kim's room. He would make a decision about what to do later. At the moment he needed to relax; to divert his thoughts away from the Service, his assignment, and the absent Israeli Intelligence officer.

When he entered her room, Kim literally exploded into his arms. "They printed my pictures of Khan esh Shih in the *International Herald Tribune!*" she said, excitedly waving the newspaper in her hand as she let go of him.

"Let me see." He looked at the paper, wanting very much to be part of her happiness. There were two pictures at the bottom of the page: one of a shelled building, gaping holes gouged out of its side; and the other of a cemetery with gravediggers readying the earth for the dead. Under the pictures was the by-line: K. Johnson. If Ari had any trace of doubt about her being who she said she was, it was now erased. Though he found himself unable to share in her success, he kissed her. At least it might help reduce the tension within him.

"But you haven't heard the best part," she said, pushing him away. "Somebody from the Foreign Ministry called and asked if I would like to take pictures of Israelis captured in border skirmishes since the October '73 War. It seems the American government has been pressing the Russians to get the Syrians to let the Red Cross in and visit the prisoners. It's a little complicated, but the man who called was very impressed with the coverage in the *Tribune*. He's invited me to photograph the Israeli prisoners to show that they are being treated within the confines of the Geneva Convention." She took his hand and held it in hers. "Newspapers and magazines all over the world will be beating at my door just to get a chance at printing the pictures. I'm so excited, this is such a lucky break." She rested her head on his shoulder, then jerked it up again, too agitated to settle in one place for more than a few seconds.

Ari sat down, marveling at her exuberance, vaguely jealous that he was never able to get that excited about anything.

"When are you going to take these pictures?"

"I don't know. He didn't say. But it sounded like it

would be soon. He told me he would call again tomorrow morning."

"Who was it that phoned?"

"I don't know. He mentioned his name, but I was so excited I forgot to write it down." She frowned. "Do you think it matters?"

Ari lit a cigarette, slowly waving the match in the air until the flame went out. "No, as long as he intends to call you again, it shouldn't make any difference if you remember his name or not." He hesitated for a moment, then looked up at her. "Did he mention where the Israeli prisoners you're to photograph are being held?"

"Yes, but it was something in Arabic. I don't recall it; those names are hard to remember."

"Does Tadmor or Sigin al-Mazza sound familiar?"

"Al-Mazza prison, that's it!" she said excitedly. "How did you know?"

"There was an article on the Syrian penal system in *Le Monde* a few days back," he lied. "It said Israeli prisoners are usually kept in Tadmor in the north or al-Mazza, just outside Damascus." He knocked a bit of ash from his cigarette into the wastebasket near the dresser. "The Syrians obviously don't know you're half Jewish."

She shrugged. "I've never been involved in any Jewish activities, my name's not ethnic, and on my visa application under religion I put down Unitarian." She smiled. "I'm not quite sure what a Unitarian is, but I figured the Syrians wouldn't know either and probably wouldn't bother to ask."

If she expected him to laugh he disappointed her.

"Are you going to be able to talk to the prisoners in addition to photographing them?"

"I don't know. I assume there will be a translator and some sort of communication."

Ari thought about Dov. The Nazis had been less than anxious to discuss the details surrounding his penetration of the German colony and subsequent arrest. He doubted he'd be able to get much information out of them; they seemed embarrassed by the whole affair. But, if Dov was at al-Mazza, there was a possibility Kim could contact him and find out how much he had told his interrogators.

"There's a specific prisoner I'm interested in who very likely is at al-Mazza penitentiary," he said, weighing his every word for the effect it would have.

"Then you were lying to me about the *Le Monde* article. You knew about al-Mazza before we came to Syria."

He nodded.

"How? Why are you interested in Syrian prisons?"

He recalled the Colonel's casual, last-minute request for information about Dov, realizing again how important an accurate report would be. It was worth the risk. The mission was falling apart; he had to salvage something, and there was a good chance Kim could reach Dov. He took a deep drag off his cigarette, holding the smoke in his lungs for a long time before exhaling. "I know about al-Mazza because it holds more than a dozen of my countrymen," he said. "I'm an Israeli. My real name is Ari Ben-Sion."

She stared at him in disbelief. But after a few seconds the surprise in her eyes faded. "Ari Ben-Sion." She repeated the name. "Now everything makes sense: why you were in Jerusalem, why you're so secretive, so distant."

She rushed toward him.

"Don't," he commanded, halting her in place. He didn't know why he threw up a barrier after having told her so much. Maybe it was because he was vulnerable now, both as a spy and as a man; and men, when vulnerable, tend to retreat behind harsh exteriors.

She dropped back on the bed, a shadow of pain clouding her face. "But I don't understand, if you're an Israeli, then . . ."

"Then what?"

"Then—we're both Jews."

"Ironic, isn't it?"

"Oh Hans," she said. "I mean Ari. Now I understand. You came to Damascus because of this Israeli in al-Mazza prison." She paused, suddenly excited. "I'll probably be going there in a few days. Maybe I can help. Maybe I'll see him or can get a message to him via one of the other prisoners. I'm not afraid. I'll try anything. Just tell me what to do."

He moved toward the window and looked out at the sun-scorched city. "The Israeli's name is Dov Elon but I did not come to Damascus because of him." He was stalling; he didn't want her to realize the only reason he'd told the truth about himself was to use her.

"I don't understand." It seemed to Kim that he had offered to let her help, then abruptly snatched the opportunity away. "If you're afraid you can't trust me, why did you bring up Dov Elon in the first place?"

"I said Dov is not the main reason I'm in Damascus, which has absolutely nothing to do with trusting you."

"Then you're in Syria on some assignment for the Israeli government."

"I'm a spy," he said matter-of-factly, the way other men stated their profession as a doctor or a lawyer.

She looked up at him, fear reflected in her eyes. "That means if you're caught, they'll execute you."

"Precisely." He ground out his cigarette with the same casual indifference the Syrians would display in snuffing out his life if he were captured.

"Ari, I'm scared."

He slowly took out a fresh cigarette, tapped the butt

161

on the armrest to pack in the tobacco, and lit it. "I'm scared too."

"What is it?" she asked nervously. "Why are you in Damascus? If you're arrested and hung I don't think I'll be able to stand it unless I know. It must be something important or you wouldn't risk your life like this."

"You will be much safer if I don't tell you. No interrogator can extract information you do not possess. I prefer not to involve you any more than I need to—it's too dangerous."

"What do you mean not involve me!" she said angrily. "You talked me into traveling here with you. I've been seen repeatedly in your company. Everybody in the hotel knows we're together. I am involved!"

"Kim, I can't tell you anything else."

"Then get out of here," she said coldly. "I'll take the first available flight to Europe."

Her sudden harshness stunned him. He sat there, on the verge of losing her, unable to do anything about it. At a loss for words he rose, not wanting to leave, but he had no choice. He couldn't tell her about the children.

"Damn it, where do you think you're going?"

"You told me to leave."

"So now I'm telling you to stay."

"Kim, I just can't tell you anything else; you have to trust me."

She stood up and faced him. "Okay, okay. I'll trust you. I'll just stand here like a little china doll. I won't ask questions or learn too much about anything—that way we'll be sure I won't break. Of course upon request I'll spread my legs, that is if you're sure your penis won't shatter me."

He slapped her across the face, the crack of his hand against her cheek slicing through him like a knife. He stood there, his arm hanging awkwardly at his side. "Kim, I'm sorry . . ." Apologizing made him feel even cheaper; his words were so inadequate.

Tears tumbled from her eyes. "That's all right," she said, forcing a smile. "The china doll didn't break."

He wrapped his arms around her waist and held her against him. "You mean so much to me," he said, reaching down to kiss her.

She let his lips meet hers, but that was all; she didn't respond. He kissed her harder. She drew back and looked at him. "Why do men always try and make love to a woman after they've hurt her? Do you really believe the pain will dissolve at the touch of your lips?"

He dropped his hands. "I guess it's a way of hiding, of escaping from guilt."

"But you are really arrogant enough to think that you can slap me across the face, then kiss me, and I'll feel better?"

"I guess I'd like to fool myself into thinking that."

"Can you?"

"No."

"Your slapping me hurt you more than it hurt me; it showed on your face. Every time I get close to what's locked inside you, you erect a barrier between us and crouch behind it. Even when we're in bed, when you're deep inside me, you hold back, as if you feel guilty about making love, or loving itself."

He fidgeted uneasily.

"You remind me of a lion cub who wants to be petted, but who lashes out at everybody with his claws before they can touch him. And I don't know what you're afraid of or what it is you want from me. But we can't go on like this, I'm certain of that. Either you let whatever is inside you out, or I'll leave. And this time I won't come back."

He bit his lower lip. There were so many things he wanted to tell her about his past, about the Service, about what it was like existing inside a hostile community, living year in and year out with the fear and the strain and the isolation. He hesitated, took out a cigarette, then returned it to the pack.

"Kim, it will take time."

"I have plenty of time," she said, sitting on the bed.

"But I don't. At least not now, not until we're out of Syria. I have a mission to complete here and I must channel all my energy into it. Afterward there will be time to explain, as much time as we want. I've decided this is going to be my last assignment, but I'm here now and I can't be diverted by personal considerations. I've got to see it through successfully and I know my limitations. I won't be able to function efficiently if I crack myself open and show you what's inside. I'm just too tired. I don't have the strength to do both at once."

He wasn't quite sure if he believed his own excuse.

She removed her watch and set it on the end table.

"What about this Dov Elon? You said he's not the main reason you came to Damascus but that means he must be connected to some secondary reason. Is there anything I can do to help while I'm at al-Mazza?"

He nodded; he was about to bring up the subject himself. "If you find Dov and can manage to get rid of your guide for a few moments, just tell him the Colonel needs to know if Sarraj forced him to talk."

"But will he trust me? Won't he think I'm a Syrian agent trying to trick him? Isn't there a password or something?"

She was right. He'd already anticipated her question and realized there was only one thing she could tell him that would guarantee his trust.

"There's no password," he said painfully. "Just tell Dov you know Ari was responsible for his capture. There's no way a Syrian could have that information."

Kim looked up at him, her eyes wide. But she said nothing.

SIXTEEN

SEPTEMBER 19

FROM ATOP the minarets wailing voices pierced the morning, waking the somnolent city, calling the followers of Muhammad to prayer. After a few minutes the undulating chant ceased and Damascus fell silent again. Inside the towers the guardians of the faith turned their record players off and reset the needles in preparation for the next appointed hour of prayer. Worship of the cult of civilization had struck even here. The cries beckoning believers to Syria's mosques were prerecorded by professional muezzins in Mecca.

Ari lay awake. Noises had kept him up most of the night—noises he knew were not there. He looked over at Kim, wanting to stroke her soft skin, yet not wanting to wake her. Curled on the far edge of the bed, she was sleeping peacefully. He flipped over on his back and stared up at the ceiling. It would be selfish to disturb her, he decided. So, moving closer to the wall, he let his thoughts turn to the absent Shaul Barkai.

The phone rang and he snatched at it. A call so early might be the contact he was waiting for.

"Hans Hoffmann?"

"Yes." Ari sat up excitedly. The voice was familiar. This could be it. Finally.

166

"Sorry to disturb you so early, it's Franz Ludin."
Disappointment.

"Good morning," Ari said, forcing cheerfulness into his tone.

"I didn't wake you, did I?"

He glanced at Kim; she was still sleeping. "No, I've been up for a while."

"Good. Listen, if you have nothing planned for this morning let me make you an offer. Ludwig Streicher and I are meeting for breakfast in a restaurant next to the Ministry of Justice. Why don't you join us?"

"I don't know," Ari hedged. He wanted to decline the invitation. Streicher was suspicious of him and another meeting might afford the Wehrmacht colonel the opportunity to penetrate his cover.

"We are going to discuss a topic I'm sure will be of great interest to you. Colonel Streicher specifically suggested I ask you to come along."

He had lost his chance to decline graciously. "In that case I would be delighted to join you."

"Excellent. We will expect you at the Safar Pacha Restaurant in about an hour. It's right next to the government buildings in Marjeh Square. You can't miss it."

"I'll be there."

He bid Ludin good-bye and hung up.

Kim was still sleeping. He touched her gently on the shoulder and whispered her name. She stirred, opened her eyes briefly, then retreated back into her dreams.

"I'm going out for the morning," he said.

She turned toward the wall.

As he climbed out of the bed and headed for the shower he realized she hadn't heard him.

Ari walked into the Safar Pacha Restaurant and moved

167

immediately toward a corner table where Ludin and Streicher were waiting. The restaurant was clean but by no means elegant. Plain wooden tables were arranged along the four walls as well as in the center of the room. Arabs, wearing dark suits, sat around them eating hurriedly. From their dress and manner Ari assumed the Safar Pacha was a meeting place for low-ranking government officials.

"Please sit down," Ludin said, as he approached the two Nazis. Ari smiled and chose the empty chair across from Streicher. He wanted to face his adversary squarely.

"Are you enjoying your stay in Damascus?" Streicher asked.

"Very much so."

"Your purchase of merchandise is proceeding satisfactorily?"

Ari nodded. "I have already sent several shipments to Europe. All indications are that olive wood articles will sell in large quantities, particularly hand-carved backgammon sets. There seems to be an almost limitless market for them. Although the quality of Damascene textiles turned out to be somewhat disappointing, I would have to say that overall my stay here has been quite productive."

"And not only from the business aspect," Ludin added, smiling.

Ari's face reddened; little pinpoints of heat pricked his cheeks.

"Franz tells me you are especially fond of, shall I say . . . kosher meat."

"What are you driving at?" Ari pushed his water glass across the table, watching a damp trail form in its wake. "Franz knows what I want from the Jews. I told him so myself."

"It just seems unusual that after spending so much

time with an attractive American, you still find it necessary to drag the dirt from the gutter into your bed."

"I cannot see how my sexual proclivities are of any concern to you gentlemen."

Ludin drummed his fingers on the edge of the table. "Why did you go to see Rachael Khatib?"

"Because I wanted to fuck her," Ari said angrily. "I get a thrill out of screwing Jewesses. I don't understand why. I wish I could feel the same way about other women, about Miss Johnson, but I don't." He looked into Ludin's eyes. "You think I like it this way? You think I'm happy that in order to find sexual relief I have to haunt the Jewish ghettos of every city I visit, searching out the dregs of humanity? How do you think I feel afterward? Like some conquering hero? Like a wild stallion? No! I feel like an ostrich who has to bury his head underground. I want to smash the bitch's face, relight the crematoria and throw her in. But that feeling soon fades. After a while the hunger returns, gnawing at my guts until I have to go out and satisfy it again."

Ari was breathing heavily. Hate burned in his eyes; hate directed not at the Nazis sitting across from him, but at the Jews. For a brief moment his real self submerged into the void and he became Hans Hoffmann. He saw the Jews as the assassins of Christ, as murderers who stealthily stole up behind Christian children, slit their throats, then drained the blood for use in the baking of Passover matzoth. For a sickening second he saw the Jews through the eyes of the rest of the world: invading aliens, more cunning than clever—different, dangerous, and deserving destruction.

"How long have you felt like this?" Streicher asked.

The sound of the Nazi's voice snapped Ari back into his cover story. "Ever since I was a teenager in Stuttgart," he said, head bowed. "There was this Jewish girl, Eva Gruener, who lived next door to my family. She kept flaunting her body at me. I followed her home from school every day begging that she let me make love to her. Finally she said yes. I brought a blanket to the park and we undressed in the middle of a dense clump of trees. When it was time I couldn't do anything. She started laughing. I was so embarrassed I picked up my clothes and ran. Later she told all my friends I was impotent."

"So then you really do understand your obsession with the Jews," Streicher said.

Ari nodded. "Sometimes when I'm screwing one of the bitches I see Gruener's face. But she isn't laughing any more." Ari looked at both Ludin and Streicher. He couldn't tell if they believed him.

Suddenly Ludin laughed and turned to his companion. "Now that he has explained himself, his behavior makes sense. I think your suspicions are unwarranted, Ludwig. I must admit I find no reason to doubt that Herr Hoffmann is who he says he is."

Streicher grunted. "In that case I'm sure he would not object if I contacted a member of the ODESSA underground in Stuttgart and had his identity verified."

"Of course not," Ari said.

Before Streicher could continue the waiter arrived carrying a metal tray loaded with dishes. Effortlessly he lowered the plates of eggs, rice, fresh figs, and sweet al-Juban cheese to the table. Then he hurried back to the kitchen, promising to personally brew their coffee. The three men ate in silence punctuated only by the sound of their forks scraping the heavy plates. The espresso arrived and they began talking about Hafez Assad's liberalizing reforms and the effect they'd had on the Baath Arab Social Renaissance Party. Finishing his breakfast,

170

Streicher abruptly put down his silverware and excused himself, claiming that he was late for an appointment. Ari sensed that he was lying, that he had wanted to begin checking his credentials. Immediately.

"You must try and understand my colleague," Ludin said, after Streicher had left. "Ever since Soviet military personnel moved into Syria the Wehrmacht advisers here have been relegated to such tasks as supervising the clean-up of latrines and the laundering of enlisted men's uniforms. The Communists refuse to have anything to do with us—it seems the twenty million Russians we killed during the war is a little difficult for them to forget. Ludwig is bitter; in the late 1940s he helped forge a bunch of bedouin, camel breeders, and frightened city boys into the fighting force now known as the Syrian army. But one of the conditions the Soviet Union set before they began supplying Syria with sophisticated weaponry was that all Wehrmacht personnel be purged from positions of authority. In 1957, in the aftermath of the Suez War, President al-Kuwatli dismissed scores of German military advisers to make way for the Russian and Czech missions. Streicher was decorated for *outstanding services to the Syrian nation,* then promptly relieved of active duty. That's one of the reasons why he's so suspicious of you and everybody else. Questioning your credentials gives him something to do. It swells his head with memories of the power he once wielded."

"I see," Ari said quietly. Streicher, the twice-deposed, twice-frustrated Nazi was on the verge of exposing him because he had nothing better to do than chase after faint scents in the wind. This time, however, Streicher had edged his nose too close to a flower, without first checking to see if a bee wasn't waiting there, poised, ready to explode in his face.

"But how do you stay in favor with the Syrians if the

Russian influence is so strong?" Ari asked.

"I maintain a privileged position because the Syrians consider Brunner, Wolff, myself, and the other SS officers far superior to the Russians in dealing with the Jews. They compare our concentration camp statistics to the Soviets sending tens of thousands of their Jews to Israel each year. Need I say the Arabs prefer our solution to the Jewish problem."

Ari nodded understandingly, but something Ludin had said stuck to the edge of his thoughts. He was beginning to see a way to steer the conversation around to a discussion of Dov.

"You said one of the reasons Streicher is suspicious of me is because questioning my credentials makes him feel like he's engaged in important work. But I sense there is more to it than that. He seems ill at ease, as if he's worried about something."

"You are quite right, my friend. Something has all of us worried. It started with that Eli Cohen business in 1965, with the shock that we are vulnerable, even here. Then, earlier this year, two former German officers, Captain Rainer Kriebel and SS Standartenführer Walter Remmer, were found murdered in their apartments. It appears there is another Israeli agent operating in Damascus."

"But at the dinner party you said the Second Bureau had caught the Israeli spy."

"An Israeli, but not *the* Israeli. We are certain that this Dov Elon was not in the country when Remmer and Kriebel were killed."

"Interesting. Then there were two of them, and you think one is still in Damascus." Ari sipped from his glass of water. "But where does Streicher fit in? I remember Wolff saying that Ludwig knew the captured spy."

"That is a slight understatement. Streicher and Elon

became fast friends. Elon claimed to be an associate of Streicher's dead brother. He knew everything about him. Ludwig was highly embarrassed when he discovered he had been unburdening his soul to an Israeli agent."

"So that's really why he's so suspicious of me. He doesn't want to get burned again."

Ludin nodded.

"But what about Elon, can't he be made to divulge the identity of the other Israeli?"

"He is in the hands of the Second Bureau. The Syrians are most brutal and Suleiman Sarraj is one of the worst. Only Yussaf Fuad, chief of the General Security Service, has outdone his excesses. Between the two of them they should be able to persuade the Israeli to talk."

"Then you don't know if they've succeeded yet?"

"No."

"Is there any possibility the Israeli is dead? That could explain the Second Bureau's silence."

Ludin shifted position in the uncomfortable chair. "Sarraj is a very careful man. He would not let Elon die until he had the information he wanted. If the Israeli has not talked, he is still alive."

"Some of those bastards are unusually stubborn. He might hold out indefinitely."

"I doubt it. Every man can be broken—can be pushed to the point where his mind refuses to endure more pain. When this happens he'll betray his country, his lover, or his family. Some resist for days, others for months. But George Orwell was right—under a skilled interrogator in the end they all submit."

"Or lose their sanity."

"Yes," Ludin agreed. "Unfortunately sometimes that is the case."

Ari realized it was pointless to press Ludin for details about Dov. The German knew little. The Second Bu-

173

reau, undoubtedly furious at Dov's successful penetration of the German colony, had probably decided to keep the Nazis in the dark about the interrogation. He would gain no information from his current maneuver. His only hope of finding anything out lay with Kim.

Ari took the cloth napkin from his lap and placed it on the table. "Franz, you really will have to excuse me, but I promised al-Husseini's assistant I would meet him a half-hour ago. He has been tremendously generous with his time and I don't want to keep him waiting any longer."

"Of course," Ludin said, rising. "But we must get together again soon. I will speak to Ludwig about you, I'm sure that he can be reasoned with."

"That's not necessary, I have nothing to hide." He snapped to attention and reached for Ludin's outstretched hand, which felt warm and clammy.

As Ari left the restaurant he looked at the green, white, and black Syrian tricolor floating limply over the Ministry of Justice, and thought about the plan the Colonel had devised to insure the children were safely smuggled out of Syria. But where was Lieutenant Barkai? Why hadn't he shown up? The timing of Operation Goshen was critical. The Colonel had honed the movements of the two Israeli agents with the precision of a Swiss watch. Nothing should have gone wrong, yet obviously something had. With the transmitter lost, and time chewing away at the days, Ari knew there were few alternatives open to him. He could claim he needed to check on his European outlets, fly to Frankfurt, and phone Jerusalem directly from there. But that would consume precious time he didn't have; the children were scheduled to be taken out of Syria in seventy-two hours. It would look suspicious if he remained in Europe for only a day or two. Otherwise he could wait for Barkai and continue to

174

ignore the Colonel's orders—which had been explicit: if there was serious reason to believe that the Second Bureau was onto him, he was to abort Operation Goshen.

Back in his hotel suite Ari bolted the door, drew the curtains, then went into the bathroom. Removing a fresh bar of soap from the medicine cabinet, he peeled off the Yardley wrapper, thankful for the Mossad training that taught him never to carry all his equipment in one case. Though he had lost the Rhinehart bar of soap that contained the material he really needed, the substance embedded in the Yardley would serve as an adequate substitute. With a pocket knife he cut through the soap approximately four centimeters in from the right edge. He tossed the carved-off piece into the wastebasket, returned to the bedroom, and sat at his desk.

The yellow soap had been dyed to blend with the color of the explosive concealed inside it. Ari measured another five centimeters and cut through the bar, this time carefully placing the segment of camouflaged chemical into the ashtray. He measured off another two centimeters and sent his knife slicing through the soft soap again. Discarding the useless sliver, he held the remaining section of the bar up to the desk light and gingerly picked at the center with the tip of his knife. In a few seconds he extracted a small metal firing pin. Placing it on the blotter, he took the tetryl out of the ashtray and scraped off the outer layer of soap, leaving a small quantity of malleable, claylike plastique.

From the desk drawer he withdrew a ball-point pen with the advertisement *Banque de l'Unité Arabe* printed on it in French and Arabic. Removing the ink cartridge, he put the tetryl in its place and set the firing pin, held under pressure created by the pen's spring, above the charge. Along with a business card he'd picked up from

175

the bank manager's office on Maawia Street, he slipped
the lethal weapon into an envelope. He would have preferred to make a conventional letter bomb that would
explode upon opening, but the potassium nitrate and
stabilizing ammonium oxalate he'd need had been lost in
the toiletry case. However, there was little cause for concern. The recipient would inevitably snap the plunger at
the end of the pen, sending the firing pin into the tetryl
—detonating the fatal charge.

Later that afternoon he dropped the envelope addressed to Ludwig Streicher in the "Damascus Only"
slot at the main post office near the Sérail.

SEVENTEEN

SEPTEMBER 20

ARI SAT at the desk in his hotel room chain-smoking, waiting for Kim to return from her tour of the Syrian prison system. On the floor by the bed lay the English-language *Daily Star* from Beirut, the crossword puzzle face up, the boxes completely filled in. A pot of coffee, laced with Scotch, rested on the dresser half empty. Ari closed his eyes. He didn't want to sleep, nightmares invaded his dreams regularly now, but if he could just rest for a few minutes . . .

The phone rang, jolting him awake. The sound felt like a splinter of ice cold metal as it pierced his skull. There was pain inside his head and the back of his neck ached from the position he'd assumed, slumped over in the chair. Groggy and disoriented, he picked up the receiver, more to stop the strident ringing than to discover who was calling.

"Hans, it's Franz Ludin." The Nazi sounded distraught. "The Jews have gotten Streicher!"

"What happened?" Ari asked, shaking his head, trying to clear the haze from his brain.

"Some kind of letter bomb. The German colony's in pandemonium. None of us is safe! If a package, a letter, even a note arrives that at all looks suspicious, call the

177

police before you open it." The words raced out of his mouth—panic was pushing them.

"Is Streicher dead?"

"I don't know. He was rushed to the Mojtahed Municipal Hospital. I haven't had time to call over there. I've been busy trying to alert the Germans living in Damascus."

"Then I better not keep you. Thanks for the warning. I'll be careful."

Ari hung up, immediately got the hotel receptionist on the line, and asked her to connect him with patient information at the Mojtahed Hospital. When the connection was completed Ari inquired about Streicher's condition. After a pause the clerk came back on the phone.

"I have good news for you," she said. "Colonel Streicher was not seriously injured. He is conscious and out of danger. You may visit him tomorrow if you like."

"Thank you very much. I'll do that."

"Can I tell him who called?"

Ari slowly dropped the receiver into place without responding. Something had gone wrong. He must have prepared the charge improperly—it should have killed its victim. Now he was in real trouble. Streicher, already suspicious, would make the connection between the attempt on his life and his probing of Ari's credentials. It was now a race with time. Somehow he would have to see to it that Operation Goshen was executed on schedule, in forty-eight hours—hopefully before Streicher was well enough to push his inquiries about Hans Hoffmann any further. But how could he possibly complete the mission alone?

The escape valve, Operative 66. He could contact the deeply placed Israeli spy. The muscles inside Ari's stomach contracted. But would the Colonel want him to take the risk? What would the head of Israeli Intelligence say

178

later, at his debriefing? Ari reached for the bottle of Chivas Regal he kept perpetually near him now.

The transmitter was gone, Rachael had been arrested, the Syrians were probably onto him, Barkai hadn't shown, Streicher might have an answer from the ODESSA at any time. Ari gulped down the Scotch, hardly tasting it. As the last of the last resorts, the Colonel had said, if and only if a desperate emergency arises, you can contact Operative 66. Ari could hear the pudgy man's voice. He stared at the bottle of Scotch, then quickly refilled his glass. He was scared, afraid of the guilt that would haunt him if he inadvertently led the Second Bureau to Operative 66. He would not be able to bear it, not now, not on top of everything else. But hesitating was pointless. As the days spun away his clutching back after them grew increasingly more futile. Everything had come apart. It *was* a desperate emergency.

He decided he would contact Operative 66 as soon as the sun descended and night offered a measure of protective cover.

There was a knock on the door and Ari rose to answer it, noticing that his legs did not move quite as fast as his mind wanted them to. Kim fidgeted in the hallway, impatient with the nervous energy of the young who, unlike those worn by life's disappointments, can't wait very long for anything.

She entered the room, closed the door behind her, and leaned back against the wood.

"What about Dov?" he asked quickly.

"I was able to speak to a pilot alone for a few minutes. His English was bad and I'm not sure I understood him correctly."

"Did he know anything about Dov?"

"He wasn't sure. He said there was one Israeli pris-

179

oner just brought down from Tadmor who was kept in a separate cell."

"Did he know his name? Had anyone seen him?"

Kim shook her head. "I'm sorry."

"Did you ask him why this prisoner was kept apart from the others?"

"Yes, but he didn't know."

"What about the other prisoners?" he pressed anxiously. "Didn't they know anything? Hadn't anyone spoken to him?"

She moved close and touched his shoulder. "There were guards with me the whole time. It was only by luck that I managed to speak to even one prisoner alone. My escort returned after a few minutes and stayed close the rest of the afternoon."

Ari spun around and her hand fell away from him. It was Dov. He was certain of it. Biting his lip, he stared at the blank wall. He'd hoped Dov had found a way to commit suicide, to end his ordeal.

"Ari," she said softly. "Maybe I can get permission to go back. The man from the Foreign Ministry liked me. In fact he liked me a lot. He made it perfectly clear that he would do anything he could for me if we pursued our relationship. Maybe if I offered to discuss my photography at his home one night he might do some checking on Dov. I'm sure I could think of a way to ask him without his getting suspicious."

Ari stiffened. She moved behind him and began working her fingers into his tight back and shoulder muscles.

"Don't," he said, though he didn't want her to stop.

She ignored him and dug her fingers deeper into his knotted flesh. He turned around to face her.

"Kim, I don't want you to do it. I need to find out about Dov, but not that way."

"Why not?" she said angrily. "You told me you believe

180

in results, not in rules. Well, I'm offering you results. Please don't tell me you're trying to protect my honor, I wouldn't want to laugh. I'm not exactly a virgin and if you were too preoccupied to notice let me assure you that you were not the first man I've climbed into bed with. In fact I'm pretty well broken in. One Arab minister more or less would hardly make much difference. I could probably knock him off two or three times and get him to do anything I wanted. These Arabs are crazy about blondes. They think we're some kind of exotic sex goddesses just because none of their women are fair-skinned. I wouldn't even have to put out much of a performance. I could just lie back and let his male ego ravish me."

"Stop it!"

"Why?" she said loudly. "You've offered me nothing but vague promises about what it will be like after we leave Damascus. And now you want exclusive control over my body. Aren't you being a bit presumptuous? I'm going to sleep with whoever I want and if I feel like screwing some fat Arab to get information to help you, goddamnit I'm going to do it."

He backed away, bumping into a chair.

"No."

"I don't understand. I thought it meant a lot to you to find out about Dov. You said the Colonel wanted to know, that because of you he . . ."

"I didn't come to Damascus to find Dov!" Ari said. It took a great deal of effort to push what was forming in his mind into words. "I came on a mission that must be completed in the next two days or else it will be too late. I have to forget about every other distraction or else I'll fail, and the price of that failure will be the destruction of seven lives. I told you before I cannot let personal considerations affect my better judgment and that judg-

ment says concentrate on my mission and drop everything else."

"What are you trying to tell me?" she asked.

He knew that he had to tell her to leave, that he needed
one hundred percent concentration for the next forty-
eight hours and that as long as she was near some part
of him would be thinking about her and not the mission.
Besides, she was in danger. Her association with him
could bring the Second Bureau crashing down on her.
Everything he had learned in the Service demanded he
send her away.

He started to speak but stopped. He couldn't do it. He
had to tell her to leave but the words wouldn't come out.
They just wouldn't.

"Just be patient for a few more days," he said. "Don't
ask any questions and don't do anything for me on your
own. If all goes as planned I'll be leaving Syria Saturday
night. You can meet me in Jerusalem. Just go to Eighteen
Ruppin Street and ask for the Colonel. Can you remember that without writing it down?"

She nodded. "But what if everything doesn't go as
planned?"

He said nothing, the answer implicit in his silence.

"What about Dov, can't I at least try?"

"Forget about Dov," he said loudly, but without menace in his voice. "There's no time. I don't want . . ."

Suddenly he was powerless to push back the emotion
rising in his throat. He was responsible for Dov's capture, for the suffering the boy had endured all these
months. He and he alone. Ari cried softly, surprised at
what was happening—he had thought himself as incapa-
ble of crying as he had been of loving. Detachment was
the rule of life in the Service. He had always followed that
formula, knowing no other. Now, suddenly, his whole
world had pitched on its axis.

182

Kim remained where she was—silent, waiting.

He said nothing for a long time, vaguely aware that the flow of tears had carried away some barrier inside him. Finally he looked up. She moved close and kissed his face, drying his tears with her lips.

Tumbling onto the bed, they undressed and made gentle love, staying locked together a long time, not wanting to start the rhythm that would inevitably end too soon. Kim ran her fingers to the nape of his neck, swirling up eddies of excitement. He tried not to anticipate the ecstasy he felt as her fingernails slid with barely perceptible contact around his waist, up his sides, and outward along his upper arms. Feeling pressure in his groin he slowly withdrew from her—they were not ready yet. She leaned over and ran her tongue along the same route her fingers had explored. The excitement churned into joy. Her lips danced along his skin so softly that he could not tell when she touched him and when he felt only the warmth of her breath. She worked her way over his stomach. He lay back. After a few minutes she stretched out on top of him. He felt the wet warmth between her legs as they came together again.

When his breathing slowed, he brushed her forehead with his lips. "Nothing is going to keep us apart."

Smiling, she outlined his nose with her forefinger. "I don't want to be left here. Can I come with you when you leave Saturday?"

He hesitated. He didn't even know if Operation Goshen was still viable. In either event it would be safer for her to travel by commercial airliner, alone.

"Maybe, we'll see," he said.

They lay entwined in each other's arms for a long time without speaking. The sheets were soft and the touch of her skin, smooth and warm. But he couldn't stay. When it grew dark he silently got up and made his way into the bathroom, trying to shake the haze from his brain. He'd been half asleep.

The cold spray of the shower brought his body into painful submission. After a few minutes he was alert and thinking clearly. To insure that he was not being followed he would have to proceed along the prescribed route with the utmost care. There could be no slipups. He dried himself and went into the bedroom to dress.

"Are you going out?" Kim asked.

He turned and looked at her. "No more questions."

She dropped her head onto the pillow and watched him. "Can I ask what time you'll be back?"

"No."

When he finished putting on his clothes he stood over the bed. Kim lay naked on top of the sheets. She hadn't bothered to drape anything over herself.

"Just be patient," he said. "If all goes well tonight we'll be leaving Syria in a little over forty-eight hours."

She smiled.

He turned and headed toward the hallway, an uneasiness building in his stomach. He hoped he was doing the right thing. Reaching the elevator, he pushed the down button. The white plastic knob turned red. While he waited for the doors to part he ran over in his mind the procedure he was instructed to use to contact Operative 66. The Colonel had made it clear that, if necessary, he expected him to move along the predesignated route with the utmost caution. Ari was to turn around if he even suspected anyone was following him. Operative 66 was not to be jeopardized, under any circumstances.

EIGHTEEN

SEPTEMBER 20

PATTERNED ON its French counterpart, Le Deuxième Bureau de l'Etat Major—the Second Bureau of the General Staff, Syria's military intelligence service—remains separate and distinct from the Mukhabarat, Syria's general security service. These agencies, in bitter competition, duplicate and often sabotage each other's work so that their leaders might achieve a further measure of personal political power. Directors of the Second Bureau and the Mukhabarat often become chiefs of staff, ministers of defense or interior, or presidents of the republic. Rarely do the two services even attempt to work together. So it was not without a certain uneasiness that Yussaf Fuad, head of the Mukhabarat, agreed to join General Suleiman Sarraj in his Second Bureau office on a matter Sarraj said was of urgent concern to both of them.

The structure just west of the walls of the inner city that houses the Second Bureau looks much like the other Kanawat district office buildings that flank it on either side. They are all under a dozen stories high, with white stone and stucco façades blackened by the exhaust spewing from the cars and buses passing noisily below them. The entrance to the underground garage below 14 Taadil Street is squeezed between the Café Tingiz and a barber shop, and signs advertising the businesses housed inside decorate the stone front of the building. There are buttons for floors one through nine in the elevator next to which a directory reveals the names and office numbers of various trading companies, insurance firms, consulting agencies, and similar corporate concerns. However, if one was inclined to count the number of stories from the outside an unlisted tenth floor would appear. In the elevator under the alarm buzzer is a slot, which, when fitted with a special key, powers the elevator to the Second Bureau offices at the top of the building.

The room in which Suleiman Sarraj and Yussaf Fuad sat displayed an opulence that would have angered the average Damascene taxpayer had he known of its existence. A thick Persian carpet blanketed the floor and ornate tapestries hugged the walls—against them hung rows of silver plates inlaid with gold. Sarraj's large desk was of polished mahogany; on the corner a pair of hand-carved gazelle bookends supported an illuminated edition of the Koran. The suite also contained the only air conditioning unit in the building.

General Sarraj stared at the file folder that lay open before him. The Second Bureau chief was conservative and calculating; his operations meticulously planned, and executed according to a preset timetable. He despised spontaneity and treated any deviation from his exact orders with a ruthless vengeance. The fifty-six-year-old graduate of the Gendarmerie, the Homs Military Academy, and the French General Staff College had built a career on his ability to foresee the demands of the future and accommodate himself to the needs of the present. He had spied successfully on the French for the British, on the British for the French, then on the French and the British for the Germans. His prowess at adapting to changes of regime was particularly important in Damascus, the scene of so many rapid and abrupt shifts of power. Physically Sarraj's appearance was in total harmony with his temperament. His dark hair was combed to one side, each hair set in its proper place. He exercised regularly, which caused his face to bear a youthful appearance that hid his actual age. His plain brown suit hung on his narrow shoulders with an effortless grace—a grace that did not carry over into his interpersonal relations. Sarraj was self-conscious about being short, particularly in the presence of powerfully built men like Yussaf Fuad.

Extracting an 8 x 10 photograph from the folder on his desk, the dark-eyed, moustached general handed it to the Mukhabarat chief. "This is Major Ari Ben-Sion of Israeli Intelligence," he said.

Fuad, tall, heavy-chested, wearing an olive green military shirt without a jacket, took the picture in his large hands and stared at it. Fuad had propelled himself through army ranks by virtue of his viciousness, eliminating his rivals when it was necessary, and often when it was not. He produced results, no matter what the cost—monetary or otherwise. His Mukhabarat, unlike the Second Bureau which operated in Western countries, was exclusively concerned with questions of security inside the Arab world. He personally controlled the Makatib al-Khassah, a special internal police force which yearly spent more than a million Syrian pounds on some 8,500 political informers.

Fuad tapped the picture on the edge of the desk, then set it down. "And Major Ben-Sion is in Damascus now?"

Sarraj nodded. "Under the guise of Hans Hoffmann, an importer of furniture and textiles. The Zionists do not know that the Russians broke his cover some time ago." He picked up the photo and snapped at it with his forefinger. "This one did us much harm before we found out about him and his weakness."

"His weakness?"

Sarraj smiled. "Women—he seems to have become rather susceptible to them. It happens sometimes, when an agent's been allowed to remain in the field too long. The prolonged, utter aloneness begins to take its toll. A need for warmth arises, interfering with the ability to function effectively. A little over five months ago he was diverted by one of my agents near Kyrenia." Sarraj slid another photograph toward Fuad. The Mukhabarat chief laughed lasciviously at the picture of Michelle and Ari in embrace. "But do not be fooled by his falling so easily into my trap on Cyprus. This Ben-Sion is a clever one. He eluded the Russian, Czech, and Arab intelligence services for years, and did us quite a bit of damage in the process. The KGB finally broke his cover. I don't have the details, but somehow they tied him to the assassination of an important Egyptian agent in London."

"You have him under surveillance?"

"Of course," Sarraj said. "Lucky thing too. Three Palestinians jumped him in an alley off the Suq el-Bzouriye. Nearly bashed his head in. We had to remove them."

"Did Ben-Sion see your men?"

"I don't think so," Sarraj said. "He was unconscious at the time."

Fuad broke into a broad grin. "How long has he been in Damascus?"

"Fifteen days. I've had him watched since he boarded the plane in Frankfurt. One of my agents sat directly across from him, but something very strange happened. When he arrived in Damascus one of his cases was stolen by a baggage boy."

"What's so unusual about that?" Fuad said. "The

188

street urchins who work at the airport are hardly of high moral integrity. I'm sure it was not the first time an arriving passenger was relieved of his belongings."

"Of course. However, this seemed more than just a simple case of theft. I have not been able to locate the culprit or discover his identity, but I did find out he appeared at the airport specifically to meet the plane from Frankfurt and that he had never been seen there previously. Furthermore, the operation was engineered with professional precision. The boy ran out of the terminal and was picked up by a waiting vehicle. One of my men got the license number. It turned out to be a rented car registered to a nonexistent company."

"You suspect Kessim's Public Security Service or Nahlawi and the Police—or possibly my Mukhabarat?"

"I don't know," Sarraj said. "To be quite honest about it, I'm at a complete loss. I have been unable to determine what was in the case or who stole it."

Fuad leaned back and rocked in the chair. "This is very odd, but go on. What can you tell me about the Israeli's movements in Damascus?"

"Ben-Sion carried a letter of introduction to the Trade Bureau from the Syrian ambassador in Bonn. It seems our illustrious diplomat was duped by the Zionists. He will be recalled as soon as this business is over. We would not want to bring him back now and risk tipping off Jerusalem."

Fuad nodded in agreement.

"He has spent a considerable period of time purchasing Damascene textiles, furniture, and handicraft and shipping the merchandise to Frankfurt," Sarraj continued. "As I said, he is clever. After being here only two days he tricked that Nazi windbag Ludin into having a Jewess sent from the *haret* to his hotel room."

"I guess he wanted to taste one of his own kind. You

189

did mention a weakness for women." Fuad lifted the picture of Ari and Michelle off the desk, looked at it again, and smiled.

"Possibly. But he also has been carrying on an affair in the New Ommayad with an American photographer. In this case I think he may have been making contact."

"Then as yet you do not know why he is here," Fuad said.

"No. We had the girl from the ghetto picked up, but unfortunately my men became a little overzealous. Her mind snapped before she could tell us anything."

"In that event, why don't I have this Ben-Sion arrested? My men will not make that kind of mistake. I will have anything you want out of him within a week."

"I don't think so," Sarraj said. "His history indicates he is not the type to break under physical pressure. Besides, I have something else in mind." But he was not willing to share his plan with Fuad. Instead Sarraj straightened the papers in front of him and looked directly at the Mukhabarat chief. "Have you made any progress in determining how state secrets are still finding their way to the Israelis?"

"What?" Fuad said. "I thought after the discovery of Eli Cohen and the subsequent arrests and executions that . . ."

"Please do not play the simpleton with me. I know that there is an Israeli operative in the highest echelons of the Baath Party and that you are on his trail."

Fuad's facial muscles tightened. "You have informants in my service," he charged indignantly.

"As you do in mine. Let us not play games with each other. We are similar men with similar ambitions, otherwise we would not occupy the positions we do. The political situation in our country is unstable. Since 1946 we've had seven major military coups, and twice that number

190

of minor ones. Inevitably those on top will be deposed, and I for one intend to prepare myself to serve Syria at the highest levels if I am called upon."

Fuad laughed. Suddenly he understood why Sarraj was offering to share information with him. He needed a major success to boost his ascent to greater power. "You are hoping that this Ben-Sion will lead you to the other Israeli."

"Precisely. With the information you possess on—how is he called?"

"Operative Sixty-six."

"Yes, on Operative Sixty-six, and with my knowledge and directing of Ben-Sion I think we can work together without bothering the Internal Security or the Police and Public Security Services."

"I think such an association could be mutually beneficial," Fuad agreed. "Now, what do you propose?"

Underneath his composed exterior, Sarraj was beaming. He had Fuad exactly where he wanted him. The Second Bureau chief would gain a wealth of information in exchange for very little. He would not tell Fuad about the painstaking operation he had launched against Ben-Sion. When the laurels came, they would be heaped on him alone.

"First we must pool the resources of our two services," Sarraj said. "You must share with me the information you have on Operative Sixty-six and I will hand over to you the dossier on Ben-Sion. Then together we will work out a mutually acceptable plan. In the meantime I propose to continue to chart every step the Israeli makes, foiling his forward progress, until he is forced to go to Operative Sixty-six for help."

"And if that does not work?"

"Then," Sarraj said, flipping the file closed, "I'll let you try and beat the information out of him."

NINETEEN

SEPTEMBER 20

THE ELEVATOR carried Ari down to the lobby. When the doors parted he slowly stepped out and moved across the worn carpet. Then he saw something that pushed his uncertainty into alarm: the short, squat Arab who had been staring at him the time he was on the phone with Ludin was sitting in the far corner of the room reading a newspaper. Ari noticed the man's eyes fell to the lines of print only *after* he had glanced in his direction. Ari hesitated for a split second, then continued walking. There was one obvious thing to do—leave the hotel. If the Arab followed he would know for certain he was being watched. If so, he could alter his plans accordingly.

He was almost at the door when the concierge called out from behind the desk, beckoning him near with a sweep of his arm. Ari swore under his breath, but finding no way to ignore the hotel employee, he turned and headed back through the lobby.

"I'm so glad I saw you," the concierge said nervously. "There's an emergency call for you. I've been ringing your room but there was no answer."

Ari's pulse quickened. "Who's it from?"

"I don't know. The caller just said that it's urgent, that I had to find you. You can take it over there." He pointed to a white phone at the far end of the counter.

Ari moved quickly to the phone and picked up the receiver, leaving little deposits of perspiration on the desk as his hand brushed over it. "Damn heat," he mumbled to himself. Then he spoke into the receiver:

"Hello."

"Hans, it's Franz Ludin. I've got to talk to you." His voice was tense, distraught.

"Can't it wait until morning? I was just on my way out. I have an important appointment."

"This is more important!" Ludin half shouted. "Stay where you are! I'll be over in fifteen minutes." He hung up, leaving Ari standing there, listening to the hum of the dial tone. Ari replaced the receiver, the buzzing still ringing in his ears. For a moment he considered ignoring Ludin and continuing to Operative 66 but he decided against that course—he did not want to risk further arousing the Germans' mistrust. Wiping his hands on his pants, he headed toward the bar. Streicher was closing in on him, that had to be it. The Mossad had not anticipated his credentials would be questioned by the Nazi colony in Damascus. Ari was instructed to socialize not infiltrate. On that level, the Colonel assumed, no suspicion would be aroused.

Assumed wrong, Ari thought angrily, inhaling his J & B and soda. Yet something didn't make sense. If Streicher was on the verge of exposing him, why was Ludin so overwrought? He had nothing to fear from Ari's arrest, except maybe guilt by association. Possibly that was it: Ludin would be held culpable for befriending an Israeli spy he assumed was a former Nazi. But if that was the case why was Ludin coming to see him? What could he possibly gain from a confrontation?

Ari closed his eyes. Confusion compressed his brain, the blood in his head pulsating. Rachael, Saliha, Barkai, the children, Streicher converged in his mind, then blurred. He heard their voices, covering each other.

Ari slipped off the bar stool, drink in hand, and stood in the entrance to the chandeliered lobby, trying to lock his thoughts to the moment. He would spot Ludin as soon as the older man entered the hotel. Hearing the elevator doors pop open across from him, Ari instinctively glanced over. A lone woman stepped out and strode intently toward the front door.

He was about to call out to Kim when something stopped him. He noticed that the short, squat Arab who had been watching him earlier folded his newspaper and quickly scanned the room. Hidden in the bar's entrance Ari was out of his field of vision. As Kim moved toward the street the fear inside him froze into terror. Casually the Arab placed his red headlined *al-Ahrar* on the arm of the chair, stood, and followed Kim out the door.

Ari rushed to the bar, threw his glass on the counter, and ran into the lobby, ignoring the high-pitched cursing of the bartender. The hell with Ludin. He had to follow Kim. She was in danger—obviously his cover was pierced. The Second Bureau was capable of anything. Destroying Kim to get to him was the type of tactic the Syrians employed with relish. He had to eliminate the Arab and rush her out of the country.

Ari burst out of the hotel and stared down Maysaloun Street in both directions. The sidewalk was deserted— there was no sign of Kim or the Arab. He stood rigid. They couldn't be gone. It was impossible. He'd been only seconds behind them. They could not have disappeared that quickly unless . . .

Unless someone had been waiting outside with a car. The Arab's partner. The Second Bureau. Kim was his soft spot, his Achilles' heel, and they knew it. He would be contacted soon and a trade offered: Kim for his cooperation, Kim for the disclosure of what he was doing in Syria, Kim for the details of Operation Goshen. He would have to refuse and then they would torture her—slowly, methodically, protractedly. The American Embassy would be powerless. The Syrians detested the Americans and a young Jewish photographer in liaison with an Israeli agent—that was espionage. His lips felt dry and the Scotch had left a bitter aftertaste in his mouth.

As Ari moved toward a vacant taxi parked in front of the hotel a voice called out:

"Hans."

He spun around like a cornered alleycat. It was Ludin. Ari had completely forgotten about him.

"Were you getting into the taxi?" the Nazi asked, a note of surprise in his voice.

"No, I was restless. I was just pacing until you got here."

Ludin grunted. Ari noticed that his face was pale and the creases in his soft flesh had deepened. But the look in his eyes answered any questions Ari had. They were glazed and dilated. Ari had seen that look before: the look on the face of the hunted. Just then a donkey brayed from a nearby street, a very unnerving sound in the silence.

"Where can we talk?"

"My room," Ari said quickly, remembering that previously Ludin had always designated their place of meeting. He attributed the change to the abandon of the defeated. The Second Bureau must be tightening a noose around the Nazi's neck. But why? He would have to hear Ludin out, then get rid of him. For a second Ari wondered if it wouldn't be better to talk outside the New Ommayad, in some out-of-the-way place where the Second Bureau would have difficulty finding him. Immediately he rejected the idea as foolish. The Second Bureau, cognizant of his true identity, would be following every movement. Getting to a *safe* location would consume precious time, nullifying the purpose of seeking an alternate place of meeting. As Ludin followed him into the hotel Ari glanced behind him. He saw nothing.

"Do you have anything to drink?" Ludin asked nervously as they entered his room.

"Some arak."

"Nothing better than that?"

An unexpected calm enveloped Ari as if he had battled his way into the eye of a storm and could relax, rest a moment, before plunging back into the tempest. He moved toward the phone. "I can order a bottle of Scotch."

"No," Ludin said. "The arak will be fine."

Ari poured two glasses and added water, which turned the liquid from clear to milky white. He handed one to the Nazi, who was shaking. Clutching at the glass with both hands, he brought the contents to his lips, spilling some of the liquor on the carpet.

"I'm sorry," Ludin said, scowling at the glass as if somehow the arak were responsible for spilling itself.

Ari set his drink on the dresser untouched and sat on the edge of the bed, indicating that Ludin should take the chair near the desk.

"I've never seen you like this, Franz. What's the matter?"

Ludin gulped down the arak. "Somebody's trying to kill me. Letter bombs, two of them. They sent one to my office and another to my home. Just like with Streicher."

"What!" Ari said, not having to feign surprise. He had nothing to do with these additional explosive devices.

"It had to be the Israelis." Ludin stared down into the

empty glass, then held it out toward Ari. "Get me another one, will you?"

He refilled Ludin's glass only halfway. The Nazi's hands were still shaking.

"I don't understand. Why, after so many years, would the Israelis suddenly attempt to assassinate two Nazis here in Damascus?"

"Three Nazis," Ludin said in a hushed tone. He looked from his drink to Ari. "The police security team found another letter bomb in the main post office late this afternoon."

"Who was it addressed to?" He didn't know why but for some reason he expected the third recipient to be Heinneman.

"You."

The single word hit him like a sledgehammer. It was impossible. Ludin had to be mistaken, yet Ari knew he wasn't. "Are you sure?"

"Positive."

Ari stared at the untouched glass of arak on his dresser. The eye of the hurricane had passed, the backlash of the storm striking him full force. The Syrians would not trouble themselves with letter bombs. Interrogating an Israeli agent would be a pleasurable diversion from the banal rigors of intelligence life—not to mention the potential information to be gained. No, they would hardly throw away the opportunity to question him. Then the lens inside Ari's mind brought everything into focus. The Syrians had not tried to kill him, at least not yet. That left only one possibility, sordid and ugly, yet a living sacrament of intelligence life: to produce the desired results even one's own agents are expendable.

The realization of what had befallen him numbed Ari. For reasons he could not even begin to fathom, it seemed his own Service wanted him dead. It must have been planned from the beginning and Barkai's not turning up was part of it, part of a plot to see that he didn't leave Syria alive. But why? Agents were not done away with unless there was a reason, unless there was something to be gained. Ari realized if he was to escape from Damascus he'd have to discover what that reason was and eliminate it—before the Syrians closed in or the Israelis struck again.

Even if he was rushing into the hands of his executioner he wouldn't alter the decision he'd made before. He had no other direction in which to turn. As soon as he got rid of Ludin he would find, contact, and then confront Operative 66. His own life had to be spared, at least long enough to smuggle the children out of Syria.

Then a sickly feeling of disgust, pain, and hate caught in his throat. What if he was being used? What if Operation Goshen didn't exist at all? What if the whole thing was a cover for another operation and the children, like Ari, were to be sacrificed to some higher priority objective? What if Rachael had suffered for nothing? White anger burned inside him. If that was the case he swore to himself that somehow he would get out of Syria, make his way back to Israel, and beat the Colonel to the ground with his bare hands.

"What are we going to do?" Ludin asked, breaking the wanderings of Ari's mind.

"I don't know." He shook his head. He had to snap back into his role as a German commercial businessman, and fast. "Maybe we should get out of the country, find someplace safe."

"Where am I going to go?"

"How about Peru or Argentina? The ODESSA should be able to provide the necessary papers."

"I'm too old to start over," Ludin snapped, wringing

his hands. "I've been in Syria for over thirty years—coming here was difficult enough. I wouldn't survive the move to South America."

Ari wanted to laugh. The Nazi propagandist's quaking before an Israeli spy, whining about how he was too old to run from the Jews, had a comical aspect to it.

"In that case I suggest you hire a bodyguard," Ari said. "Someone to stay with you twenty-four hours a day."

"Do you think the Israelis would give up if they saw I was being protected?"

"Maybe, maybe not." Ari was enjoying himself now. "But I wouldn't feel too confident in any case. The Jews are everywhere. Every time you get in a car you'd better check the rear-view mirror and make sure no suspicious vehicles are following you. The same goes for the streets. Also I wouldn't accept food or anything to drink from anyone except a close friend. Restaurants and bars are out—I wouldn't go near them. You can never tell who's been paid off to slip something in your food."

The shaking in Ludin's hands spread to his entire body. Perspiration dripped down his wrinkled forehead. "What are you going to do?"

"Get out of Damascus as soon as possible."

Ludin inhaled deeply, trying to calm himself. "I'd better go now."

"You're right. It's probably dangerous for us to be together. A double target might tempt the assassin."

Ludin shook his head and stood up—he hadn't thought of that possibility. Ari brushed past him and opened the door. Ludin muttered something unintelligible that sounded like thank you, and literally ran out of the room, lumbering down the hall with awkward strides.

"Good luck," Ari called after him.

He didn't respond.

Ari closed the door to his suite and stood in the hall

199

until he was sure Ludin had left the New Ommayad. When a full five minutes dissolved into the backwash of time, he strode toward the elevator—strengthened by a surge of energy, granted by the realization that the end was nearing.

As he stepped out of the hotel he stopped and stared down Maysaloun Street, as if by an act of will he could cause Kim to reappear. But the street was deserted, the shops shuttered, their windows dark. It was almost beyond hope that he could do anything for her, but he would tell Operative 66 what had happened; make him listen, help.

Ari jumped into a taxi and ordered the driver to proceed over the short distance to the intersection of Port Said Street and Farouk El Awal Boulevard. When he got out of the cab he casually glanced down the street to see if any vehicles had stopped to discharge their passengers. None had, but that meant little. Those following him would be careful. Ari crossed the wide boulevard, darting through the rush of oncoming cars, whose drivers chose to swerve around him rather than brake to a halt. Looking back across the muddy Barada, he saw the tall, twin minarets of the Tekkiyeh of Suleiman the Magnificent.

The sidewalk on Port Said Street was crowded. Ari blended into the flow of people and headed for the red marquee of the Al Ahram Cinema. At the cashier's window he bought a ticket and went inside. The Arab film, already in progress, had no subtitles. As Ari's eyes adjusted to the lack of light he settled into an end seat. The rustling of paper, the crunching of chickpeas, and the shouting of advice to people on the screen drowned out the dialog of the actors. It was not so different from Israel, where patrons noisily rolled Coke bottles down the concrete aisles. After a while he realized why there

200

was so much noise—it was not necessary to listen in order to follow the plot. The action centered on a heroine, wearing a chenille dress, who strolled through an oasis singing songs, unaware that she was being pursued by three villains intent on murdering her. As a sheik's dagger poised above her veiled head a woman next to Ari jumped up in excitement and spilled chickpeas into his lap. Then suddenly the hero arrived on a white stallion and charged toward the sheik. A great sigh escaped the audience.

Approximately thirty-five minutes later he rose and eased his way down the aisle toward the corner of the theater and a green neon sign that read SORTIE. He pushed a heavy wooden door open and stepped into a dimly lit alley. His back pressed against the red brick wall, his heart pounding, he waited; but nobody followed him outside. Breathing easier, he proceeded along the alley toward the residential Baramke district and away from anyone waiting for him on Port Said Street. The sounds of his footsteps echoed through the still night. Quickening his pace, he hurried through a series of mazelike alleys that eventually opened onto the square in front of the Hejaz Railway Terminal.

Chestnut and fruit vendors stood behind carts on the cobbled pavement, but they had no customers. Passing them, he entered the huge four-story terminal. Inside, a glance at the information board confirmed that a train to Homs, Hama, and Aleppo was scheduled to depart in forty-five minutes. Ari bought a ticket and climbed the refuse-litt`red steps to Track Four. He would wait.

With the squeal of metal grating against metal the train moved out of the station. The journey to Homs would take an hour and ten minutes, but Ari had no intention of remaining on the train that long. He looked out the window as the locomotive slowly picked up speed and headed northwest toward Mount Kassioun, nearing the spot where he had picnicked with Kim. He closed his eyes; that afternoon seemed like a lifetime ago. The train maintained a steady forty-five kilometers per hour as it crawled through the city. The locomotive would not pick up speed until it penetrated the fringes of the desert.

When the train entered the small bridge that forded the Tora River, Ari made his way to the back of the car, opened the door, and stood out on the platform. Tall, leafy eucalyptus trees lined the banks of the river. The winds had shifted suddenly, the Mediterranean breezes temporarily succeeding in pushing back the summer siroccos.

The night was cool and crisp. Broken points of stars scattered in the sky winked through the treetops as the train wound along the edge of the al-Ghutah apple orchards toward the Yazid River. Two miles away, nestled under the protective cover of the slopes of Mount Kassioun, was the exclusive Mohajirine district. Composed of handsome houses and gardens, the quarter was built by Ottoman aristocrats in search of clear water and fresh winds, away from the heat and grime of Damascus. As the train slowed to climb the hill leading to the bridge over the Yazid River, Ari jumped.

He hit the dirt at the orchard's edge and rolled, letting his whole body absorb the shock of the fall. Seconds later he was on his feet and peering back at the train. No other forms flung themselves off the moving vehicle. He was alone.

Quickly he plunged in among the trees, stopping only long enough to pick an apple. He was hungry. Events were moving with inconsiderate haste—he had not eaten since noon. Listening to the sounds of the river flowing past in the darkness, he bit into the apple and continued northeast toward the Mohajirine district, relishing each

202

mouthful as he slowly chewed and swallowed it.

Emerging from the orchard, he looked up at the slopes of Kassioun. In the pale moonlight he could make out the red-domed Koubbet el-Sayyar mausoleum and higher up the tall steel tower that beamed the programs of Syria's single television station down to the city. It took him a little over half an hour to reach Jarir Street, a small avenue lined with myrtle saplings, located behind the brilliantly lit, H-shaped presidential palace. Approaching number seventeen he cautiously surveyed the exterior of the villa. The answers to all his questions, the removal of all the uncertainties, were just seconds away. At least he had not been followed. He was sure of that.

He entered the outer courtyard and moved past a fountain, brimming with water and surrounded by lemon trees. The soft scent of the fruit floated in the air. He tapped on the oak door, uncertain if the sounds his knuckles made would penetrate the thick wood and be heard within. Reluctant to knock again, he waited. Just as he was about to ring the bell, the legendary Operative 66, a man so completely integrated into his background that even he wondered sometimes whether he was Jew or Arab, swung the door open.

Ari stood in the darkness, momentarily blinded by the bright light thrown out from inside the house.

"Sabri al-Alazar?" he asked, blinking rapidly, trying to accustom his eyes to the light.

"Come in, Ari," al-Alazar said in Hebrew. "I've been expecting you for several days."

TWENTY

SEPTEMBER 20

THE TAPPING on his office door woke the Colonel. Groggily he lifted his head; it hadn't done him any good to fall asleep slumped forward on his desk. As he sat up pain arched through his back. It hadn't done him any good at all. He rubbed his eyes, then groped blindly for his glasses, knocking over an ashtray and the remains of a half-dozen or more smoked cigars. "Shit," he mumbled out loud.

The knocking at his door intensified, then stopped, and a voice spoke to him from the hall:

"Colonel, it's six A.M. Lieutenant Barkai is on his way up."

"Thank you, Sergeant," the Colonel said, listening to the sound of his bodyguard's footsteps fade as the Sergeant moved toward his desk at the far end of the corridor.

The Colonel picked up the file folder on Suleiman Sarraj, over which the cigar ashes had spilled. Gingerly he brought it toward the wastebasket and knocked the manila folder against the side of the can, jarring the fragments of ash off the paper. A few specks of gray remained. The Colonel brushed at them with his hand— rubbing the ashes into the paper instead of propelling them to the floor. Angrily he snapped the file shut and threw it on his cluttered desk. Yawning, he reached for the mug in front of him, brought the heavy porcelain cup to his mouth, and drank. The coffee was cold. What time had he made it—three, four A.M.? He should have asked the Sergeant to bring him a fresh cup, but it was too late now. He took one last sip, rubbed his tongue against his palate, then pushed the mug to the far end of the desk and out of his way. The cold coffee left an unpleasant taste in his mouth.

For possibly the hundredth time in the last twenty-four hours the Colonel picked up a single soiled piece of paper and went over the timetable for Operation Goshen. The *Hanit,* one of the six fast attack craft paid for in 1968 and secretly spirited away from Cherbourg during the French arms embargo two years later, would depart the Atlit Naval Base north of Caesaria on the twenty-second. Armed with 76-mm. Oto Melara AA guns and eight Gabriel surface-to-surface missiles, the *Hanit* would leave Israeli coastal waters at seven-thirty P.M. Saturday night. At exactly one-fifteen A.M. the lone boat would rendezvous with Lieutenant Barkai in a little cove at Ra's al-Basit, eighteen miles south of the Turkish border. The Israelis had never sent their navy that far north before and evidently the Syrians expected no incursions near Ra's al-Basit. Operative 66 reported a total absence of military activity in the area. Syria's Soviet-built "OSA" patrol boats were heavily concentrated thirty-two miles south of Ra's al-Basit, at Latakia, where Russian cargo ships docked to unload MIG-21s, T-54 tanks, SAM missiles, and other heavy war material. The Colonel was counting on the *Hanit* being able to skirt around Latakia and slip in and out of the designated cove unobserved.

On the back of the heavily creased sheet of paper the Colonel had drawn a rough sketch of the main lines of

Damascus's sewer system. The city's refuse, discharged into the lower Barada River or the Yazid and Tawrat streams that issue from the Barada, flows below the streets by way of a series of underground canals built by the Turkish governor Nezem Pacha between 1908 and 1932. By the 1960s the narrow Tawrat tributary had become so polluted that the raw sewage spilling into it had to be diverted directly into the lower Barada, via a newly constructed channel. The old channel, now dry, leads from the walled city to the Tawrat tributary, passing directly under the Alliance Israélite Universelle School. Shaul Barkai would drop down into the city's sewer system, enter the school's basement through a passageway dug in 1966 by escaping Jews, and guide the children through the underground cavern to a car he would leave in the desert, walking distance from where the concrete canal opened into the Tawrat.

A knock on the door suddenly severed the Colonel's train of thought. "Come in," the head of Israeli Intelligence said.

Shaul Barkai entered wearing a light gray suit, custom tailored for him by a Jewish firm on Bond Street in London.

"What time does your plane leave?"

"Eight-ten."

"And the connecting flight to Damascus?"

"It departs from Heathrow at two this afternoon."

The Colonel nodded, wondering why he'd bothered to ask Barkai about the flights, when he'd already gone over the lieutenant's schedule three times that morning. He cleared an empty space on his desk, set the ashtray in the middle of it, and lit a Montecruz. "So far everything has proceeded as planned. There were some problems associated with Major Ben-Sion, but the matter is being taken care of."

Barkai seemed to stiffen as he stood before the Colonel. "What problems?"

"Nothing that you need concern yourself about. Your mission will not be affected." He flicked the ash off the top of his cigar. The constant questioning by this young breed of intelligence officer, their forever wanting to know things that were unnecessary to the fulfillment of their assignments, irritated as well as worried the Colonel. But he betrayed none of this in his manner or expression.

Barkai sat in the chair across from the desk, though the Colonel had not asked him to do so. "What if I run into Ben-Sion in Damascus?"

"You won't."

"What if I do?" he persisted.

"Then ignore him."

"What if he insists on speaking to me?"

"He won't."

An uneasy quiet filled the gap between them, punctuated by the sound of the wind rustling through the trees outside.

"Are you scared?" the Colonel asked suddenly.

Barkai wanted to say no, to show the Mossad chief that he was tough; but he knew he couldn't lie to the Colonel and get away with it. The man was too damn perceptive.

"Yes," he said softly.

"Good. You'd be a fool if you weren't."

Barkai managed a smile.

"Is there anything else we need to go over?" the Colonel asked, gathering the papers together on his desk. "Otherwise I think you'd better pick up your luggage and head for the airport."

"One thing."

The Colonel lifted his eyebrows. "Yes," he said,

caught off guard. He had not expected the lieutenant to raise any questions at this late date.

"I'm still worried about something we discussed at the policy board meeting with the Shin Beth in Tel Aviv. I lived in Damascus for eighteen years. I know the Syrian police, they're vicious when they're in the kindest of moods. When they've been humiliated by the Jews they turn on the *haret* like mad dogs. If we succeed in smuggling the children out of the country it is quite likely that the government will vent its anger on their families. I'm afraid they might take drastic measures to get back at us."

An almost audible silence breathed in the room. Barkai's warning was not lost on the Colonel; he always had shared the lieutenant's concern, privately pondering the possibility of retaliation at great length.

"It's a calculated risk," the Colonel said, clearly forming each word in his mind before he spoke it. "A risk that Nissim Kimche and Ibrahim Sassoon chose to take. It is their children—their families who will suffer if reprisals come. Remember, they requested Operation Goshen; we did not initiate it."

"But don't we have a responsibility to evaluate their personal request in terms of our larger picture?"

"That's exactly what we've done. The heads of Modiin and the Shin Beth agree—we need the children for their propaganda value. Those American television programs describing the idyllic coexistence between Jews and Arabs in Damascus have crippled our attempt at organizing international opinion to support free emigration for Syria's Jews. Pressure must be put on Assad and the Baath party. Publicly presenting seven suffering youngsters who chose to leave their parents rather than endure the hardships of life in Damascus will provide the political leverage we need to offset the harm done us by the

American broadcaster. I plan to have photographers and cameramen at the dock when the *Hanit* comes in. And I'll have those kids sobbing and crying, if I have to order them spanked while they're still on the boat. I won't see this story buried. Too much is at stake!" He snuffed out his cigar and threw the butt into the wastebasket. "Now swallow the rest of your questions and get out of here. You have a plane to catch."

Barkai nodded and rose.

As he hurried out of the room the Colonel's thoughts turned to Ben-Sion.

TWENTY-ONE

SEPTEMBER 20

ARI FOLLOWED Sabri al-Alazar through the bright corridor, cascades of confusion rippling through him. Al-Alazar's tone implied he had been waiting, not for days as he conceded, but for weeks—expecting his plea for help even before Ari arrived in Damascus. A sinking despair pulled at him. It seemed he had been set up.

Operative Sixty-six quickly guided him through a swinging door into the kitchen, motioning at a table nestled in a corner alcove as he drew the curtains over the draining board. Ari approved of the choice of sites. The alcove was small and intimate. The kitchen, with rococo designs running along the tops of the walls, provided a touch of warmth a larger room would not have.

He stared at al-Alazar as they sat down. His host's face, taut and weather-beaten, seemed chiseled from a characteristic Semitic mold. He had wavy black hair slightly worn away by years, a high forehead, heavy eyebrows, and a neatly trimmed moustache. But what was distinctive about him were his eyes. They were chocolate brown and large, giving Ari the impression that al-Alazar was watching him even when his head was turned to the side. Ari put his age at fifty, fifty-five—roughly the same as his.

"Are you sure no one followed you?" al-Alazar asked.

"Don't worry. I haven't forgotten how to shake a tail."

"Are you positive, the Syrians might . . ."

"I wasn't followed!"

Al-Alazar nodded, then glanced over at the window. He couldn't tell because of the curtains, but he was pretty sure he'd remembered to close it.

"Would you like something to drink or eat?" he asked, returning his attention to Ari.

"I'd prefer to know why you tried to kill me."

Al-Alazar looked puzzled for a second, then a spark of understanding flickered in his eyes. "Oh, you mean the letter bomb. It wasn't intended to kill you."

"Only maim, blind, or permanently damage?"

Al-Alazar shook his head. "You don't understand. I only wanted to make it look like the Israelis were trying to murder you. I felt fairly certain that after your attempt on Streicher's life the Syrian Internal Security Service would set up emergency procedures to screen all letters passing through the central post office. There seemed little doubt that they would detect the bomb."

"What if they didn't?" Ari asked, the anger in his voice cutting through his words.

"Then I assumed you'd be perceptive enough to recognize the letter as one of our own explosive devices before you opened it."

"And if I wasn't?"

"I was sure you were. In any event I had little choice in the matter. Streicher told the police he was certain you were the Israeli agent who had attempted to kill him. They were going to pull you in for questioning. They would have penetrated your cover story. I had to act immediately." Al-Alazar paused for a moment to let the impact of his words soak in. "By the way, that was a very sloppily made pen trap you mailed him. You must have set the firing pin too low."

"So you sent booby-trapped letters to Ludin and to my room, hoping the police would drop their suspicions about me," Ari said, quickly changing the subject, embarrassed about the bomb that had hardly harmed the Wehrmacht colonel.

"Exactly. You have been seen several times in the company of Ludin and Streicher. The police made the logical leap and assumed that Operative 66 had tried to wipe out the three of you. Streicher's suspicions were dropped, which was imperative for us. We could not let the police arrest you and rob the Second Bureau of the caged bird they had trapped so carefully. That would have spoiled everything."

Al-Alazar's words hit him like a sledgehammer. "What?" Ari said, realizing that for weeks he'd been a pawn being moved by a skilled chessmaster in a game much different than the one he thought he was playing.

"I will explain everything in due course. But first let me make us something to eat. I'm famished and I suspect you have not eaten this evening. I'll just fry some eggs; it will take only a few minutes. This whole conversation will proceed a lot better if we continue on full stomachs."

Although he didn't feel like eating, Ari nodded.

Al-Alazar rose and moved toward the refrigerator. He was delaying the inevitable—what he had to tell Ari would crush him, and he was by no means in a hurry to do that.

As the sound of eggs frying in oil filled the room, Ari tried to push all thoughts out of his mind. The Second Bureau was closing in on him and the Colonel had arranged it. But why? Why?

Al-Alazar slipped the eggs in front of Ari, a plate of yellow eyes that seemed to stare up, mocking him. He dashed the yolks with his fork, but the laughter ringing in his ears only intensified. It wasn't the right time to ask

212

about Kim, but that didn't matter. No time was right any more.

"A friend of mine has been picked up by the Second Bureau," he said with strained equanimity. "I think they're going to use her to get to me. If they harm . . ."

"What makes you think Kim Johnson has been detained by the Second Bureau?" al-Alazar interrupted.

Ari stared at his host in disbelief, but his surprise dissolved after a moment as it became clear that al-Alazar was aware of every move he had made over the past two weeks.

"There's been a man watching me, a short, squat Arab. When Kim left the hotel this evening he followed her. I ran after them but by the time I reached the street they were gone. It had to be planned. The man was a Second Bureau agent, his partner was waiting outside. The short, squat Arab must have forced her inside a car; then the three of them sped off."

Al-Alazar rose. "Let me make a call and see if I can find out what happened. I'll be right back." He moved through an ornately engraved door at the far end of the kitchen and entered the living room. On an inlaid rosewood table next to a backless Ottoman sofa lay the transmitter Ari had attempted to bring into the country. Al-Alazar's transmitter had broken a little over a month ago. Without knowing it, Ari had brought him a replacement.

The senior Israeli agent picked the wireless up, placed it inside a chest in the corner of the room, and closed the top. His task was difficult enough, there was no need to let Ben-Sion know the full extent of the Colonel's duplicity. That job completed, al-Alazar went to the phone and dialed quickly. He didn't want to keep Ari waiting too long. After receiving the information he requested, he hurried back into the kitchen.

"Well?"

"She's in the hotel, apparently waiting for you."

Ari breathed a sigh of relief. "Thank God."

Al-Alazar knew no way to do what he had to do gracefully. "You were right, though. She was picked up by Second Bureau agents. They drove her to an out-of-the-way café where she was questioned by Second Bureau chief Suleiman Sarraj and Mukhabarat head Yussaf Fuad."

"And they let her go?"

"I'm afraid I'm not making myself clear. They didn't let her go, they gave her further instructions. Kim Johnson is an Egyptian agent. She's working with Sarraj."

The color drained from his face. His mouth went dry. A muffled scream escaped his throat.

"It was no accident that you met her," al-Alazar said. "Sarraj arranged it."

"Impossible!" Kim was in love with him. She couldn't have been faking everything.

"I can prove my allegations if you really want me to."

"No!"

Ari stared at the ceiling, reliving their meeting that first afternoon in Jerusalem. He had suggested she accompany him to the Old City. She had hesitated, explaining that she wanted to go back to the hotel. He'd had to work hard to persuade her to have dinner with him, to convince her to alter her plans and fly to Damascus instead of Cairo. He recalled her offering to find out about Dov, her unexpected trip to al-Mazza, her demanding the right to sleep with an Arab minister to get additional information.

The memories slashed through him, one after the other, smothering him beneath them. He relived her running out of the dining room in tears when he told her he was a Nazi. Remembered her fears and uncertainties. It had all been an act! A cold, calculated maneuver. Un-

214

derneath that veil of pain she had been confident that she had him dangling off the edge of her bed, that rather than be left alone, he'd run after her and confess being an Israeli. Even her protesting that she wanted to leave Syria was false, designed to suppress any subconscious suspicions he might be forming. Suddenly he understood the source of her insight and intuition. She had been able to penetrate his personality so quickly because she'd been thoroughly briefed on him!

He cringed. She had played her part flawlessly; she had made a fool out of him without his suspecting a thing. He tried to hate her, but he couldn't. He was too full of self-disgust.

But something was still unclear. Kim had stepped into his life in Jerusalem, before he'd been given a new assignment. How was it that the Second Bureau had broken his cover so early? There was only one possible answer—someone had tipped the Syrians off.

"Why did the Colonel set me up?" There was a quiet, menacing anger in his voice.

Al-Alazar saw by the look in Ari's eyes that there was no sense in denying it; he would have to explain more than he had intended to. But not everything. There were certain details it was best Ben-Sion not know yet. "The Syrians have been aware for several months that there is an Israeli spy operating somewhere in the upper echelons of the Baath Party. Both the Second Bureau and the Mukhabarat are on the verge of discovering Operative Sixty-six's identity. It is only a matter of time before they do so. There are signs of an imminent shift of power here in Syria and for certain reasons the Colonel would like to see Suleiman Sarraj discredited when President Assad reshuffles his regime. What you have been doing the last two and a half weeks is leading the Second Bureau chief to me. My sources report that, based on his manipulation

215

of you, he is so sure he'll succeed he has promised the Syrian High Command that Operative Sixty-six will be in prison by the first of October. He cannot back down; he has invested his entire political prestige in capturing me. What you will do now is discreetly let Sarraj know I am Operative Sixty-six, but we will flee Syria before he has a chance to arrest us. Our escape will require split-second timing and coordination, but both the Colonel and I are convinced it can be accomplished successfully. Sarraj will be left with nothing to show for his boasting. He will be blamed for allowing two Israeli spies to get away with state security secrets. Public humiliation is inevitable. And, you know what losing face means to an Arab, he will either resign or be deposed. Most likely he will resign."

Anger burned inside Ari. Not only had Kim's words veiled her true intentions, but the Colonel's briefing had been spurious, purposely designed to mislead, maneuver, and manipulate him.

"What about Operation Goshen?" He didn't even attempt to hide the disgust in his voice. "Have I been banging my head against the wall for nothing?"

"On the contrary. Lieutenant Barkai arrived in Damascus this evening. Saliha Maaruf, though not a strong person, was able to contact Nissim Kimche and relay your message. The children will be in the basement of the Alliance School Saturday evening. If all goes as planned you and I will leave Syria tomorrow night. Our departure should prove an effective cover for Operation Goshen. We'll be traveling south, over the Golan. Because of us a major part of Syria's security forces should concentrate in that direction. They'll never suspect we're running another operation to the north twenty-four hours later."

Some of Ari's anger seeped away. He resented being

216

used, but the Mossad chief's plan was a masterful one. He couldn't help but marvel at it. He decided then and there that the first thing he would do upon seeing the Colonel again was deck him, then reach down and help the venerable bastard up. That is, provided he lived through the next forty-eight hours.

"I have just one question," Ari said. "How am I going to tip off Sarraj and still leave us enough time to stroll out of Syria without getting shot to pieces?"

"I'm glad you asked that," al-Alazar said, smiling. It was the first time he allowed himself the luxury of relaxing since Ari had entered his house. "First of all, if my source is accurate, you have told Miss Johnson that you are an Israeli agent, but you have not divulged your purpose for being in Damascus or any of the details of Operation Goshen. Is that substantially correct?"

Flushed with embarrassment, Ari nodded—wondering how al-Alazar knew so much about his conversations with Kim, information that would not normally be available to a member of Parliament.

"We calculated you had too many years of intelligence life ground into you to discuss details of a mission even with those," the Israeli agent hesitated for a moment, "with whom you were most intimate."

Ari's stomach muscles contracted. He'd lied to al-Alazar about Kim, the same way he'd lied to the Colonel about Michelle. But he couldn't admit to this senior agent that he'd told Kim his assignment was to be executed on the twenty-second, he just couldn't.

"This may be unpleasant for you," al-Alazar continued. "But the key to our success lies with Miss Johnson. When you return to the hotel tonight I want you to try and act as normal as possible. She must not suspect that you know she's working for Sarraj. Then tomorrow evening, confide in her—tell her you're meeting a high-placed Israeli agent Saturday night and that you'll be ready to leave Syria immediately afterward. Act nervous, excited. She'll probe for more information. Give it to her, make up any reason you want for meeting Operative Sixty-six. It doesn't matter as long as she believes you. But don't be too anxious to discuss your assignment. Part with the information reluctantly. Make her work for it. Drink, talk about how the Israelis have pulled one over on the stupid Arabs. Have a good laugh on the Syrians, on the fact that a member of their Parliament is an Israeli spy. Let my name slip out naturally. Then pull back in fear, horrified at what you've done. Act as if everything has suddenly become clear, let her know you realize she's an agent who has been working for weeks just to get that information out of you. The codes of your profession demand you kill her to protect my cover, but she's your lover, you can't do it. Tie her up and leave her in your room. Then get to a pay phone in the lobby and call this number." Al-Alazar removed a slip of paper from his shirt pocket and handed it to him. "I'll be waiting to hear from you. Try and make the call as close to nine P.M. as possible, that's important. It's crucial that you time the entire evening so that you phone from the hotel lobby between nine and nine-fifteen, the closer to nine the better. But you must call within that quarter-hour span, otherwise we'll never get out of Syria alive. A Golani paratrooper rescue unit will be waiting for us at a pre-designated spot in the desert from nine-forty to nine-fifty. They can't risk remaining there for more than ten minutes. It will take us twenty-five minutes to reach them. We must be out of Damascus by nine-twenty-five at the absolute latest."

Ari stared down at the floor, then looked into al-Alazar's eyes, and spoke in a voice just above a whisper: "I lied when I said I didn't give Kim any details about

Operation Goshen. She knows whatever I came to Syria to do will be attempted on the twenty-second."

For a long moment the room was quiet. "I'm aware of that," al-Alazar said softly.

Ari's face registered the surprise that bounded through him. It seemed impossible that al-Alazar could have obtained such specific information about what he'd told Kim, yet somehow he had.

"The Second Bureau's knowing your assignment is scheduled to be completed on Saturday does not present a problem. Sarraj will conclude that upon discovering the Second Bureau is onto you, you fled Syria a day early, aborting your mission in the process. It will appear that with my cover blown, I was forced to escape with you. To make it look like I ran out on a moment's notice I intend to leave all my equipment and codes behind, intact."

"And in the wake of what looks like a broken operation, Lieutenant Barkai will lead the children out of Damascus."

"That's what I'm hoping."

Ari paused for a moment. The whole damn thing just might work. "But how am I going to get from the hotel to you without being followed?"

"I was just coming to that. From the lobby you proceed into the dining room as if you are going to have a late supper . . ."

As al-Alazar outlined his proposed escape route, Ari fought an inner war, trying to keep his attention riveted on al-Alazar's words, and away from drifting into thoughts of Kim. He wanted so much to scream *betrayal,* to hate her with every fiber of his being, to retreat behind a tirade of angry invective and threats of revenge. That was the ego-salvaging reaction of the victim of self-deception—he could have no part of it. She had not made a fool out of him; she had allowed him to make a

219

fool out of himself. And the Colonel had based an entire operation on the assumption that he would behave that way. That's what really hurt.

Ari winced. He accepted being used—at this point he had little choice; but he didn't understand how the Colonel could have anticipated in advance his becoming involved with a Syrian spy. Then something in him snapped. After al-Alazar finished speaking, Ari looked across at him.

"How could the Colonel be sure Sarraj would send a girl after me and that I would fall for her?"

"I don't know," he answered, a bit too quickly.

"You're lying."

Al-Alazar paused, then spoke expressionlessly. "With your history it was inevitable."

And suddenly it all became clear. "Michelle," the name slipped from his mouth. "She was an agent."

Al-Alazar nodded. "One of Sarraj's best."

"And the Colonel knew the whole time, that's why he selected me for this assignment."

"Yes," al-Alazar said as gently as he could. "Though the Syrians did surprise us by sending Kim to Jerusalem. We expected you'd accidentally meet a young lady here in Damascus."

Ari's attempt to hide his humiliation did not succeed. His expression betrayed everything he felt.

"I should have suspected something. It was too much of a coincidence that I was lured to a remote part of Cyprus exactly when an important message was coming over the transmitter."

"What about your escape route from the hotel, is it clear?" al-Alazar asked, as if he hadn't heard his confession.

"I think I'd be more comfortable if you went over the

details one more time," Ari said. He liked al-Alazar. He was compassionate, a rare quality in an agent.

Al-Alazar meticulously went over the steps Ari was to take to insure they met unaccompanied, without showing the slightest trace of annoyance at having to repeat himself. This time Ari cemented every word into his consciousness. Al-Alazar would not have to go over any part of it a third time.

Completing his briefing, al-Alazar leaned back and stretched.

"Ari, I've told you as much about our operations in Syria as I dare to at this point. The rest the Colonel will explain in Jerusalem, we owe you that much." He paused for a moment and shifted uneasily in his chair. "I know how you must feel about the way you've been . . ."

"Don't," Ari interrupted.

Al-Alazar nodded. "Then I think it best you start back to the hotel. The number thirty-two bus at the corner of Adnan el-Malki and Omar Safar streets will take you directly to Marjeh Square.

"I know."

Al-Alazar groped for something to say to cushion the blow his words had inflicted. "You have no idea how important what you're doing is to the security of Israel."

"Spare me the platitudes," Ari said. "I've been an agent long enough. I know the price tag our life carries."

"I'm sorry, I was just trying to make it easier."

Ari rose. "I will phone you from the hotel lobby tomorrow night—exactly at nine."

Al-Alazar nodded. "Come, let me walk you to the door."

Silently they moved through the hallway, each man immersed in his own thoughts.

In the courtyard al-Alazar looked into Ari's eyes,

searching for a sign of weakness. "We're going to make it," he said, finding none.

Ari grunted and stepped out into the night.

Suleiman Sarraj and Yussaf Fuad sat impatiently in Sarraj's office waiting for the phone to ring. Fuad sipped his coffee slowly; Sarraj's cup sat at the end of the desk, untouched. Nervously clicking his amber worry beads in one hand, he was too angry to drink. Those bungling fools of his had lost track of Ben-Sion. The Israeli might have contacted Operative 66 and left the country by now.

Suddenly the phone rang and Sarraj snatched at it.

"He's back at the hotel," a voice said hurriedly.

Sarraj did not allow himself a sigh of relief. "I want the watch on him doubled," he shouted into the phone. "I want four teams of men following him at all times. And I do not want them to be seen. Do you understand?"

"Yes, general."

"Good." Sarraj slammed down the receiver and turned to Fuad. "Ben-Sion's back at the hotel. He must have made contact with Operative Sixty-six. Whatever they're planning has probably been set in motion. We must put a stop to it immediately."

Fuad set his cup and saucer down on the desk. "I still think it would be less risky if we arrested Ben-Sion and let my men question him in their own delicate manner."

Sarraj shook his head. "I'm afraid he'd die before he talked." Besides, Sarraj added to himself, the success was to be his, not the Mukhabarat chief's.

Fuad bared his white teeth. "There are ways of keeping the Israeli alive while breaking every bone in his body one by one. The effect is most excruciating. I assure you, no man can withstand the pain."

"No," Sarraj said loudly. "Your methods will be employed only as a last resort. I've studied this Ben-Sion carefully. He is not the type who will betray a fellow agent under physical pressure. He would welcome death first. I'm certain a much higher percentage of success lies with Kim." Under the threat that Fuad would intercede and arrest Ben-Sion if more information was not forthcoming, Sarraj had been forced to divulge the details of his entire operation.

Fuad folded his hands on his lap. "I am becoming impatient with your Miss Johnson."

"Without her we would not have known that what they're planning is set for the twenty-second," Sarraj said.

Fuad leaned back in his chair. "Two months' work and that's all she's been able to come up with. I'm hardly impressed. Let me remind you that the twenty-second is the day after tomorrow. We cannot exactly afford to just sit here. I will give Miss Johnson twenty-four more hours. If she does not produce results by then I will order the arrest of the Israeli. I will not wait until the twenty-second, when it may be too late."

"All right," Sarraj said, slamming the table with his fist. "We're meeting again in the morning. I'll tell her she must induce him to talk without further delay. But you must give her time."

Fuad stood and moved toward the door. "We have already given her too much time as it is. My personal opinion is that she is growing fond of Ben-Sion and that she will never obtain the information we desire. Didn't you notice the way she spoke about him this evening, the way she kept calling him Ari? I think she's as much in love with him as he is with her. If we don't arrest him soon, the two of them will probably escape together and you'll receive a wedding invitation postmarked Tel Aviv."

"She'll have the information out of him by tomorrow!" Sarraj shouted.

"I hope so."

Fuad smiled and left the Second Bureau offices.

Ari slipped the key into the lock in the hotel door and pushed himself into the room. Kim lay sprawled on his bed reading last week's Sunday supplement of the London *Times*. At the sound of his entrance she rushed over and flung her arms around his neck. He felt her breasts rubbing against his shirt.

"I'm so glad you're back," she said, kissing his ear.

The touch of her lips sent a rush through him. His reaction irritated him; he shouldn't be feeling that any more. He laced his arms around her. He had to maintain his cover, he told himself, but he knew that was only part of his reason for holding her. He wished she could tell him that what al-Alazar had said wasn't true, but he dared not ask—for al-Alazar was right. He saw it now in her every movement. Why else would such an attractive, vigorous young woman be interested in him? He'd been so blind.

"You meet with anybody tonight?" she asked, sitting on the edge of the bed as he pulled away from her.

Instead of answering he began to undress.

"Did you do anything interesting this evening?" she repeated, rephrasing her question so that it sounded less like she was probing for something specific.

"No."

Moving close, he pushed her onto the mattress. Roughly lifting her negligee over her head, he stared at her naked body, reeling from the fact that the brief moment of happiness she'd given him had been false.

224

"Ari," she protested.

"Just be patient," he whispered to himself. "Tomorrow night I'll tell you everything you want to know."

Abruptly he thrust himself between her legs, driving his anger down through his loins and into her. She tried to respond as best she could. Seconds later, it was over.

As he slipped out of her she shifted position. "I hope that's not it for the night," she said.

He forced a smile.

Later, after several attempts to elicit information that he blunted with the excuse of being too tired to talk, he tried to enter her again. But he couldn't. Using the tips of her fingers she enticed his body into cooperating. Once together he worked for a long time, unable to achieve release. Finally, he fell away, drifting into a morose fog that robbed him of real sleep.

TWENTY-TWO

SEPTEMBER 21

ARI WOKE slowly. First he heard a sound in the hallway and then he was aware it was morning. Even with his eyes closed the bright rays of Middle Eastern sun slanting in through the window shot through his lids, causing his head to pulse. His mouth was sticky and his throat parched. Outside the cry of the muezzins rose, held for a long breath, then fell away. He stared at the cracked ceiling; the lines seemed to be dancing in the air. He flipped onto his stomach. Pressed tight against the mattress he pulled the sheet over his face. He lay there, sweating, afraid to get up. An hour passed, then another. He drifted in and out of a nightmare. His mouth grew drier. Finally, forcing himself out of bed, he shuffled toward the water faucet in the bathroom, suddenly realizing that Kim had left already.

He felt a little better after he showered and ate. Faced with the prospects of what he hoped would be his final day in Damascus, he phoned Mustafa Suidani and arranged to be picked up at one-thirty and shown several glass factories in Kissoué, a village on the road to Amman, twenty miles south of Damascus. Ari's interest in hand-blown glass vases registered just below his interest in withered ideas and last year's insights. Yet he was

226

anxious to accompany Suidani, not because spending the afternoon shopping for exportable merchandise would draw suspicion away from his intention to flee the country that night, but because haggling with Arab manufacturers promised to chew away at the hours. Cramming activity into his day would divert his thoughts—and help him resist the depression overwhelming him.

For a long time Ari had sensed that he was being watched. Except for the short, squat Arab in the hotel lobby he had not actually seen anyone suspicious; but the feeling was there nonetheless, a palpable certainty that pairs of eyes followed his every movement. As he stepped out of the hotel to wait for Suidani the feeling intensified. They had lost him the night before when he jumped from the train. They would not be so careless again. Ari casually glanced around him, sensing that he was being monitored from the street, from cars, and from the roof across the way. He just hoped al-Alazar's escape plan worked. They would not have a chance to try an alternate one.

Despite the shift in winds it had been an oppressively hot afternoon and Ari was exhausted by the time they returned to the New Ommayad. The car wasn't air conditioned and they'd been forced to drive with the windows down, the sand and dust flying in their faces. A thin line of mud ringed Ari's hairline where he sweated. As Suidani switched off the ignition key a group of school-age boys, wearing heavy flannel military uniforms, trudged toward the Tajhiz Secondary School.

"Saika guerrillas—they're in training," Suidani explained, catching the perplexed look on Ari's face.

"But why are they wearing such heavy uniforms in this heat?"

Suidani started to get out of the car. "Their clothes are

227

specially designed to toughen them for the struggle against the Zionists."

Ari nodded and stepped out onto the sidewalk, looking at the waves of air behind the Renault's exhaust pipe, thinking about the eighteen- and nineteen-year-old boys training in Israel. There are few things more sad, he believed, than the sight of young people who are preparing to kill each other.

Suidani thanked him verbosely for his generous investment in Damascus glass, giving his assurance that the merchandise would be packed and shipped with the utmost care. Ari promised to phone him in a few days, said good-bye, and walked toward the lobby. Inside, he went directly to the house phone and asked for Kim's room. To his dismay there was no answer. He had intended to set a specific time for them to meet that evening, but Kim had left early, before he had the chance to arrange anything. Now he started to worry. What if she didn't return to the hotel before nine? He knew the answer to his own rhetorical question. Al-Alazar's timetable would be destroyed—and both their lives with it.

Before going up to his room he asked the desk clerk to phone him as soon as Miss Johnson returned to the hotel. To insure that the young man's memory did not fail him Ari tore a ten-pound note in half and stuffed one piece into his breast pocket.

Once in his room he poured himself some arak and though he should have taken only a few sips, just enough to insure that his breath smelled of alcohol, he drained the glass. After pouring another and drinking it he went into the bathroom, taking the bottle with him. He looked into the mirror and mussed his hair. Exhaling listlessly, he returned to the bedroom, set the bottle on the nightstand, and prepared to wait.

Hundreds of times over the years he had gone through

these same motions, preparing the room for the target, readying himself for a duel in deception with his adversary. But this time he felt different; no sense of animal joy bounded through him. The exhilaration that had always electrified the moment before he sliced the rope that sent the trap crashing down on his victim was absent. A heaviness pervaded his movements. He was tired and sad and ready to go home.

When the phone rang he checked his watch before answering it. Eight-eleven, there was plenty of time.

"Monsieur Hoffmann, this is the front desk. The American, Miss Johnson, just entered the hotel. I took the liberty of mentioning that you were interested in speaking to her. I hope that . . ."

"That's fine," Ari cut him off. "You'll have the other half of the bill in the morning." He hung up without waiting for a response.

A few minutes later Kim entered the room, a smile brightening her face. She knew the door would be unlocked so she hadn't bothered to knock.

"I see you've been bribing the hotel staff to report my whereabouts again."

"Do you mind?"

She hung her leather handbag on the chair. "No, actually I'm flattered you're so anxious to see me that you're willing to throw good money away."

He smiled, took a sip of the arak, and held the glass out to her. "Would you like some? I'm afraid I've already had a little too much."

She took a small sip and settled on the bed next to him. "What are we celebrating?" she asked, looking over at the half-empty bottle.

He took the glass from her hand and drank off the remaining contents. "We're leaving Syria tomorrow night—the two of us."

"Oh, Ari." She hugged him with unbridled excitement. "Then you finished what you came here to do?"

Resting her head against his shoulder, she was the perfect actress. There wasn't the slightest hint of duplicity in her manner. He held her tight against him; he couldn't bear to meet her eyes, that's what he'd been so angry about last night. He despised himself for the feeling that still darted through him when he looked at her.

"No, it's not quite over yet," he said. "I have to meet Operative Sixty-six tomorrow. He's gathered some crucial intelligence on Syrian Scud missile emplacements. It's imperative that the information be sent on to Jerusalem—that's why I came to Damascus, to serve as an intermediary." Ari stared across the room at the blank wall. At least he had steered the Syrians away from Operation Goshen.

She unbuttoned his shirt and played with the hair on his chest. "Operative Sixty-six. I don't understand. What's that?"

He forced a laugh. "Not a what but a who. He's a man, a high-placed Israeli agent called a sleeper—a spy who is stationed in an enemy country to lie dormant for five, ten years, or until he's needed. In the meantime he works himself into a position of power, totally unsuspected by those around him because during the entire period he's *sleeping*, he has no contact with his mother country."

"And Operative Sixty-six is a sleeper?"

"He was a sleeper," Ari corrected her. "The Israeli Secret Service planted him in Syria in 1961 intending he remain buried until the 1980s but they hastily activated him when the Yom Kippur War broke out." Ari laughed, the abandoned hilarity of the drunk. "I bet some heads would roll around here if the Second Bureau ever found out that a high-ranking member of the Syrian Parliament was an Israeli spy." He was irritated at himself, the touch of her fingers rolling over his chest aroused him.

"A member of Parliament," Kim gasped. "That's unbelievable. I wonder who he is?"

"What does it matter? I don't want to talk about him. Come on, let's go to bed." He started unbuttoning her blouse. Make her work for it, Al-Alazar had said.

"I'm not in the mood right now." She pushed his hand away. "Besides, I want to hear more about this Operative Sixty-six; he sounds fascinating. What kind of a man would bury himself in a hostile country and live there for more than a decade without once being contacted by those who sent him? Wouldn't he worry that his superiors had forgotten about him? What if the person who sent him died?"

Inwardly he bristled at her feigned naïvité. "There are always files," he said, shaking off his irritation. "It's impossible that any service would lose track of one of its sleepers, even by accident. Those agents are placed with extreme difficulty. The fruits produced by their long period of gestation are the sweetest intelligence life bears."

"Tell me, what is he like, this Israeli member of the Syrian Parliament?"

Ari smiled. "Al-Alazar, well he's . . ."

The expression on her face altered abruptly. She was shocked, surprised that after so long he'd slipped, letting Operative 66's name drop so casually.

Ari pounced on the opportunity, jumping up in mock horror, forcing hatred to burn in his eyes. "What have you tricked me into doing?" He knocked at the bottle of arak and sent it reeling on the floor. "The whole evening, all you've been interested in is getting me to talk about Operative Sixty-six! Why?"

"I don't understand. What are you talking about?"

He grabbed her by the neck and pushed his thumb up under her Adam's apple, compressing her trachea, momentarily blocking the air supply.

"You're lying," he said.

She realized instantly by the look on his face that he knew, that any attempt to convince him of her innocence was futile. "Oh Ari, I'm so sorry," she said, choking. "Suleiman Sarraj forced me into doing it. Kill me if you want to, but it won't do you any good. The room was bugged after you slipped away from Sarraj's agents. As soon as the Second Bureau retrieves the tapes they'll know who Operative Sixty-six is."

He hesitated for a second, then threw her on the bed. "What do you mean Sarraj forced you into doing it?"

She curled up into herself, shaking. "I had no choice. I would have been sent to prison if I didn't agree to help him!" She tried to fight back her tears, unsuccessfully. "You have to understand. I graduated from New York University with a degree in sociology. I couldn't get a job, not even as a secretary or a salesgirl. I was over-qualified. There was a recession, everybody was getting laid off, no one was hiring. My parents are dead. I went to college on a scholarship. I hadn't worked so I couldn't collect unemployment. All I had was my camera, but nobody would buy any of my pictures. I was living with this man I hated. He beat me, but I couldn't leave. I had no way to support myself. Finally one night he got drunk and hit me over the head with a lamp. I landed up in the hospital. When I was released I had no money, no place to go. I had to sell my body to eat!"

He stood there silent, immobile.

"A young Arab, Muamar Gamasy, picked me up one night in a bar. He was very kind and understanding. He took me home and introduced me to his father, who turned out to be a security officer in the Egyptian consul-

232

ate in New York. A few days later the senior Gamasy offered me a job as a secretary. I grabbed it, anything to get off the streets. Eventually he asked me to do a few favors for him, to join some Zionist groups and report on the meetings. Being legally Jewish nobody suspected what I was really doing. At first I only wanted to make enough money to move to California, but before I knew it I was involved too deeply. I couldn't quit. The Egyptians and Syrians even paid off various magazines and newspapers, getting them to print my pictures so I'd be happy. But when Gamasy asked me to fly to Israel and do a big job for him there, I refused. Then some people at the consulate brought out these movies they'd taken of me in bed with customers, complete with my taking money for my services. It was no coincidence that Muamar showed up in that bar, it had all been carefully planned from the beginning. Later his father presented me with a choice: either I flew to Israel or I went to prison for prostitution."

Hate scorched his throat. "Why didn't you go to the authorities in Jerusalem? They would have protected you."

"I was afraid. I had to report the progress I was making to a Palestinian terrorist leader in Jericho twice a week. He said they were watching me, that if I went to the police I'd be killed. You have to believe me," she said. "After I got to know you I tried to get out of it. Remember when I said I went to Aleppo—that was a lie. I really drove to Lebanon. I thought maybe I could fly to Europe and hide so that Sarraj couldn't make me hurt you. I got as far as the airport in Beirut. They brought me back and threatened to throw acid in my face if I tried escaping again." She reached out to touch him. "I didn't want to do it, but I was so frightened. You have to believe that. I care about you. Don't leave me here."

233

He wanted to smash her face into the wall. What kind of fool did she think he was! She was lying; her only concern, finding Operative 66. Disgust and anger fused together inside him. He no longer cared to control his emotions. He'd give her what she wanted. He'd take her to meet Operative 66—for two seconds. Then he'd blow her fucking brains out.

"Get into the bathroom and wash your face. You're coming with me." He looked at his watch. It was three minutes to nine.

She jumped up and followed his instructions. When she returned he led her out of the room and down the hall. As they waited for the elevator Kim clung to his arm for support. He felt each of her fingers individually. Once in the lobby he crossed to the pay phones. Nobody stopped them; the Second Bureau would want to follow him to Operative 66. He inserted a brass five-piaster coin in the slot and dialed the number al-Alazar had given him. The senior Israeli agent answered after half a ring. Ari spoke the single word "Go," then hung up.

"I'm hungry, why don't we get something to eat," he said.

"Fine," Kim responded. She would agree to anything he suggested.

The pounding of his heart beat in his ears as the maître d' seated them. Ari opened the menu, keeping a close eye on his watch. Exactly four minutes after he had called al-Alazar he got up and motioned to Kim to follow him. Walking up to the maître d', Ari spoke in a quiet voice:

"Do you think you might be able to introduce us to the chef? Miss Johnson is very interested in watching him prepare her meal."

The maître d' frowned. "Such a request is highly irregular. I'm extremely sorry, but I don't think . . ." Ari handed him a fifty-pound note. The maître d's face registered no reaction. He simply took the bill and slipped it into his pants pocket. "I think something can be arranged. Please follow me."

He guided them across the dining room toward the kitchen. As soon as the swinging doors closed behind them Ari grabbed Kim's hand and pulled her past the surprised maître d'. "Come on," he shouted, dragging her through the maze of cooks, food, and counters. Seconds later two men burst into the kitchen. Spotting Ari and Kim fleeing out the back door, they ran after them, knocking the perplexed maître d' to the ground as he protested loudly.

Ari and Kim dashed into the alley behind the hotel, where an empty Triumph Spitfire was parked, its motor idling. As Ari leaped over the door of the convertible, Kim jumped in beside him. Quickly he threw the car into gear, sending the vehicle racing down the alley with the screech of rubber grating against asphalt. The two Second Bureau agents ran out of the kitchen just in time to get the car's make and license number.

Ari drove quickly, aware that the police would have an all-points bulletin out on the Spitfire within minutes. To Kim's surprise, instead of heading down side streets he followed Brazil Avenue into Farouk El Awal Boulevard, Damascus's main thoroughfare, and turned left, toward the crowded Marjeh Square district. Veering around a donkey pulling a chestnut vendor's cart, he drove through the main entrance to the Ministry of Justice, around the building, and into a back parking lot that was empty, except for a green Fiat. He parked the Spitfire against the building where it would not be seen and got out, carrying a dark tarpaulin in his hand. "Help me cover the car," he said.

Kim hurriedly stepped out of the convertible, took one edge of the camouflaging canvas, and pulled it over the bright yellow vehicle.

"The Fiat's ours," he said, instructing her to follow him as he finished draping his end over the hood of the Spitfire.

Within seconds he guided the Fiat by the soot-covered obelisk in Marjeh Square and onto Farouk El Awal Boulevard, heading west this time. So far so good. It was 9:07. They would rendezvous with al-Alazar in six minutes.

"Are you scared?" he asked as they sped parallel to the Barada River which watered the spacious Jalaa Park stretching on the right side of the highway.

"A little."

He looked at her.

She leaned over and kissed his cheek. "I'm incredibly happy."

Driving just under the speed limit of sixty kilometers per hour Ari turned south, passing the domed Madrassa Selimiya, its weed-infested courtyard piled high with rusting bed frames. The eucalyptus-lined secondary road they followed wound through the suburbs toward the desert, skirting around the olive green Hamidieh barracks which serve as dormitories for Damascus University. Ari gripped the steering wheel tensely. When he was inducted into the Service, one of the first and most important rules drummed into his head by his training sergeant was not to ease up during the period of psychological vulnerability, that span of time when one appears to have succeeded but has not yet bridged all possible danger. Relaxing, even slightly, might prove fatal.

Kim touched his hand. "I love you," she said.

Moving his arm away, he didn't respond.

Soon they emerged from the suburbs and sped onto

a narrow two-lane highway that continued straight ahead, disappearing into the desert. Ari switched off the headlights. The road was dark and quiet; the bright beams might attract attention. To compensate for the loss of light he reduced his speed.

"How much longer?" Kim asked nervously.

"A minute or two."

Seconds later they passed a sign, barely discernible in the moonless night, that read: KUNEITRA 65 KILOMETERS. Ari slammed on the brakes and swung the car off the road.

"We were closer than I thought," he said.

"But we're in the middle of nowhere."

"Precisely."

As he stepped out of the car the silence seemed to quake in his ears. A quick glance at his watch informed him that they were two minutes late. She slid across the seat, climbed out, and moved next to him.

"What are . . ."

"Shush," he said. He reached into the car and flashed the headlights. The beams illuminated the desert, then darkness enveloped the barren plain again. He waited. A heavy layer of clouds blotted out the stars. An uneasy quiet descended over the desert. There were no lights, no sounds, and no signs of movement. Ari shivered. The temperature was dropping rapidly and they hadn't brought jackets.

"Al-Alazar," he called into the night.

His voice rolled over the rugged plateau, climbing toward the Heights of Golan.

There was no response, no echo, no recognition.

Al-Alazar couldn't have left; he would wait more than two minutes, he had to.

He led her away from the car, moving a few steps into the rocky plain.

"Al-Alazar," he called loudly, a note of despair ringing in his voice.

Silence. The interminable silence of Orion, the dark hunter. Ari looked up to where the constellation should have been. What was the hunter trying to tell him? What was he always trying to tell him?

"Al-Alazar!" he shouted, perspiring freely in the cold air.

"Over here," Sabri al-Alazar spoke softly from the road three feet behind them. The sound of his voice startled him. There was something in his flat tone, in the way he had snuck up behind them without being heard, but Ari couldn't mold what he sensed into clear thoughts.

Spinning around, he saw al-Alazar pointing a snub-nosed Smith & Wesson .38 caliber revolver at his chest.

Cracks formed in Ari's fragile world. He couldn't believe Operative 66 intended to kill him, but there it was: a gun leveled at his heart.

"What's she doing here?" al-Alazar asked icily.

Abruptly the anger that had flashed through him was gone. He felt stupid. Why had he brought her along? To kill her? He could have done that in his room.

Kim looked at him, realizing he hadn't believed the story she'd made up.

"You fool," al-Alazar said, moving close to them. "Her father's a professor of political science at the American University in Cairo and her mother's a Palestinian. She's been trained by the Egyptian Mukhabarat el-Amma since she was sixteen. She's probably led the Second Bureau . . ."

He snatched at her purse, opened it, and pulled out a small directional transmitter. Ari's knees buckled. His chest felt weak. Not only had he ceased to be of value to the Service, he realized he'd become a burden.

238

Suddenly the sound of car engines shattered the silence. The two Israelis stared down the road as three pairs of headlights bore down on them. Their attention momentarily diverted, Kim darted into the desert.

Before Ari could turn, al-Alazar fired. The shot pierced the back of her skull and the bullet exploded inside her brain. She fell forward, dead. Ari felt neither sadness nor satisfaction; he no longer felt anything.

Al-Alazar turned back to the road. The cars were less than a minute away.

"Shit, we'll never get out of here," he swore out loud.

"Give me the gun," Ari said.

Al-Alazar hesitated.

"Give me the gun!"

The senior agent handed it to him.

Ari weighed the light 24-ounce M-15 Combat Masterpiece in his hand. It was a good, reliable revolver, but he would have preferred a Browning automatic pistol with a multishot magazine.

"Now get in the jeep," Ari said. "I'll try and hold them off long enough for you to make it to the rendezvous point, or at least until you're out of rifle range. Those cars shouldn't be able to follow you through the desert, it's too rocky."

"But I can't leave you here."

"I'm no hero. If my life was worth anything to Israeli intelligence, I'd make you stay and I'd go. But it's not. It's important that you get out of here alive. Now move!" He shoved the smaller man toward the desert where the jeep was parked.

Al-Alazar grabbed his hand affectionately. "There are five bullets left, save the last one for yourself."

Ari nodded.

As the Syrian vehicles screeched to a stop, al-Alazar broke into a run. Ari dropped to his knees and crouched

239

behind the green Fiat. Uniformed soldiers with olive green helmets piled out of the cars clutching onto Kalashnikov AK-47 assault rifles. One of them adjusted the searchlight atop his car, scanning the desert for the two Israelis—in vain. Then Ari heard the sound of a motor starting up. Al-Alazar had reached the jeep. With a lurch the senior spy sped toward the rendezvous point. The searchlight darted toward the source of the noise, catching al-Alazar and holding him in its beam like a rabbit caught in the headlights of a car. Two soldiers aimed, flicking the rapid load on their automatic rifles. The AK-47 had an effective range of 440 yards. Al-Alazar was well within that distance.

Ari fired rapidly, three times. The first bullet shattered the searchlight, plunging the desert in darkness; the second caught the nearer soldier in the chest, but the third shot missed, hitting way wide of its mark. Before the soldier could turn and fire at him Ari squeezed the trigger and landed his fourth bullet in the man's abdomen. The sound of orders wildly shouted echoed through the darkness. A fusillade of 7.62 mm bullets ripped into the Fiat. Ari crouched low to the ground behind a tire. He had one shot left. He would use it on himself, but not until the last moment. He had to give al-Alazar every additional second.

Then to his horror he heard a jeep approaching on the highway; the slower vehicle had not been able to keep pace with the faster Moskwiches. Ari had to stop it, protect al-Alazar, salvage the mission. Bullets exploded into the Fiat, fracturing the windshield. Then there was silence. Ari huddled against the tire.

Since he hadn't fired back perhaps they thought he was dead. Then he heard it: the sound of men fanning out in all directions. They were going to surround him, then move in.

240

The jeep pulled to a halt twenty yards down the road. But Ari couldn't get a clear shot at the driver, the army vehicles blocked his line of fire. More orders were shouted in Arabic and the jeep's engine started up. The vehicle bounced into the desert, heading in the direction al-Alazar had taken. In the distance Ari could still hear the sound of his colleague's jeep. The Arab would be able to follow him! Ari had to take a chance. Now. He picked up two stones and flung them behind him. A burst of fire erupted where the rocks had landed. He ran out into the desert in the direction of the jeep, dropped to the ground, aimed with both hands and squeezed the trigger. Just as two soldiers fired at him.

The first soldier's bullet missed, but the second caught Ari's head, flipping him onto his back. Blood gushed down his face. The sky spun. The ground seemed to pitch underneath him, and suddenly he was cold, very cold. But as he lost consciousness he was quite certain he heard the sound of air escaping from the jeep's front tire.

TWENTY-THREE

SEPTEMBER 22

ARI WAS wakened by a scream echoing somewhere in the distance. Then pain exploded in his brain. He lay rigid, realizing to his dismay that he was not dead. Remaining still, he tried to diminish the pain by breathing carefully and filling his lungs only halfway.

Slowly he explored as much of the room as he could without moving his head. The upper walls and ceiling were whitewashed. The floor on which he lay had to be stone, somehow he sensed that—for he was cold, especially his feet. He tried to lift his hand and touch the dried blood on his forehead, but his wrists were bound together behind him. He couldn't move them. Suddenly he remembered al-Alazar, wondering if the Israeli agent had escaped.

The tiny world in which he was enclosed gradually crystallized into reality. The air was damp and stale and he was aware of the sour smell of prison clothes. Somewhere outside the cell he heard the sound of dripping water, or else his mind was playing tricks on him, for he was extremely thirsty. Instinctively he tried to sit up and as he did his whole body was torn with such pain that he screamed out. He fell to the floor panting and bit his lower lip until the blood filling his mouth jarred him into a realization of what he was doing. His body was stiff and bruised, his groin ached, and his feet were numb. They must have beaten him while he was unconscious. He spit a mixture of blood and saliva onto the floor, cursing the bungling soldier whose bullet had grazed his forehead and failed to kill him.

He lay there for a long time in the darkness unaware if it was day or night, if he had been in the cell hours or days. He wasn't hungry and he hadn't eaten much for dinner so he assumed it was early Saturday morning, still hours before dawn. The children were to be smuggled out of the *haret* Saturday night. He would have to hold out until then. He would not betray them, no matter what—he would die first.

Ari lay quite still and thought about the pain, daring not move lest his body start in savage convulsions again. It might be hours before they came for him. They would want him to lie there, alone, without hope—his mind doing their work for them. He knew if he was to resist he would have to gain some advantage, achieve some goal, no matter how small. He would have to find a handhold to grab onto as he slipped down the face of a cliff descending into hell. He would sit up, that was it. He would defy the pain and sit up. Then he would use that small achievement to build a psychological fortress. No matter what happened later he'd rivet his thoughts to that success.

He lifted his head off the ground. Shaking, he lifted his shoulders. His chest hurt horribly . . .

Just then the door swung open and a uniformed guard stepped in. "I see you're feeling better," he said sarcastically.

Ari strained, just a few more inches.

The guard lashed out with his foot and caught the side of Ari's skull, exactly on the spot where the soldier's

243

bullet had hit. He toppled over, drifting warmly into unconsciousness, the blood from the reopened wound forming a pool where his head struck the stone floor. He had not achieved his advantage.

The Russian-built van hit a bump in the road, jolting Ari awake. Instantly the pain from his head reached every nerve fiber in his body. He lay on the floor handcuffed and manacled. Preceded and followed by Land Rovers filled with soldiers carrying AK-47s and Samoval machine guns, the van raced along the narrow dirt road leading from the Damascus-Kuneitra highway to Sigin al-Mazza, the central penitentiary where all political prisoners were held.

The prison, erected by the French during the mandate, juts from a steep hill ringed by a deep uncultivated valley and surrounded by a barrier of barbed wire and mine fields. The entire area is dotted with military installations. As an added psychological torture, al-Mazza was built close enough to the capital so that those confined behind its walls can hear the planes landing and taking off from Damascus's International Airport.

When the van stopped inside the prison courtyard two soldiers removed the manacles bolting Ari's feet to the floor of the vehicle, picked him up, and dumped him into the dirt. He felt nothing upon hitting the ground.

"Stand up!" one of the soldiers ordered. The command was absurd, he could hardly move.

The soldier kicked him sharply in the groin.

Ari rolled onto his knees. Crawling to the side of the van, he put his handcuffed hands to the cold metal just as dawn broke over the desert. He was halfway up when the guard kicked him and he fell. Listening to the Arab's laughter, he lay there for a moment, then struggled to his feet and abruptly thrust himself forward, driving his

244

lowered head at the soldier's stomach. The soldier sidestepped quickly and Ari landed in the dirt, his damaged head striking the ground hard. He waited for the guard's retaliation, but the expected blows were not forthcoming. Instead the soldiers grabbed his shoulders and dragged him past a neatly stacked pile of palm frond lashes, into a gray-walled corridor. They shoved him in an interrogation room, shaved his head, ripped the clothes from his body, and left him sprawled on the floor, naked.

He was cold, hungry, and unbearably thirsty but he didn't call out, he didn't move. Several hours must have passed before the two guards returned. Without a word, they went to work on him. The room was bare except for a long bench that jutted perpendicularly out from the wall. They carried him to the bench, and secured his body in place with two leather straps: one at the base gripped his ankles, leaving his feet hanging over the edge of the bare wood; and the second was pulled taut around his chest and arms. The soldiers left, but returned momentarily, each carrying a palm branch with the fronds removed.

One soldier lit a cigarette as the other slowly moved toward him, beating the air with his branch. Ari squeezed his eyes. Abruptly the first blow bit into his bare soles, the thorns slicing through his skin, bloodying the green stalk. Repeatedly the guard lashed at his feet. Ari screamed, writhing in place, trying to break away from his bonds. But there was no escape. Gasping for breath, he struck his head against the wooden bench again and again, until finally he knocked himself unconscious.

Ari dreamed deliriously. *Thunder cracked above a mountain forest. Running among the trees he fell, striking his head. Torrents of rain dropped from the sky. The soil came away and muddied the waters. The whole forest quaked; trees fell uprooted*

245

and slid down the mountain, carried by a rushing river. He struggled to his feet and started running again. A bolt of lightning sliced through the trees and struck his hand.

He screamed. The first guard held his hand in a vice-like grip while the second, using a specially designed pliers, ripped the fingernails from his flesh one by one. When he finished he circled the bench and grabbed Ari's other hand as his partner lit a cigarette and stood off to the side, smoking leisurely. The anticipation of pain was too great. Ari lost control of his sphincter and the excrement flowed out of him. Squashed between his buttocks and the bench, the warm feces pressed against his skin, dribbling down his thighs and between his legs. The odor penetrated his nostrils, filling him with self-disgust. The guards ceased their torture. His physical humiliation was complete.

They untied him and dragged his unresisting body through the gray-walled corridor, past an iron gate, and down to an underground high-security cell block, making sure to scrape his feet on the stone floor. They threw him in a three-by-four-foot chamber, then shut the door, enclosing him in semi-darkness.

The room was windowless. Air found its way in through a ventilating strip at the base of the door. A pit dug in one corner of the cell served as a toilet. The sour stench rising from that direction suggested it was rarely, if ever, cleaned. A gallon can stood in the opposite corner. There was no bed, no mattress, no blankets.

Ari lay face down in the cold dirt. After a while he hoisted himself up on his elbows and dragged his body toward the gallon can, the dirt sticking to the wet excrement on his legs. To his grateful surprise he found the can was half full. He thrust his still undamaged right hand into the icy water and drank voraciously. When he'd had enough he used the rest of the water to clean himself as best he could. Not long afterward a tin was silently passed through the food trap in the door. It was filled with soupy porridge made from the roasted grains of bulgur, cracked wheat. Unable to sit up, Ari lay on his stomach and lapped up the food with his tongue, like a cat. Then he waited, his mind awash with pain. There was nothing else to think about. Nothing else in his life. Nothing that mattered. Just the pain.

Hours later the door swung open and the two guards reappeared. Ari bit his torn lower lip. It was going to start over again! The lashing at his feet. The ripping of the nails from his fingers. He thrust his undamaged hand under his stomach.

To his surprise the guards lifted him gently, slipped a brown robe around his shoulders, and carried him up a dark flight of stairs, this time making sure that his feet did not scrape against the ground. The room they took him to was small yet comfortable. It was adequately furnished with a desk and an upholstered armchair. The guards deposited him in the chair, then stood at the door. When Ari opened his eyes, the light from the window sent a fresh spasm of pain jerking through his body. He blinked rapidly, momentarily blinded. The man behind the desk said something to the guard, who moved across the room and drew the drapes.

"Is that better?" the man asked.

Ari looked up, focusing for a moment before he recognized the face across from him. It belonged to Suleiman Sarraj. Ari had seen his picture only once before but that was enough—he remembered the eyes. Sarraj's entire character was stamped in his eyes: they were small, cold, and broodingly contemplative, like Sarraj himself.

"Your welcome left a little something to be desired," Ari said, looking at the two guards.

"I'm afraid that was only the most meager of beginnings," Sarraj shrugged. "Unless you cooperate I'm not going to be able to restrain my men. They will be allowed to torture you around the clock, or until you are persuaded that any attempt at resistance is futile."

"You're a bastard."

"I suppose so," Sarraj said matter-of-factly. "Actually if it's any consolation, Yussaf Fuad wanted to pick you up some time ago and obtain the information about al-Alazar by the most brutal methods, but I opposed him. I didn't want to have to resort to hurting you."

Ari liked the fact that, unlike the Colonel, Sarraj shunned superfluous pleasantries. He began right away, trying to psychologically win him over, to exploit the natural dependency the prisoner has on his interrogator.

"But now that al-Alazar escaped and one of your top agents was killed, you had no choice but to order your men to work me over."

"Precisely."

Ari had baited the Second Bureau chief, hoping to find out if al-Alazar had successfully fled the country. Sarraj had provided him with an answer without realizing he'd done so.

"Let me come directly to the point," Sarraj said. "You came to Syria and contacted Sabri al-Alazar, your Operative Sixty-six. Why?"

Ari stared at the floor, silent—sensing from the uneasy edge in Sarraj's voice that he was rushing things, that there was someone leaning on him, demanding he produce immediate results.

"I'm not known for my patience, Ben-Sion. For your own sake I suggest you answer my question."

"If my hotel room was bugged you already know why I'm in Damascus."

"Oh yes," Sarraj said, leaning back in his chair. "The Scud missile locations. An attempt at deceiving us, but

248

I'm afraid an inadequate one. The communication of such information to Israel would not require the presence of an additional agent in Damascus. We searched al-Alazar's apartment thoroughly. We now know he was quite capable of transmitting the most complex military intelligence directly to Jerusalem."

Ari cringed, causing an intense wave of pain to roll through his head. Assuming his escape with al-Alazar was assured, he'd created a simplistic reason for being in Damascus merely to satisfy Kim—oblivious to the possibility that he might be arrested and challenged to protect Operation Goshen behind that reason.

"Let me caution you," Sarraj continued like an admonishing parent. "Further attempts at deceit will be dealt with most severely. You will make a full confession. And you will make it today." There was no menace in his voice; just cold, detached determination.

Ari closed his eyes. He felt each pulsation of his blood singly, at regular intervals. He had to produce a good excuse, one that would satisfy Sarraj until the children were smuggled out of Syria. But he couldn't think; no ideas would coalesce.

"I'm waiting," Sarraj said. "As soon as you answer there will be a doctor."

"I can't."

Sarraj motioned to one of the guards, who approached clutching a bull's tail kurbash in his hand.

"No!"

As the guard raised his arm, the wild pulsating in his head increased. Sweat rolled down his body.

Sarraj raised his hand to stop the guard and spoke to Ari. "I'll give you one last chance. What was your mission? Why did you contact al-Alazar?"

"Don't beat me any more. Please, Sarraj, I beg you." He cowered in the chair.

Quickly Sarraj said something to the guard at the door. There was a shuffling of feet and someone was pushed into the room. Instinctively Ari turned and looked. What little strength he had left melted into despair. A pallid and emaciated figure of a man staggered into the room, his face a mass of bruises, his left arm gone, a bloodied bandage covering the stump. Shock sucked the breath out of Ari. It was Dov Elon.

Before he could call out to him the guard grabbed Dov by the shoulder and propelled him out of the room. Tears crawled down Ari's face.

"You fucking pig," he shouted at Sarraj. He knew what was coming.

"Within a matter of minutes my men will shoot off his other arm," Sarraj said, choosing to ignore the invective Ari had hurled at him. "That is, unless I intervene. Ben-Sion, I'm offering you a simple trade: Dov's life for the information I want. I understand you are responsible for his capture; please don't be responsible for his death too. If you cooperate I'll have him returned to Tel Aviv immediately, if you don't . . ." He let the rest of his sentence drift into suggestion.

Ari lunged at Sarraj, but the instant his feet touched the ground he screamed and fell to the floor. The room spun. He heard shouting and the sound of footsteps running toward him—then he lost consciousness.

The touch of a damp cloth triggered the pain again, eddies of agony that swirled through his bones. He opened his eyes and found himself propped back in the same armchair.

"That was very stupid," Sarraj said, looking down at him. "I really don't enjoy seeing you suffer. It causes me great discomfort, especially when the unpleasantness is so unnecessary. Just tell me why you contacted al-Alazar, afterward I promise you a quick execution. And I am a man of my word, Dov will be set free. He no longer is of use to us. Once we have the information we want the Red Cross will be contacted and his transfer to Israel arranged. It's in your hands. Help him. Make up for the unfortunate mishap on Cyprus."

Ari pictured himself on the beach in Kyrenia with Michelle. Dov's suffering was his fault. The beatings, the bruises, the lost arm; he was responsible for it all. He had caused Dov's capture. He was to blame. Though he'd known this before, seeing the boy's bloody stump had been too much for him . . .

His will to resist shattered. Dov's suffering had to end, nothing else mattered. The boy was so young, he deserved a chance at the future. He could not let him die because of his bungling. He would tell Sarraj what he wanted to know, no matter what the price.

"No!" he screamed at himself. He had to hold out for one day, until the children were safe. Sarraj was manipulating him. He had to fight—find the strength to defy him.

Without his noticing it the room was darkened and a movie projector wheeled in by the guards.

"I think you'll enjoy this," Sarraj said, suppressing a smile.

As the whine of the projector filled the room a blurred image appeared on the wall opposite Ari. The guard focused, then turned on the sound.

"No," Ari whispered, shutting his eyes. But he couldn't block out the sound of their voices, of his telling Kim that he couldn't live without her.

Sarraj snapped his fingers and the projector was shut off. "We have some excellent footage of you two. Who killed her?"

"Al-Alazar," Ari said, whimpering.

"I thought so. I didn't think you could do it. You loved her right up to the end, even after you knew she was an agent, didn't you?"

"Yes," he shouted, his will to resist a distant memory.

"I also have a lengthy reel of you and Michelle Giroux. Would you like me to bring it in?"

Silence.

"In that case maybe Dov would like to see it. I'm sure he would find such documentation of what his liaison officer was doing while he was signaling for help quite fascinating. We could even delay the removal of his arm long enough for a full screening, in the hope that you might change your mind, provide us with the information we want, and save not only his arm, but his life."

"I can't," Ari said, holding his head with his hands. "I can't talk now. In the name of God, Sarraj, my head's . . . just let me rest. Let me have a bed."

"Tell me why you contacted al-Alazar. Then you shall have a doctor, food, and a bed. Otherwise I will show Dov the films, then I'll have his arm shot off. Do you understand? You will be beaten again, mercilessly. All that unnecessary suffering. You can put a stop to it. Dov's young, don't let him die. Give him a chance at life. Just whisper the answer to me, then you will be able to sleep."

Ari's breathing was labored. He covered his eyes with his arm, unsuccessfully trying to fight back the tears.

"Just tell me what I want to know, then it will be all over," Sarraj said gently.

Ari shook his head, crying uncontrollably, every ounce of what strength he had left focused on defying his interrogator.

Sarraj sensed he was on the verge of success. He would now break Ben-Sion finally, irrevocably. He spoke rap-

252

idly to the guards. Seconds later Dov was pushed into the room.

Ari looked at him. "I'm sorry, I didn't . . ."

"Shut up!" Sarraj said, the menace in his voice terrifying.

The guard sat Dov on the edge of the desk. He responded with detached indifference. There was a glassiness in his eyes and he didn't seem to recognize Ben-Sion. Sarraj stood, removed his FN Browning .45 caliber pistol from a drawer, and placed it pointblank against the boy's elbow.

"Tell me what I want to know or Elon loses his other arm."

Ari sobbed in agonized self-pity.

"I can't. Don't make me."

"You contacted al-Alazar. Why?"

He couldn't talk—the children.

"The first shot will shatter his arm. The second will be aimed at his knee. The third at his other knee."

Silence followed, parted after a long moment by the sound of Sarraj snapping a magazine of cartridges into the butt of the pistol.

"The bullets have grooves sliced into their tips. They expand on contact. The effect is most . . ."

"All right! All right. I'll tell you." He spoke softly now, his voice trembling. "The code name for my assignment was Operation Goshen. The Colonel thought we would be able to smuggle . . ."

For some reason he stopped and looked up at Dov. A thin line of tears rolled down the boy's cheeks.

"No," Ari screamed, squeezing his eyes shut. "I can't. I won't." He opened his eyes and glared at his interrogator. "Go to hell, Sarraj."

In angry frustration the Second Bureau chief pulled

the trigger. The sound exploding so close to Ari's ears was deafening. Pieces of wet flesh flew into his face. Dov's arm hung from the elbow by a patch of membrane, blood gushing from the open wound.

Ari fainted.

He woke hours later aware that he was back in his cell. Suddenly he remembered Dov's arm hanging by that small piece of skin. In anguish he clawed at the dirt with his good hand—then lay still. His mind ravaged by pain, he watched the door, waiting for them to come. Sarraj's interrogation cycle was clear. He alternated between physical and mental torture. They would attack his body next, most likely with the *harka*, electric shock treatment. Ari was well acquainted with the device: metal clips protruding from a power joint would be attached to his tongue and sexual organs, then Sarraj would switch on the 110-volt current. He shuddered and tried to sleep; but the throbbing in his head kept him awake. Escape eluded him.

He woke a second time, surprised that he'd lost consciousness. He had no way of telling how long it had been since Dov was shot, or for that matter how much time had elapsed since he'd been brought to al-Mazza prison. But some inner sense told him it was morning, Sunday morning, the morning after Operation Goshen was to have been executed. He had succeeded. Sarraj had not dragged the information out of him! Then with brutal swiftness despair dissolved his momentary elation. If the children had indeed escaped, Sarraj would assume he contacted al-Alazar to arrange for their safe passage. There would be no need to question him further. They would beat him now without restraint, not to elicit information, but to inflict punishment. Syrian methods were well known. The torture would be pro-

254

tracted and excruciating. It might last months. In the end they would hang him publicly in Marjeh Square.

And he still really didn't understand why he'd been sent to Syria. Al-Alazar said the Colonel wanted Sarraj discredited. If that was the reason for his venture into Damascus, the Mossad had failed. Sarraj was very much in power. Ari would die, not understanding why, or for what.

Then he heard the door opening. He pressed closer to the dirt. His muscles tensed.

The lone man who entered closed the door silently behind him and bent to the ground. Ari looked up. After a moment he recognized the face. It was Yussaf Fuad, head of the Mukhabarat. The Colonel had shown Ari his photograph.

"Ibrahim Sassoon's and Nissim Kimche's children escaped from Damascus last night," Fuad said. "Sarraj is being blamed for failing to induce you to talk in time, that's why I'm here."

Ari said nothing. The certain knowledge that the children had arrived safely in Israel filled him with joy, but his happiness was tempered. He knew what the success of Operation Goshen meant to his own life.

He bit his swollen lower lip, readying himself for a fresh onslaught of pain. Fuad's reputation preceded him. He was known to be cold, merciless, and savagely sadistic —viewing the torture of human beings as a form of recreation, a respite from the tedium of his administrative position. Unlike most secret service chiefs, Fuad administered physical torment personally, rather than relegating the task to his subordinates. It was well known that he did not care for public hangings, much preferring to perform executions in the privacy of a prison cell where he could beat his victims to death with his bare hands.

Ari cringed, waiting for the first blow to come. But it

255

never did. Instead Fuad reached over and touched his right hand, placing something in it. Ari couldn't believe what his fingers told him was true. Fuad had slipped him a razor blade!

"This is all I can do. I'm sorry I can't help you escape, but I would be held responsible," Fuad whispered in Hebrew, instead of the French he began the conversation with.

And suddenly all the tumblers fell into place. For weeks it was as if he had been trying to open a twenty-combination lock with the first nineteen digits. Now he saw that the missing number had always been there, out of reach. One by one the people in Ari's life passed before him. The Colonel, phlegmatic and unrevealing, who'd been even vaguer than usual. Michelle, who wanted to go away that particular weekend. Kim, who'd asked too many questions. Barkai, who never showed. Al-Alazar, who seemed to be warm and sympathetic but was as ruthless as all of them. After twenty-nine years in the Service this is what it had come to: his only value was as a decoy.

He realized now how al-Alazar had known so much about his relationship with Kim. Fuad had told him. Fuad was Operative 66. Ari had been sent to Damascus for only one reason: to create the illusion that al-Alazar was the Israeli the Syrian High Command sought so desperately. The Parliament member was an Israeli spy, but one of much lesser importance. Ari had been sacrificed openly to protect Fuad, to assure all concerned that they had eliminated the alien agent operating in their midst.

"What about Dov?" he asked, feeling the weight of the razor blade in his hand.

"His suffering is over. He died last night."

Tears rose in Ari's eyes.

"I must go now," Fuad said rising. "I can't risk being